HAMMER TOWN

Selina Rosen

Published by Yard Dog Press
710 W. Redbud Lane
Alma, AR 72921-7247
http://www.yarddogpress.com

Edited by Lynn Stranathan
Copy Editing by Leonard Bishop
Cover art and design by Brad Foster

First Edition: October, 2002 ISBN 1-893687-28-7
Second Edition: August 1, 2006 ISBN 978-1-893687-80-5
Third Edition: June 1, 2017 (larger size)
        ISBN 978-1-945941-07-8

Printed in the United States of America
0 9 8 7 6 5 4

For Lynn

CHAPTER 1

Tarent laughed as he looked at Mishy's face on the screen in front of him. "You threatening me, now that's rich." Tarent's eyes narrowed to slits as he glared back at Mishy's image. "What can you do to me, Mishy? You've had it, man! It's over! You're washed out. Why don't you just give up now while you still have at least one shred of dignity left? One little tiny insignificant piece of turf."

Mishy snarled back at him. He was a man walking the razor's edge. Tarent wanted him to be afraid, maybe he should have been, but Tarent had pushed him way beyond that. There was a point at which all reason just shut down. Mishy had reached that point. There was only a black burning pit of rage in his stomach, and the need for revenge in his heart. He had no other purpose; nothing else had any meaning. "Laugh your stupid black ass off, Tarent. Some things are worth more than money, or turf, or even power. My father told me, long ago, when I first took over his business, he said, *'Never take all that a man holds dear, because there is nothing in this world as dangerous as a man who has nothing to lose'.'"*

"And nothing as impotent." Tarent laughed hatefully. "What is this shit? Your last great hurrah? You can't do anything to me, and we both know it." He took in a deep breath. "Save your threats for the few people you still control, the scum that I left for you – your ever-dwindling empire. Don't waste your breath on me. I was never afraid of you, Mishy. I'm certainly not afraid of you now. Computer, close transmission."

Mishy glared at the blank screen and smiled. "The cocky bastard. It's all just a matter of time. Soon he's about to learn that the road to hell goes both ways." Mishy laughed as his chair swiveled to face the men waiting for his orders. "We'll see if I'm as impotent as he thinks I am or if I can get it up... Way up, when I have to!"

Mishy's face left the screen to be replaced by swirling colored lights and the mechanical music the dygarhythms machine produced for Tarent's entertainment.

The door slid open and his daughter walked in, short and thin, fine featured, regal and graceful. She was a brown-eyed beauty, immaculate and cultivated – a credit to him and to her dead mother. *The bitch had at least been good for genetic material*, he thought as he leaned back in his chair, which moved to accommodate him.

He looked up at his daughter. For the moment at least, she had his undivided attention. "So, Elantra, what can I do for you?"

"I wanted to talk to you about school, my residency." She sat, and the chair, anticipating her intention to sit, rose to meet her.

"What's the problem?"

"The program runs too fast for me. I'm two or three days behind..."

"No problem, just slow the program down...."

"I'd like to go to college, Dad," she said nervously, not sure whether her new approach to this old argument was going to get her any further than earlier attempts. "I think that if I could study with other people, interact with them on an academic level... Work on real patients instead of holograms..."

"How many times do we have to go through this, Laney? The answer is still no. Having all those people around is just going to distract you from your studies. As for patients, you'd never get the variety of cases in a hospital that you're getting from the program. Laney, you're only twenty-one years old, and you're seven months away from having your MD. Why change things now when you're so close to finishing? If you go into a residency program it will be two years before you get your degree. Rejoice in technology, dear. Don't fight it. It takes three times as long to do things the old way. I should know. When I was a kid the programs were different – they called it a public tutor board. It's very hard when fifty kids are all asking the terminal questions at once. The public program made learning slow and tedious, I can only imagine what it would be like if the kids had been sitting all around me as well, screaming out their answers, all asking questions..."

"Maybe I could learn something from their questions or from the answers they give and receive. Maybe they would ask questions I wouldn't think to ask, come up with answers not even the program had thought of. Treating a real patient with the flu has got to be better training than treating a holographic patient with malaria – which by the way there hasn't been a real case of in over two hundred years…"

"Elantra… You are being ungrateful. You have always had the best of everything. Maybe I should send you off to college so that you'd appreciate just how easy you have it…"

"Just let me go for a while. If it's as awful as you say…"

"The answer is no. Now I let you do this doctor thing because you had your heart set on it, but I have never really embraced the idea. The idea of anyone purposely exposing themselves to so many germs – it boggles the mind! You aren't going off to college, and that's final. Now… find something pleasant to talk about, or go to bed." Tarent turned away from her to look at the swirling colors on his screen. She was being dismissed.

Elantra had enough of her father in her that she wasn't going to be put off that easily. "I… I don't even know what people *look* like. I feel like I have spent my whole life in this building. Like some pet or house plant. Just once, I would love to step outside these walls and see just how awful it is out there. Do you plan to keep me here the rest of my life? I'm going to leave eventually, whether you like it or not… I just don't see why it's such a big deal…"

Her father laughed, but didn't turn to look at her. "You're exaggerating, Elantra. Right now is not a good time. It's not safe outside the building. The street urchins are fighting over a piece of turf, and…"

"What does that have to do with us, with me?" she demanded.

"If you'd let me finish. I'm in the middle of a corporate takeover, dear. Sometimes the competition doesn't want to play by the rules. They stir the thugs up and then none of us are safe until things cool down and the police agencies can get things back under control."

"There is always some excuse, some reason why I can't have a life…"

"I'm a villain because I want to keep you from going through the hell that I went through on the streets…"

"I'm a prisoner here!" Elantra screamed, and the chair helped her to stand up. "You can't keep me at home forever, Father." She turned on her heel. The door opened before her, anticipating that she wanted to leave, waited a sufficient amount of time and closed behind her. She stepped onto the moving walkway and it carried her to her room, where her door opened before her and closed behind her.

"Music on, " she ordered. The dygarhythms machine kicked in. "Chair up." The chair rolled up behind her and rose to meet her flopping butt. She was mad. Dealing with her father always left her feeling like a six year old. He was always going on and on about how he was sparing her from the horrors of his own youth, but she was sure the truth was he hadn't been outside a building much more than she had.

He certainly didn't leave the comforts of the building now. Tarent Powers never left Power's Tower. If he had his way neither would she, and if Tarent Powers was good at anything it was getting his own way.

She was furious, and she was bored – if it was possible to be both. "H.V. on," she commanded, and all around her colored lights began to dance. "Holo-vision, so named because of the hollow way it makes you feel," she mumbled. "Give me something to fit my mood." The computer read her body heat and heart rate, and then picked a suitable program – two people beating each other up with big sticks. She sat back and watched as the images played out her frustration and her rage. The pictures didn't really look like people, but they were close enough for most. For *most* that was, but not for Elantra. She longed for physical contact with real people. People besides her father and his well-paid lackeys.

She decided to do something drastic. She decided to go out. She dressed appropriately, grabbed her cat for company, and using all the tricks she had learned over the years made her way out of the building undetected. Feeling very smug, she called for a car. Her victory, however, was short lived. Before the car had time to arrive, three people wearing masks appeared seemingly out of nowhere. There was a smell, an awful smell, and then nothing.

Tarent rubbed at his temples. "How the hell did she get past my security system!" he screamed.

"Don't know, boss." The man rubbed at his own head, perhaps to show sympathy for Tarent's headache. "Maybe she smuggled something through on one of her tutorials."

Tarent nodded. That made sense. He inwardly cringed; he should have had the tutorials screened. After all, he screened all other data that entered his system. "Do we have a clear picture of who grabbed her?" he asked.

"Look for yourself, boss." He pointed at one of the screens that lined the wall in Tarent's office. Men in masks – they could have been anyone, but Tarent was fairly sure he knew exactly who was behind the abduction of his only child.

A third man ran into the room, completely out of breath although he probably hadn't run any further than the length of the hallway, and even then on top of the moving walkway.

"Any sign of Elantra?" Tarent asked him.

The man – too winded to talk – shook his head no, and took three deep breaths before he spoke in gasps. "We've looked all around the building and the surrounding area, nothing."

Tarent wasn't too surprised. After all, the computer hadn't found her anywhere.

"Did we at least get a make, a model, a license number on the car, anything useful?"

"They must have used some stealth thing. None of the cars the cameras picked up had Elantra in them."

Tarent's computer buzzed, and then Mishy's face filled the screen. Mishy smiled broadly at Tarent. "I told you, dick head. Don't fuck with a man who has nothing to lose." He laughed sadistically, and the transmission ended.

Tarent let out one long, loud scream.

He jumped to his feet and said more to himself than anyone else, "The bastard just wants to fuck with me." Tarent paced across the room twice then stopped. "Computer, run the agencies. I want the best one."

"You want to hire *cops*, boss?" one of the men said in disbelief.

"Like I don't own cops all over this city. It doesn't take a genius to figure out what Mishy did or why. Mishy's got Elantra, and he's going to use her to get to me. As much as I know about Mishy and the way he operates, the cops know more. Any of you know your way around Slum Town?" The other men were silent. "I didn't think so."

James Rank took a double take. Powers was the last person you expected to see on a police agency terminal. Unless of course you were accessing his file to see if he was most probably involved in the crime you were investigating. Tarent Powers was the biggest crime lord in Freight City. Everyone knew it, but try as they might they could never get anything on him. The bastard owned way too many politicians for that. Tarent was a smart crook. He stayed holed up in his building, running everything and never actually getting his own hands dirty. It was hard to prove someone was guilty of a crime when all you had to prove it were a few vague computer files.

"I got to tell ya, too happy to see your ugly mug I ain't. What the hell do ya want?"

"I realize that you people at the police agencies all suffer under the delusion that I am some sort of criminal master mind, but you've yet to turn up any evidence to prove your pathetic theories. I'm clean, Rank. I'm clean, I have the money, and by law you have to take my case…"

"You were never fuckin' clean, Powers, not even on the day you were born. Just good at coverin' yer ass. I know the fuckin' law, Powers, and I don' have to take your fuckin' case unless you've already been turned down by every other agency in town – and that ain't what my terminal is tellin' me…"

"You'll do what I tell you to do, punk…"

"Ya threatenin' me, Powers? Cause if ya are I can haul your ass in and we can charge the city a small fortune for gettin' yer sorry ass out ah yer buildin'…"

"I'm not threatening you, Rank," Tarent said through gritted teeth. He wasn't used to kissing anyone's butt, much less the police. Unfortunately he was between a rock and a hard place. "Mishy took my daughter…"

Rank choked on his laugh, but cut it short. "Now don' tell me yer surprised 'bout that considerin' what ya did ta Mishy. Hell, I'm surprised it took him this long ta do somethin'."

"I didn't do anything to Mishy."

"Nothin' that we can prove. Nothin' at least that will hold water in court. Apparently Mishy has all the proof he needs. One of these days, maybe today, yer gonna step your ass over the line one too many times, and one of the agencies is gonna grab ya. I only hope it's us. I could use that kind of money right now. But who knows? Maybe Mishy will take care of ya for us. Either way we win."

"I'll give you twenty million dollars to find my daughter, return her to me safely and bring Mishy in."

"Ya pay us twenty million dollars, we find your daughter and return her to ya, same price alive or dead. Ten million up front, ten million on delivery. As for Mishy… we leave Mishy where he's at..."

"Mishy kidnapped my daughter..."

"I doubt Mishy left any more evidence of what he did than you do. Jus' cause no one can prove what ya did don' mean ya didn' do it, and both of us know what ya did to Mishy. I'm not about to get in the middle of your fuckin' turf war. I'd lock ya both up and pocket a bunch of money if I could. But as long as you're runnin' around free an able, I'm sure not goin' to be the fool to lock up anyone who's a thorn in yer side. We're not stupid, Tarent, we know that if we take out all the little guppies there's jus more shit fer the big fish in the cesspool."

"Quit talking shit, Rank. That's no deal! It's a bunch of threats and innuendoes. You're wasting minutes and my daughter may have only seconds. I'm not an idiot. You really expect me to pay you a small fortune to *maybe* rescue my daughter and you let her kidnapper go scot free?"

"That's my deal, Powers, take it or leave it. I doubt any other agency is going to offer you anything any better. Thanks ta people like you we have plenty of business, and we're not hurtin' for work."

Tarent seemed to think about it for a minute, then he nodded. "All right, Rank, but it's ironic that you're the one who's calling me a crook. I want this kept as quiet as possible. I have many enemies, lots of people besides the police agencies who would like to take me down. I want my daughter back in one piece, Rank. But I can't afford to lose face. If everyone knew that my daughter was taken right in front of my own home..."

"Don' tell me how to be a cop, and I won' tell ya how to be a crook. I'll work for ya 'cause ya have a legitimate case. But if ya think I'm gonna take orders from ya like one of yer goons, then yer outah yer fuckin' tiny little mind."

James listened to the computer drone its data for the tenth time. No matter how many angles he came up with, no matter how much information he fed the computer, it always spit the same name back in his face, and he was running short on time. According to the computer not one of his other detectives had more than a twenty percent chance of retrieving the girl alive. Only one of his agents had a ninety percent chance of success. He sighed as the computer droned the name again, "Conner McVee."

"Well?" Jason Hunter asked, sliding into Rank's office on a moving walkway. He had been hovering around the office for ten minutes like a vulture waiting for something to die. He very much wanted the computer to say that he was the one to lead the assignment, no doubt because whoever did it was going to get a huge cash bonus. "Well?" he asked again.

"Everyone's on the case, Jason." James sighed, he wished the computer had chosen Jason – or *anyone* else for that matter.

"But am I *assigned* to the case. Is it my case?"

"Sorry, but no," James said.

"Who?" Jason asked, all the wind taken out of his sails.

"McVee," James answered.

Jason laughed. "Conner "The Hammer" McVee! She's never going to take this assignment, and thinking she would is just ludicrous. Would you do it if you were her?" Jason didn't give him a chance to answer. "Come on, boss, give the job to me. You know I can do it, and you know Hammer isn't going to."

"The computer gives you a less than twenty percent chance of success, and it gives Hammer McVee a clear ninety. No one has the kind of connections in Slum Town that McVee does, or anythin' close to her arrest record. As for McVee not takin' the case... Unlike yerself, Hammer is not a cop for the money. She's in it 'cause she has a very well-defined sense of what's right, an what's wrong, an she wants to help make things right. Tarent may be the scum of the earth, and McVee may have good and personal reasons to hate him, but this girl has committed no crime. I doubt even Hammer wants to see Tarent punished bad enough to see an innocent woman killed."

"Yeah, right." Jason laughed.

"Tell you what, Jason. Get out on the street. If you get the girl before Hammer does, I'll give you the bonus."

"Thanks, boss!" Jason smiled and left. As he stepped onto the moving walkway it anticipated which way he wanted to go and started moving.

James watched him move away. The smug little bastard was sure he could do the job, but then he didn't know Hammer or the streets the way James did. It might take some talking, but in the end she would do it – if it could be done.

"Chair up." The chair pushed up so that it took him as little effort to stand as was possible. He got onto the walkway. "Garage," he ordered. In a few minutes he was in the garage under the building, and he'd maybe had to walk a grand total of ten feet. "Computer, send car." In seconds his car stood before him. "Door, open." It did, and he got in. "Door, close." It did, and his restraint slipped on automatically. "Take me to 148 West Street in Hammer Town." The car took off. "Play music." The dygarhythms started to play. He sat back and relaxed. Ten minutes later he entered Hammer Town.

The whole place gave him the creeps. It was like walking back in time. He saw a bunch of Constructionists working with anachronistic tools to build a home, of wood no less! Their air hammers made a loud piercing sound as they shot things called nails into the wood. Not many steel or plastic homes here. Not many computers, either. In fact, very few machines of any kind.

The Constructionists were a religious cult that believed that man was never meant to live in a push-button, computerized world. They believed hard work and personal contact were all important if one wanted to live a righteous life.

McVee lived in Hammer Town. That's how she had gotten the nickname Hammer. Well, that and the fact that she used an air hammer as a weapon.

James liked McVee, but he didn't understand her religion, and he didn't understand her.

The car stopped in McVee's driveway, an open thing with no roof or walls. In fact everything in Hammer Town was just kind of open and airy. If he thought about it too much it would give him nightmares.

He walked up to her door. "It's James Rank," he told the door. It didn't open. "James Rank," he said again. The door remained closed, and it took a second for him to realize why. Then he remembered where he was. He looked for and found the little button that was by the door. He pushed it and it made a noise inside the house.

"Come in!" He heard Hammer scream from inside.

He looked at the round thing on the door at waist level and tried to remember how it worked. Finally he grabbed hold of it and turned. After a moment he remembered to push and the door opened. He walked through and kept going, then remembering that the door wouldn't close itself he went back and shut it. He could never get used to this shit.

"I'm in the kitchen!" she hollered.

James walked through the house – under his own power – to the kitchen.

The kitchen was a real trip. The Constructionists got in their cars and drove to these places and bought their food, or they grew it themselves in these things they called yards. Their appliances were all separate, and they prepared and cooked their food themselves. There was this thing called a sink that always fascinated James. Water ran into it from a tube, and it held water – for what purpose he had no idea.

As weird as James thought the Constructionists were he couldn't help but admire them. They lived a very hard life.

McVee stood at the sink holding a container under the metal tube to fill it with water. When it was full she shut the water off by hand and then walked over and poured it into this little machine. "Rank, good to see you," she smiled. "So were you talking to my door again?"

"Yes. Fer the life of me I don' know why you live like this."

She laughed and pushed a button on the machine. It started making tea. James could smell it. It smelled good. That was the one thing he liked about Hammer Town – all the smells – food cooking, wood, grass. Computers just couldn't replicate it.

"You want some tea?" she asked.

"Ah..." He'd never eaten there before, and he wasn't sure that it was safe, but it smelled so damn good. "Yeah."

"Well, sit down take a load off."

She waved towards a chair at a table, and he sat down. The chair didn't rise to meet him, and he hit it so hard he almost fell over. McVee laughed.

"Primitive," he mumbled. She poured two cups of tea, set one in front of him, and sat down with the other across the table from him. "You know if you would keep your computer on I wouldn't be forced to travel out here every time I have an assignment for you."

"And what does it take? Ten, maybe fifteen minutes of your precious time?" she asked.

"In some cases that fifteen minutes can be the difference between life and death," James said.

She shrugged and took a sip of her tea. He tried his carefully, then smiled and sighed.

"Good?" she asked.

"Out of this world," he said.

"So everything about us is not so bad?"

"I don' have any trouble with Constructionists. I don' understand why ya would choose to make so much work for yourselves, but I don' have any problem with it."

"If God had meant for us to live in a push-button, computerized world, It wouldn't have given us opposable thumbs. You think we're lunatics, but where is the sanity in having the computers and the machines do everything for you so that you have to go to the gym three times a week just to keep your body from atrophying?"

And that was basically the foundation of their faith.

"So... what's the problem with this job that you know that I don't want to do it?" she asked, suddenly changing the subject.

"Oh, God! I wish you wouldn' do that," James said, a bit unnerved.

"Hey, don't blame me. The agency was the one that pushed me to get the empathy implant," Conner said with a smile.

Conner McVee was a shop job, a cyborg, a relic from a time before they made shop jobs all but illegal in the trade. Even after eight years of working with her he still wasn't sure just what she was capable of. How much was flesh and how much was machine. He wasn't even sure how much of her ability was her and what had been mechanically enhanced.

Back in the old days when Conner McVee had first started out, the business had been very competitive. Brakston Agency, which James ran for the corporation as his father had before him, had used everything at their command to make them number one. Conner McVee had made them a lot of money, and the company had put a lot of money into her.

"James?" she prompted.

"You ain't gonna like it, but the computer says yer the only one with an acceptable success ratio."

"And we all know that computers are never wrong," she scoffed, making a face.

He ignored her. "It's a good payin' job. Your part will be two million up front, five on completion."

"God in a car, man! What the fuck's the job?" she asked suspiciously.

A more eloquent man would have found some gentle way of weaving into it. He had never been a man of many words. "Tarent Powers' daughter was kidnapped from right outside

Powers Towers by some of Mishy's hired thugs. Now I know that..."

"I'll do it," she said too quickly. Her hand was shaking, but that was the only sign that she was feeling anything.

"I expected a fight..."

"Why? The girl didn't do anything to me."

"It needs to be discreet."

"Yeah right," she laughed. "By now everyone and his dog knows that she's been kidnapped. Hell, she may already be dead."

"All the more reason to get right on it," James said. "If the girl's still alive she isn't likely to be much longer."

"I'll load my gear, jam up my computer, and I'm on the road."

"I've got everybody on it, and you'll all be linked in," he said. "We'll keep a trace on ya." She glared at him then with her one eye, and he felt like his dick was crawling back into his body. He had hit an extremely exposed nerve. One of her implants allowed them to monitor her every movement for a fifty mile radius. It was an extremely sore spot because it was the one piece of hardware in her body that she hadn't authorized.

"Don't get too close. If I need help I'll yell. Otherwise stay the hell out of my way."

"I never put the trace on ya unless you're workin'," James said.

"That's not really the point is it, Rank?" she said through clinched teeth. "The point is that you can do it *any time you like.*"

He nodded his understanding. "Are you going to be all right with this? Because I could put..."

"If you could have thought of anyone else who could have done it, you would have assigned them already. I'm fine with it." She got up from the table. "I'll get my gear up and you can put me on line." She left to get ready, and he drank his tea. He looked around quickly, saw that she wasn't coming and drank hers, too. It was good. He went and got another cup and drank it, too. He was about to get another one when Conner walked out in full pack. "I'm out of here. Get back to the office and line me up."

He nodded and followed her out to the driveway. "Door open," he said. His car door opened. As he got in he saw

McVee open the door of her primitive car manually.

So much wasted energy.

"Car, drive back to the agency." Suddenly he had to go to the bathroom very badly, and he shuddered to think what that might be like in Hammer Town. "Car, go faster."

CHAPTER 2

He stuck the girl in a tiny cage with rusty metal bars in the middle of a smoke-filled room. Her cat was curled up beside her. She was starting to stir.

"Why'd ya take the fuckin' cat?" Jakelord asked. His every nerve was on edge. This whole thing had been a big mistake. He didn't really see any way out alive. He silently damned the day that he had decided that money was his god. "I said... Why'd ya take the fuckin' cat!"

The man he was talking to shrugged, and Jakelord smacked him. Why the hell had he done this? He hadn't wanted to do it. He didn't want to tangle with Tarent Powers. He was a little bitty bad man and he didn't really play the big leagues. But sometimes you had to make a stand. Tarent had gone after Mishy, and if he succeeded at getting rid of Mishy, little Jakelord couldn't be far behind.

Besides, Mishy had paid Jakelord a butt load of money, and there was that worshipping money as a god thing that he had to deal with.

Just a few more minutes and he could relax. He didn't have to kill the girl. Waiting for weeks for her to poke her head out of the building had been the hard part. They had gotten away undetected with the help of some of Mishy's high tech guys and his own skill as a computer jumper. All Jakelord had supplied was the code busting and some muscle. The girl had come out on her own. All he had to do now was wait for Mishy to come and get the girl, but the longer he sat here with the girl waiting for Mishy, the more likely it was that Tarent's boys would find him first, and no amount of money was worth dying for.

He didn't think.

The girl was wide-awake now, and she trembled with fear as one man licked the bars of her cage. "Can we fuck her?" he asked Jakelord.

She cringed.

"No, you can't fuck her." Jakelord ran over and kicked the

man. "Just leave her the fuck alone till Mishy gets here. Whatever's going to happen to her, Mishy's going to do it. Not me."

"She's beautiful, man," another man said looking with lust at the half-dressed woman in the cage.

"Yeah, and she's going to stay that way at least until Mishy gets here," Jakelord said. He took a deep breath and let it out. "Where the fuck is he anyway?"

Elantra pulled her shirt tighter around her. It had torn at some point. The place stank and it was dark. There were only two small windows at the very top of the wall and Elantra could see that it was dark outside. There was one small bulb burning in the middle of the dank room, and a rickety wooden staircase with no rail led down to the floor from a door twelve feet above them. There were about a dozen rough-looking men and women in the large room sitting on what might have once been nice furniture but was now filthy and disgusting. Several of them were wearing weapons in plain sight, dressed in clothing in not much better repair than the furniture they sat on.

Elantra swallowed hard. These didn't look like the people her father did business with. These looked like... well, they looked like... not very nice people.

"My father is going to be very angry," she said. She got shakily to her feet and picked up the cat.

"No shit!" Jakelord said, and all his men laughed hysterically.

"I say we fuck her, and then we kill her," one of them said.

"Dead people don't talk," another one agreed.

"And if we're going to kill her anyway we might as well fuck her."

"Why don't we kill her, and then we can fuck her," yet another said.

"Shut the fuck up!" Jakelord screamed. "We ain't gonna fuck her, and we ain't gonna kill her. Not in any order. We're going to sit here and pray that Mishy gets here and takes her off our hands before the cops or Tarent's hired goons come and blow our fucking asses away."

Elantra held her cat in front of her like a shield. "My father doesn't have any goons. I'm sure that if you gave me back now, my father would be willing to make sure that the police give you a fair break."

They all laughed. "Little girl, what do you think your daddy does?"

Elantra never had been really sure. "I think... I *know* he's in imports and exports..."

They rolled with laughter.

"Yeah, he imports drugs and programs and exports hookers and programs," Jakelord laughed.

"What do you mean?" Elantra asked, confused.

Jakelord walked up to the cage. "You really don't know? Honey, your daddy is the biggest gangster in Freight City. Hell, if he has his way, eventually he'll own the whole damn place."

"My father is a legitimate business man." She pulled her blouse even more tightly around her.

They all laughed. "And I'm the fuckin' president," Jakelord said.

There was a knock on the door at the top of the stairs, and suddenly the room got very quiet except for the sound of people jumping to their feet and the cocking of guns. Elantra, feeling that it might be helpfull, started screaming. Jakelord cocked a rifle and stuck it through the bars into in her face. "Shut the hell up!" he hissed. "Or I'll blow your pretty head off." She was quiet.

A voice screamed through the door, "Jakelord!"

Jakelord looked relieved and lowered the rifle. "It's Alex. Let him in," he ordered.

One of the thugs started to open the door. Someone on the other side kicked the door open, and the man opening it was slung off the stairs. He fell screaming to the ground and landed with a thud. He screamed out in pain as his leg broke in two places. A man, apparently Alex, bloody and badly beaten was held like a shield in front of the person who walked in behind him. Then Alex was tossed down the stairs to land at Jakelord's feet. The injured Alex looked up at Jakelord with a mixture of fear and apology.

A woman stood alone at the top of the stairs. Elantra stared at her in disbelief. She was like a character the computer might generate; tall, thin, well muscled, and not quite real. Her long, straight hair was jet black. Her skin was well tanned, and her one eye was the brightest blue Elantra had ever seen. There was a patch over the other eye. She was wearing a

simple tank top and what was left of a pair of pants. She held
a weapon that looked like it was capable of eliminating everyone
in the room with a simple sweep of her arms. There were
primitive tools hanging from a belt she wore around her waist.
She looked at Elantra, and Elantra felt like she could no longer
breathe.

The woman scanned the room until she saw Jakelord.
Then she smiled a smile that made Elantra's flesh crawl. Before
she could speak, Jakelord muttered in a voice filled with respect
and fear, "Shit! It's the Hammer."

The woman fixed Elantra with a stare then, and Elantra
looked away.

The Hammer turned her attention back to Jakelord. "I
have no beef with you, Jakelord. We have been friends a long
time, family. I came for the girl, and if you give her to me we're
OK."

"Hammer... It's not that easy, man. Mishy's gonna have
me killed if I lose the girl."

Hammer smiled. "I'm takin' the girl, Jakelord. Don't get in
my way."

A man in the corner moved to fire his weapon. With a flick
of her wrist and without turning to look, Conner aimed and
fired. A sixteen-penny nail smashed into the man's forehead,
blowing up most of the man's skull in the process. He gasped
once and fell to the floor, his body erupting in a fit of spasms.

Elantra couldn't control the scream that was ripped from
her lungs.

Jakelord shuddered. "Let the girl go! Let her go!" he
ordered. One of his boys started unlocking the door. "Hammer...
what do I tell Mishy?"

Hammer started down the stairs, talking as she went.
"Tell Mishy I came and I took the girl. Tell him I said I'd make
it right. Tell him I said if he did anything to you, I'd kill him."
She reached in, grabbed the girl by the arm, and dragged
Elantra out of the cage. She looked at the cat Elantra held and
made a face. "Come on." She dragged her up the stairs and
out of the basement, and Elantra knew in that instant that
nothing was ever going to be the same again.

Jakelord watched them go.

"What we gonna do, Jakelord?" one of the boys asked.

"Hope that Mishy's as afraid of Hammer as I am," Jakelord

answered.

"What did she mean... tell him she'd make things right?"

Jakelord smiled broadly. "I think it means Tarent isn't going to get his little darlin' back till The Hammer gets what she wants."

Mishy and two of his thugs walked into Jakelord's den. Mishy looked around, surveying the destruction left in Hammer's wake.

Jakelord was nervous; it was hard to tell how a man like Mishy might react. "The Hammer showed up..." Jakelord started to explain.

"No fuckin' kiddin'." Mishy bent down and pulled the nail out of a pool of gray matter by the dead man's head. "What did she say?" he asked, throwing the nail onto the stiff's chest and wiping his hand on one of his goon's jackets.

Jakelord repeated Hammer's message in its entirety.

Mishy looked at Jakelord and smiled. "It must be nice to have friends in the police business... Ya done good, kid. You'll get full payment." He rubbed Jakelord's head then looked at his hand in disgust and rubbed it on the goon's jacket again. "I'll be in touch." He laughed all the way out of the basement.

Jakelord sighed with relief. "OK, you dickheads get rid of Ryan's body and let's go celebrate. The girl's gone, we're not dead, and at least for a couple of weeks we're filthy rich."

Tarent waited impatiently at his terminal. Needless to say the transmission he received was not the one he wanted. "Mishy," he hissed, "what the hell have you done with Elantra?"

"I thought I'd have to wait longer than this to taste revenge." Mishy laughed. "The best part is I don't even have the little bitch. I really never did."

"I'll kill you, Mishy. If you so much as touch a hair on her head..."

"Touching her hair was never on the agenda." Mishy leaned closer and continued. "Thanks to you, Tarent, I welcome death, I long to embrace it. I live for one purpose and one purpose only, and that's to see you go down in flames. If I go down, I will take you all the way down before I go."

"I didn't kill your family..." Tarent said, his voice sounding as desperate as he felt.

"Then why did you take credit for it? You did it, and now

you're going to pay. And the rich thing is that I don't have to do another damn thing."

"What the hell do you mean?"

"Five years ago it was my little sister Peggy you killed to make a point. No one could prove that either. You didn't really know Peggy; she was a bit of a flake. A Constructionist of all things. You know, those whacked out people that believe computers and technology are basically evil. So you see her personal life doesn't really show up on the web. It's a shame, really, because if it had maybe you would have learned that Peggy had a lover, in fact a legal partner. A big ole dyke cop with enough implants in her to build a small car. But then you didn't really care about Peggy or her personal life, did you? No, all she was to you was a way to get at me. A way to scare me so that I would back off and let you have what I busted my ass to get. It didn't work, just pissed me off. So then I killed some of your people, and you killed some of my people, and I killed some more of your people. In the end Peggy was dead, I still had my shit, and you still had your shit, but my sister was dead. Now you've killed my son, and I asked myself, if I had backed off – let you win after you killed Peggy – would my boy still be alive? And the answer is that it doesn't matter now because I didn't and now he's just as dead as Peggy, and the business doesn't matter to me any more but I've got nothing else worth living for. So the only thing that matters to me now is seeing you burn... And now as my sister the Constructionist used to say, 'All the chickens are coming home to roost'.'"

"What the fuck is that supposed to mean?"

"You pride yourself in being a smart man, Tarent. You hired a police agency to find your daughter. Peggy's partner was a cop. A cop named Conner McVee. Why don't you call your police agency and see who they sent out to save your daughter?" Mishy laughed as the transmission closed.

Tarent stared at the computer screen for a minute. "Computer, call James Rank." In a second James Rank was on his screen.

"Not yet, Tarent. I'll contact you as soon as we have the girl," Rank said plainly

"Who did you assign to retrieve my daughter from Mishy?" Tarent demanded.

"The computer spit out only one name, and I sent that agent. I assure you that if anyone can return your daughter in one piece, it's her."

"Who the fuck did you send!" Tarent demanded.

"Conner McVee."

CHAPTER 3

The car had to be driven manually. Elantra had never seen such a thing in her life. She'd sure never seen anything like Slum Town. The machines here were old and in bad repair if they worked at all. The buildings didn't look much better. And everywhere there were neon signs and holograms showing pictures of people doing things they shouldn't have been doing in the public eye and certainly not without a very heavy screen. She wasn't an idiot, and she'd seen some of the more unsavory programs the HV had to show. She knew what these places were; they were clubs, clubs that sold alcohol and drugs and sex, or at least something very close to it. She stroked Mr. Buttons as she looked out at the strange streets. "What is *fuck?*" she asked.

Conner choked on her own laughter. "Intercourse," she answered using a word the young woman was likely to understand.

Elantra shuddered. "That's what I thought... It's funny. Just tonight I wanted to get out of the building so bad that I bypassed my father's security system and slipped out. Now all I want to do is get back home. How long will it take?"

"I'm not taking you home, not yet anyway," Conner said matter-of-factly. "Your father wants you taken to a safe house. He's afraid they'll come after you again."

"They *who?* I mean... who were those men? I don't understand. You are a cop, aren't you?"

"Of course I'm a cop." Conner nodded towards the agency tattoo on her shoulder and the girl nodded. "It's really very simple. Your father has been trying to take over Mishy's operation for years, but he hasn't succeeded. Tarent recently had Mishy's wife and son killed. Apparently he thought this would completely demoralize Mishy and then he could easily take over Mishy's turf. What he didn't count on was that Mishy now feels he has nothing to live for, and he's putting all of his efforts into taking your father down. Taking you was only the first step in his plan, and things aren't likely to be safe around your father for a very long time."

"This is all a mistake!" Elantra laughed nervously. "My father is a business man. He does something like import-export of... things. He could never kill anyone."

Conner stared out at the night, brooding and silent.

"Well he couldn't," Elantra explained.

"Isn't it hard to breathe with your head so firmly stuck up your ass?" Conner asked with a sly smile.

"That would be physically impossible, so I'm assuming it has some double meaning, and I'm thinking it's probably not nice," Elantra said hotly.

"Forget about it."

"Where are we going? We're not staying here, are we? I don't like it here."

"No one actually *likes* it in Slum Town. But, no, we're not staying here." She ignored the girl's first question.

"I don't want to go anywhere with you. You take me home. I want to go home."

"The apple doesn't fall far from the tree," Conner mumbled, then turned an angry face on the girl and said in a low hiss. "I don't give a good do-diddily-damn what *you* want. *I* do what *I* want – you get that? I only *ever* do what *I* want. I don't take orders from you. I don't take orders from anyone."

The computer in the car buzzed up. "Hammer. Man, what are you doing?" Jason asked. "You're heading further into Slum Town."

"Leave me alone, Jason," Conner hissed back.

"You have the girl, don't you?"

"I said leave me alone, Jason," Conner said in a more menacing tone.

"Oh, God, man! What the fuck do you think you're doing, Hammer?" he asked in a panic, then ordered, "Car! Drive faster."

"I have to do what I have to do, Jason. Transmission close." The computer screen cleared.

"What's going on?" Elantra asked suspiciously.

"Cop shit. Don't worry about it," Conner answered.

James had just assured Tarent that all was well when Jason Hunter's panicked face filled the screen. "Boss! Hammer's gone off the end."

James took a deep breath. "What do you mean?"

"She's got the girl, but she's running into Slum Town. Boss, I think she's kidnapping the girl herself."

"Stay on her, Jay. Computer, find Conner McVee." Conner's face appeared on the screen, and she smiled broadly at him. "McVee, what the hell are you up to?"

"Tarent asked me to keep the girl out of the way until things with Mishy cool down. By the law he can hire me out from under you without me giving you notice. I'll come back to work for the Brakston Agency as soon as this job is done, don't you worry. The money is just too good to pass, you understand..."

"I know what you're doing, McVee. Do you really think you can cover your butt..?"

"If I have a big enough net, sir." She smiled. "Computer, terminate link with central."

"McVee! Damn it, McVee!" The transmission ended and all attempts to link back up with her were a waste of time. "Computer, find Jason Hunter." Jason appeared. "I'm transferring the trace signal from Conner's body to your computer. Don't lose her, the device only works on short radio frequency and it has no GPS capabilities..."

"What! Why the hell not?"

"Because if it did anyone including the bad guys could find her at any time. It's there to help us locate her in case of an emergency, not them."

"But this way... it's damn near useless!"

"Not if you don't lose her."

Jason sighed and watched his computer; he smiled when a little blip appeared on his screen. "Transfer complete. Boss, what's Hammer up to?"

James thought about it only a minute. "Tarent hired McVee to protect his daughter until Mishy cools off."

Jason laughed. "Isn't that a little lame?"

"That's the story, Jason."

Tarent called Mishy, and Mishy looked gloatingly back. "What will she do to Elantra?" Tarent asked in a defeated tone.

"Conner loved Peggy a lot. At Peggy's funeral she told me she wouldn't rest until you paid for what you did, and I don't think that she has. She's spent most of the last five years trying to put your ass away, or kill you, but of course you cover your ass too well and you never stick your cowardly neck out of your hole. So nothing – that's a lot of frustration. They threw this opportunity in her lap, and she's running with it..."

"But what do you think she's going to do to Elantra? She's just a girl. She knows nothing about the business, nothing about me, nothing about the world out there..."

Mishy shook violently. "My son was only ten years old. Do you really think you can do whatever you like and that nothing will ever happen to you? Peggy was a wonderful person; she wouldn't have hurt a fly, a true innocent. She had her whole life ahead of her and everything to live for. If you want to know what's going to happen to your daughter, I suggest you try remembering what you did to my sister. The way I remember it, Conner and I had to identify the pieces. Transmission close."

The screen returned to swirling colors. Tarent took in a deep breath. He remembered what he'd had done to Peggy Mishy. "The sins of the fathers," he muttered.

"What's that, boss?" Wayne asked.

"Nothing, Wayne. Computer, get me everything you can call up on a police agent named Conner McVee."

Conner looked over at the girl. She was sound asleep and snoring in a not very lady-like manner. She'd probably gotten more exercise last night than she'd had in her whole life up till then, not to mention more excitement.

The sun was starting to come up and Jason Hunter was still on her tail. They were in the middle of nowhere – or at least they were fifty miles out of Freight City. She had shielded her car against such things as the global positioning system long ago. If Jason lost her now, there would be no way for them to use the tracer on her. If she got rid of Jason she could buy herself some time; maybe enough time.

She pulled over onto the shoulder and stopped. She got out, grabbing her nail gun off the back seat as she went. As Jason pulled in behind her she set her gun on high, aimed and fired. First the tires, and then the block itself. The girl started screaming. "Get down and shut up!" Conner ordered. She walked over to the car with a hammer, and kept hitting the side window of Jason's car until it smashed. Jason was cringing in the front seat screaming at his computer.

"James! She's fucking lost it, man! She's..." He looked at

Conner's smiling face as she reached in the broken window of his car and opened his door. Jason reached slowly for his gun. "Now, Hammer, I don't want to have to..." She took his weapon away from him and threw him out of his car in one motion. With the hammer in hand she smashed his entire computer console. Jason picked himself up off the dirt. "Damn it, Hammer! What are you playing at?"

Conner turned slowly around and in those few awful seconds Jason imagined all sorts of horrors. He fully expected her to kill him with one of her primitive weapons. She didn't, she just stared at him with her one eye full of contempt. She had never liked him, never liked the kind of cop he was, and if he hadn't known it before he knew it now as she looked him up and down, as if trying to decide whether he was worth killing or not.

Finally she hissed at him, "Tell Rank. Stay the fuck away from me. I'm going out of tracer range and I'm taking the girl. If anybody asks, I'm working a protection job for Tarent Powers. It doesn't matter if he denies it. Don't come looking for me. If you do I'll kill ya. Leave me the fuck alone. I've given a lot to Brakston, and I've given a lot to the citizens of Freight City. Now it's time for them to give something back. If this works I'll take Tarent Powers down and ensure Brakston Agency stays on top, but Rank is going to have to trust me. You all are."

Jason nodded, not daring to disagree with her. "How am I going to get back to town?"

"God gave you feet so that you could walk." Conner turned, walked to her car, got in and drove off.

Jason watched her drive away and then screamed after her. "You... Fucking religious fanatic!"

The girl was still screaming. She might have even been saying something. Conner didn't know because she wasn't really listening. Conner popped a CD in the player, turned it up on high, and started singing along. The girl stopped screaming. After a moment she moved to look into Conner's mouth.

"What are you doing?" she asked, obviously confused.

"I'm singing."

"Machines do that for us," she said in disbelief. She stared at the CD player. "What's that?" she asked pointing.

"It's a CD player. There's music by live performers, and

you record it on the disk and then you put it in and you get to hear them sing."

"The same thing over and over again!" Elantra asked in disbelief.

"There are usually five to ten songs on a disk, but yeah over and over again."

"Why? A dygarhythms system will play music on voice command, and it never plays the same thing twice."

"Well that's a good reason all in itself. Besides, it sounds like shit and there are no words, no soul. You can't sing along with it. Hearing it doesn't remind you of the time you were laying this really hot blond chick under an oak tree. Not that a budding building brat such as yourself would know the first thing about nostalgia," Conner hissed. She took in a breath and tried to conjure up some patience. "Didn't you ever hear a tune that you wished you could hear again?"

Elantra thought about that for a second. "No," she answered truthfully.

"Because all you've heard is that dygarhythms crap!"

The girl was silent just staring at Conner. "What the fuck are you looking at now?" Conner hissed when the length of time and the intensity with which she was looking at her started to annoy Conner.

"If fuck means sex, I don't understand the use of fuck in that sentence. You have a lot of scars." If she was upset at all about Conner's' screaming or apparent bad temper she wasn't letting on, but then what could you really expect? She was Tarent Power's brat.

"So nice of you to point that out," Conner said through gritted teeth.

"I was only wondering why you hadn't had the surgery done in such a manner that it wouldn't scar."

"You won't understand this any more than the idea that I enjoy listening to the same song over and over again, but each one of these scars represents an event - a part of my past that may be gone but is not forgotten. Think of it as a very personal scrapbook. If God had meant for us to forget the pain of our past It wouldn't have made us scar…"

"You're a Constructionist!" Elantra screeched in disbelief.

"Well, duh!" Conner laughed.

"Where are you taking me? I… I want to talk to my father."

Conner realized that was probably what the girl had been

screaming while she had been busy not paying attention earlier. "I told you before, I don't care what you want. I'm taking you someplace safe, and when we get there I'll let you talk to your father, if I feel like it."

"I'm scared. I want to go home." Elantra started crying.

She kept crying, and Conner kept ignoring her and her stupid cat.

"I don't like you!" the girl finally screamed. "In fact I hate you!"

"Then I guess we'll hold off sending out the wedding invites," Conner said.

Elantra dried her nose on her sleeve and longed for her cleaning cabinet. She felt filthy. She stared at Conner and the cop smiled broadly back.

"I guess we could just live together for awhile first."

"If you're trying to make me vomit you're doing a good job," Elantra said in her best snooty voice.

"Oh you'll want me. Sooner or later all the girls want me," Conner said. She reached out and grabbed hold of Elantra's leg close to her hip. The girl slapped at her hand till she let go.

"I like men," Elantra said matter-of-factly.

"Funny, they all say that, too." Conner laughed at the expression on the girl's face.

"You're just trying to annoy me," Elantra said. "And succeeding beyond your wildest dreams. I don't believe you're working for my father. If you were, you'd let me talk to him. My father would never hire someone like you. My father..."

"I wonder if you're as naive as you seem, or if you know just what kind of scum your father is..."

"My father is the greatest, most noble man I have ever known..."

"How did your mother die, Elantra?" Conner asked.

It was night. She had heard a noise – *someone screaming. She stumbled through the dark. For some reason the walkways weren't running, and lights weren't anticipating her direction and going on. There was a glint of light coming from her parents' bedroom. Her father was standing there with something shiny and long in his hand. It was dripping something red on the floor. Her mother lay on the ground behind him. There was red stuff all over her, and she was still. Her eyes were open, staring at Elantra, but she couldn't see.*

Elantra knew she couldn't. Her father was screaming, "Computer! Send police! Send doctors! My wife has just killed herself." He looked at Elantra then yelled. "Elantra, go to your room!"

She couldn't move. She just stood there looking at her mother, wondering why she didn't smile at her, wondering what all that red stuff was.

"Elantra!" her father screamed again. "Go to your room!"

This time her feet worked. She ran into her room and into the corner where she sank down on the floor and started to cry. Her life had changed forever that night. Her mother had touched her, held her when she was scared. Since her mother had died... Well, her father never held her. He wouldn't even touch her. Contact made him nervous.

"My mother killed herself," Elantra answered coldly.

"Yeah, that's the official report," Conner said plainly. "They couldn't ever prove he did it. Of course, we can never prove he did anything."

"My father is not a criminal! He didn't kill my mother!" Elantra screamed at Conner.

Conner shrugged. "OK. So let's say, for the sake of argument, that she did kill herself. Did you ever wonder why?" Conner asked.

"She was unhappy," Elantra snapped back. "Who knows why someone kills themselves?"

"Or for that matter if they really did."

CHAPTER 4

"*You fucking idiot!*" Tarent screamed at James, and James for one was glad that there was half a city between them. "You sent Mishy's sister's widow to retrieve my daughter! What the hell were you thinking?"

"The computer didn't think there would be a problem. There shouldn't have been, unless of course you really had Peggy Mishy killed. Which there was no way for the computer to know since you didn' get caught if you did…"

"Damn it! You knew!" Tarent rephrased it. "You knew that Conner McVee thought I killed Peggy Mishy. You knew, and you put her on the case anyway. I swear if she does anything to my daughter…"

James clicked his tongue. "Threatenin' a police agent is a minimum five months in prison, an I don' think I have to tell ya how many enemies ya got there… I didn' know that Conner thought ya killed Peggy. I have here a contract Conner McVee just faxed through which says ya have temporarily hired her away from my agency as a protector agent…"

"I never hired that crazy bitch. She's a fucking dyke for God's sake! My daughter has grown up in the building. She's never been exposed to…"

"…the scum that people like you create." Rank finished for him with a shrug. "The contract ya made with Hammer is all on public disk. All very legal an above board. I appreciate what you're tryin' to do…"

"God damn it! I'm not trying to run a cover. I'm telling you that one of your agents has kidnapped my daughter!"

"*I have to go to the bathroom,*" Elantra said.

Conner had no doubt that she did. After all, Conner had stopped to take a leak three times while the kid was asleep.

"So you've said a dozen times. I've told you your options," Conner said with a sigh. She was tired, they were still fifty miles away from their destination, and she had to go as bad as the girl did. She pulled over. "Don't think of it as roughing it, think of it as the world is your toilet." She reached in her glove box and pulled out a roll of toilet paper.

"What's that?" Elantra asked.

"After you pee, you take a few pieces of paper off the roll and you dry yourself off."

"You're kidding me!" Elantra shrieked.

"It's the truth. You want to watch me go first?" she asked.

"No!" Elantra screeched. "Door open." The door did not respond to her order. "Door open!" When the door still did not open she said angrily, "Your crappy car is broken."

Conner sighed, got out of the car, walked around and let the girl out. Elantra glared up at Conner and Conner smiled back. "Can I watch you go?"

"Most certainly not." Elantra grabbed a few pieces of paper off the roll and marched off into the woods. Conner went in the other direction. When she got back the girl was still gone and so was the cat.

"Fucking little bitch!" Conner grabbed her gun off the back seat and started down the path the way the girl had gone. She flipped her patch up and the electronic eye under it scanned the area for signs of heat and easily found the girl and the cat. She appeared to be running. Conner pulled down her patch and ran after her. "Stupid fucking girl," she hissed. In seconds she had caught up with Elantra. "What the fuck do you think you're doing?" Conner demanded.

"Getting away from you!" Elantra tripped and fell, and the cat went flying, screaming all the way to the ground. Conner ran up to Elantra and jerked her to her feet. Tears were streaming down the girl's face although it was hard to tell if it was because she was actually hurt or if she was just that scared.

Conner shook her hard. "Look around you!" she screamed.

Elantra looked. All around her were green plants, some in bloom, and huge trees – a dense forest. To her left there was a creek flowing over rocks. She saw birds, real birds flying. "It's beautiful!" she gasped.

"Yes it is," Conner said with an impatient sigh. "And just how long do you think a Freight City building brat like you could live out here?"

"I'm scared," Elantra cried. "I'm scared. I just want to go home."

"And you really think you can get there from here without me? With that fucking cat... Do you even have any idea where you are? Do you even remember which direction the road is? Once you got to the road, how would you get a ride, and how do you know whether the person you are about to ride with isn't one of Mishy's boys? How do you know they won't rape you or steal your cat and kill you? Besides which, there just isn't that much traffic. How many cars have you seen on the road today?"

"One, maybe two..."

"Exactly. No one travels anymore. That's why the roads are in such shitty shape. Even if they absolutely have to travel they get on a plane or a rail and they fly there. No one has time to drive. Do you see a fucking airport or rail terminal here?"

"No, but..."

"But what, girl? There are no buts. I'm *it*. I'm your only ticket back to civilization. Right now if it wasn't for me you'd be dead. Right now I'm the only thing keeping you alive. I'm your only friend, sugar, and you by God better remember that. Now come on, we've wasted enough time." Conner started pulling her back towards the car, her hand clamped firmly to the girl's upper arm.

"Where's my cat?"

"Fuck the cat!" Canner screamed.

"You can't make me," Elantra said defiantly, and stopped dead in her tracks so that Conner would have had to drag her to get her back to the car.

"Come on, chick, don't make me carry you."

Elantra ignored her. "Here, Mr. Buttons! Come here, Mr. Buttons!"

"Mr. Buttons!" Conner's laughter momentarily washed away her anger. She let go of Elantra's arm. "Mr. *Buttons*?"

"When he was a kitten he used to like to play with the buttons on my blouse," Elantra defended.

"This kid I used to hang with told me that when he was a baby he used to play with the shit in his pants. I'm thinking he ought to be thanking God that he didn't come from your family."

The cat ran up to Elantra, and she picked him up.

"Let's go," Conner ordered.

Elantra followed without further prodding. "Can I talk to

my daddy now?" She asked as she climbed in the car.

"For the last time... You can talk to him when we get where we're going."

Like most Constructionist towns Wrench Town got its name from a common hand tool. Elantra had only seen anything like it in her virtual reality history vid. It was like being on another planet, or more accurately, in another age.

Conner opened the window, took in a deep breath and smiled. Elantra smelled it, too. It was the smell of food, but it was much stronger and more vivid than any food she had ever smelled before. Her mouth watered. It was a new sensation, or at least she couldn't remember it ever happening before, but then she'd never been hungry before, either.

Conner pulled up in front of a restaurant and stopped. She turned the key and the car's engine was silent. She pulled the keys out of the ignition.

"What are those?" Elantra asked.

"They're called keys. They're used to turn the car off and on."

"Wouldn't it be easier just to say, 'Car, start'?"

"Yes, but I prefer sticking things in to places, working them around and pulling them out." Her lewd remark was wasted on the girl – who obviously missed the double meaning. There was an edge of disappointment in Conner's voice when she said as she got out of the car, "Come on. Let's go get something to eat."

It was two hours after the morning crowd and about two hours before the lunch crowd, so the place was pretty empty. First Elantra had bitched about leaving the cat in the car, then she had bitched that her blouse was torn and she was hardly presentable to be in public. Once in the restaurant she had bitched about how unsanitary it was to eat someplace where total strangers ate, and that she wasn't about to eat food that had been touched by human hands. Conner had ordered for her anyway and then she had bitched that she was never going to eat anything that came out of a chicken's butt. She had now eaten everything on her plate and was slowly working on what was on Conner's. "Do you mind?" Conner asked.

"I'm very hungry," the girl said. Conner pushed her plate

towards the girl and went to pay the check.

"Haven't seen you in Wrench Town for awhile, Hammer," the waitress said taking her money.

"Haven't felt much like vacationing since Peg died. Keep the change, Helen."

"Thanks. So, is that what they're wearing in the big city?" Helen asked nodding her head towards Elantra.

"You know building folk, not a bit of sense."

"So... is the building brat your new lady?"

"No, just a friend interested in learning our ways. She's thinking of converting. Do you know if Doc Pherson's in town?"

"Why? You got trouble with an implant?"

"You might say that. Is he around?"

"He went to the lake, but he should be back in a couple of months. His intern's taking care of his patients here, but I don't think he knows a damn thing about implants. Is it bad?"

"It's not life threatening. It's just something I should have had taken care of a long time ago."

"You want me to have some supplies sent to your cabin?"

"You know, Helen, that completely slipped my mind. Yeah, I could use some supplies. I'll make a list."

Elantra came over and watched intently as Conner made lines on the paper. "What are you doing now?"

"I'm writing. It's a lost art of the audio computer age. We read, too." Conner smiled at the look on Elantra's face. "You'll find we do most things differently here. What size do you wear?"

"Six..."

"And your shoes?"

"A nine..."

"Lord you got big ole feet for such a tiny little girl. Helen, get this girl some sensible clothes and shoes, too. Everything she's got... Well, you can see it's not appropriate for Constructionist life."

"Will do, Citizen." She took the list Conner handed her. "Good to see you again, Hammer... You gonna come by the club tonight?"

"Does a baby shit yellow?"

They drove another five minutes into a completely wooded area. In the woods ahead of them, Elantra saw a small house that appeared to be made from dead trees stacked up. Around it were huge, living trees.

"Peg and I used to come up here to reaffirm our faith. The cabin is pretty primitive, but if you'll allow yourself to leave your prima donna bullshit here in the car I think you'll enjoy your stay, and we should be fairly safe here."

Elantra followed behind Conner. She watched as Conner put one of those key things into the door and turned the round thing. Conner pushed and the door opened. As they walked in, the cat yowled and jumped out of Elantra's arms. Conner flipped a switch on the wall, and the lights came on. Conner sighed. It really had been a long time. There was dust everywhere. The cat walked right into the fireplace, dug a hole in the old ash still there and took a dump. No doubt it looked like the self-cleaning shoot he was accustomed to using at home.

"Fucking beautiful," Conner mumbled. She was not about to tell Elantra at that point that the shit was not going to clean itself up. Conner was tired and she wanted to sleep. "This is the living room, there's the kitchen, there's the bathroom, and there is my bedroom. You can either sleep here on the couch or you can sleep with me. I won't promise not to take advantage of you, because I most probably will. So if you want to have sex, sleep with me, and if you don't, then sleep on the couch, but I'm not giving up my bed."

"I'll take the couch," Elantra said. She was too tired to protest Conner's vulgar comments, but not too tired to bitch about the house. "This house is dirty and it smells bad."

Of course it smells bad your fucking cat just took a dump in the fireplace. Conner smiled and said, "Bitch, bitch, bitch..."

"What's that mean?"

"It means you complain too much." Conner opened a trunk and pulled out some bedding. "Here." She threw the girl a pillow and a blanket. "Sleep good." She took her bedclothes and headed for her bedroom.

"Hey!" the girl hollered. Conner turned an unhappy, tired face towards her.

"Hey what?"

"What's your real name?"

Conner figured that wasn't too much to ask. "My name is Conner McVee. My friends call me Hammer."

Elantra nodded. "My name is Elantra Powers, my friends call me Lanny," she said nervously.

"Yes, I know." Conner smiled and went in her room, closing the door behind her.

Elantra stared at the computer box Conner had removed from her car. Conner had said she could talk to her father when they reached their destination, and they were here. She was about to walk over and get the computer when Conner's door opened. She walked out, walked over and picked up the computer. Elantra stared at her in dumbfounded disbelief, and Conner smiled broadly.

"Yes. I know exactly what you're thinking." She took the computer and went back in her room. "It will take some time to make a clean link. I'll do it when I get up. I need some sleep now."

Elantra sat down on the couch carefully. Eventually she lay down and waited for the couch to make her comfortable, but it didn't budge. She even had to cover herself up, and that wasn't easy. Her toes were either sticking out or her chest was. Finally she got comfortable. She stared at the ceiling. "Light off," she ordered. "I said light off!" she screamed. Conner walked in, flipped a switch on the wall, and the lights went off. She double checked the lock on the door and then started back for her room. "It's still light," Elantra complained.

"You're giving me a giant pain in my ass." Conner walked over and pulled the curtains over the window. Elantra watched in wide-eyed amazement.

"They're called curtains. They're used to filter the light out of the room instead of using computerized glass," Conner explained. She walked over and covered the girl up. "You warm enough?"

"Yes."

"Then go the fuck to sleep!" Conner screamed.

"What's that mean, go to sex asleep? Do you want me to dream about sex or have sex till I go to sleep, or..."

"I want you to shut up and go to sleep. It's that simple. Were you raised in a box?"

Elantra was silent. She *had* been raised in a box, what could she say? Conner threw up her hands and went back in her room; she started to close her door.

"Conner McVee?"

"What is it now?" Conner yelled back.

"I'm scared. Could you..."

"I'll leave the door open," she sighed. "Now, *please*, let me go to sleep."

Elantra watched Conner lie down. She could see her from where she lay on the couch, and for some reason that made her feel better.

Elantra was sure she'd never get to sleep with all the strange thoughts that were racing through her head, and the oddness of her surroundings. She stared at the ceiling for several minutes, finally decided she wasn't comfortable enough to go to sleep, and then she did.

CHAPTER 5

Elantra didn't know how long she had slept; she woke to some strange pounding noise. She looked up and Conner was opening the door. A dark-haired man walked in with two containers and set them down on a table by the door, and then he hugged Conner McVee. It seemed that these Constructionists didn't understand germ theory and thought nothing of bodily contact. "Good to see you," he said.

"You, too, Bud. What do I owe you?"

"Forty-seven fifty." Conner handed him something Elantra had never seen before. Round pieces of metal stamped with some design she couldn't quite make out.

"Be staying with us long this time?"

"Could be," Conner said noncommittally.

Bud looked past Conner at Elantra. "She's very pretty," Elantra heard Bud whisper to Conner.

"She's not mine, Bud," Conner said with a laugh.

"To hear the girls round these parts talk, she'll be yours if ya want her," Bud said, and then changed the subject. "House is a mess, you want me to help you clean it up?

"Nah, I got it. It will take me a couple of hours at the worst. Thanks though."

"Well, in that case I better make like a baby and go. I have a lot to accomplish before it gets dark. Have a good stay, Hammer."

"Go in peace and do good work, Citizen," Conner replied.

"May the work of your hands bring pleasure to the world," Bud answered and left.

Conner looked at Elantra. Her fake sleeping routine hadn't fooled her. "So, I suppose you're going to want to talk to your daddy."

"Please," Elantra sat up. It wasn't easy; the couch didn't make one move to help her.

"Give me a few minutes to prepare the equipment, and talk to your father myself. I'll call you when I'm ready. Until then stay in here out of my hair." Conner went into her room, got the unit and took it in the kitchen. She made sure the girl was still in the living room, and then she shut and locked the door and made the link.

Tarent glared at her, and she smiled broadly back.

"You must be Conner McVee," he said coolly.

Conner smiled her most confident smile. "Must be."

Tarent glared back and in a voice dripping acid started, "McVee, if you do anything to my daughter..."

"Hold it! Let me see," Conner made a big deal about looking around. "I have a really big vendetta, a bunch of very dangerous weapons, your daughter, and... Oh, yeah... You have no idea where I am. I thought I'd better remind you of that, because it was beginning to sound a little bit like maybe you were going to threaten me."

Tarent gritted his teeth. "What do you want from me?"

"You know what's funny? You killed the only person I ever loved, and I've spent the last five years busting my ass trying to burn you, and you don't even know who the fuck I am. Or at least you didn't 'til now. No... Wait a minute. That's not funny; it's just sad." Then Conner laughed maniacally. "Big shots like you... You just don't pay any attention to what's going on out in the streets. You're like Teflon; nothing sticks to you. You sit up there in your big steel and glass tower playing God and ruining peoples lives, and it never dawns on you that one of those little insignificant bugs you see crawling around down there in the street might actually jump up and bite you on the ass some day. You took something from me, something you can't give back. Now I have something of yours. I want you to pay for what you did to me, what you did to Peggy..."

"I don't know who you're talking about," Tarent said.

Conner's cool chipped away and her anger took control of her features. "Don't make me relive the moment when I had to go identify the pieces of her body at the morgue, because if I do... I'm going to snap and go absolutely bumb-fuck crazy, and you might be going to look at body parts and deciding whether it's your daughter or not. Save your lies for someone else! I hold all the cards, dick head. Push my hand, push it just a little bit, and I'll snap her fucking head off and mail it to you in a box. Now do you remember who Peggy was? Does that refresh your memory?"

"I didn't kill Peggy Mishy..."

"I know that." She laughed, though she was obviously not amused. "You never get your hands dirty, do you? I killed all the guys that did it." She smiled at the look on his face then. "Yeah, that's right. They didn't just disappear, and Mishy didn't do it. I did. You had Peg killed. It's the same thing to me. In fact it's worse. You're the real villain. I killed the fuckers who actually did your dirty work, but I've never been able to get to you. Now, I have."

"What do you want me to do?" Tarent asked again, his own cool evaporating in the wake of Conner's rage.

"You got two choices, kill yourself, or admit you had Peg killed and turn yourself in," Conner informed

"You must be fucking crazy..."

"I'm surprised you know that word. Your little girl sure doesn't, but I'm teaching her. I can teach her lots of things," Conner licked her lips.

"You fucking dyke, I'll..."

Conner clicked her tongue and shook her head. She held up her nail gun. "Don't make me tell you again not to threaten me."

Tarent took a deep breath and seemed to count to ten before continuing. "Those terms are unacceptable, McVee. Why would I agree to them?"

"Because you care more for your daughter than you care about yourself. I doubt that you do actually; it's a long shot. But I'm betting that when I kill her it's still going to twist in your gut, and the knowledge that all you would have had to do to save her would have been to pay for the crimes you've committed. Well, if you're any kind of man at all that would have to eat your insides. Of course I doubt you're even that much of a man, so I'll have to settle for you losing face. The great Tarent Powers can't protect his own daughter. Couldn't keep her from meeting the same terrible fate as Peggy Mishy..."

"All right! All right!" Tarent screamed. "I have to think about it."

"See, a real man would be eating a gun about now. You want to see her one more time?"

"Yes I do," Tarent said swallowing his pride.

"She doesn't know she's been kidnapped. At least not by me. She thinks you hired me to protect her. It's better for her if she continues to believe that, at least for the time being. Make it good, Tarent, because unless you turn yourself in and she comes to see you on visiting day, you're never going to see her again."

"Damn it, McVee. You're a police agent. Elantra has done nothing..."

"Peggy didn't do nothin', either. You didn't care. She wasn't part of Mishy's organization, and never had been. That didn't stop you from killing her. I'm tired of playing by the rules, Tarent. I'm tired of you running free to do whatever the hell you like, when I live in a prison of grief and loneliness that you created. Being one of the good guys has done nothing but turn me into a lonely pile of scrap metal. This is my only chance to make you pay. I've tried to do it the right way, but you just stay holed up in your ivory tower slipping right through the legal cracks. You've left me with no choices. Peggy was my life. I died when you killed her. The things you did to her I'm going to do to Elantra unless you play my game by my rules. Don't make me wait too long for your answer."

Tarent nodded.

Conner got up walked over and unlocked the door. "Elantra, you can come in now."

Elantra walked in and Conner followed her. She sat down in the chair that Conner indicated slowly, because she had figured out it wasn't going to rise for her.

Conner stood behind Elantra, out of the girl's view, but in full view of her father's terminal, nail gun in hand.

"Elantra, are you OK?" Tarent asked.

"I'm scared, Daddy, but I'm OK. I want to come home."

"Soon, baby. It's not safe now..."

"Daddy, they keep saying you're some kind of gangster. You're not, are you?"

"No, of course not."

"Terminate link," Conner ordered. The computer shut down.

"What! Why did you do that?" Elantra screamed. "I hardly got to talk to him at all."

"We had reached the time limit. Any longer and someone in the net might have fixed on our location. I'm sorry," Conner said with a shrug.

Elantra snarled back at her. "I don't think you are. I don't think you're sorry at all. I think you like to make me angry."

"Could be." Conner shrugged coolly at the girl's anger. "Why don't you get a bath, then get into some real clothes and we'll go out for awhile?"

"What makes you think that I would want to go anywhere in this awful place with you?" Elantra all but screamed.

"You're making a big mistake there. See, you're living under the delusion that I'm *asking* you. That I might actually give a damn what you want, and see... I don't really give a good rat's ass what you'd like. I'm going out, and I can't leave you here alone. So get your happy ass in there and take a shower. Once again, in case you didn't hear me the first time, *I don't care what you want,*" Conner said.

It turned out to be a bigger hassle than Conner had anticipated. She had forgotten just how differently the building people lived. She had to convince Elantra that getting water on her would not hurt her, and then show her how to get it the right temperature.

"It's barbaric! You mean to tell me you don't have a proper cleaning cabinet?" Elantra had balked after looking in.

"Yes, I do. It's called a shower. You go inside, and instead of having this horrible machine steam you and then vacuum all your pores and fluff your hair, water streams down on you. You take a wash cloth and soap like so and scrub the dirt off. Then you rinse."

"I might as well go to the gym..." She was still bitching when Conner left the room. Thirty minutes later she was still in the shower.

Elantra had been in the virtual pool a hundred times, but it was nothing like the feel of real water on your skin. It wasn't even close. Finally the water got too cool and she got out. She waited for something to turn on and dry her off, but it didn't happen. The water didn't stop running, either. She looked at the two knobs she had seen Conner McVee turn. She grabbed hold of one and twisted. The water slowed down. She turned the other and the water went off. She smiled proudly. It wasn't all that hard. But she was still wet, and it was starting to lose its novelty. She was also getting cold.

Conner McVee walked in with some sort of cloth in her hand, she made no attempt to hide the fact that she was looking at Elantra's body. She smiled, apparently liking what she was seeing, and Elantra wanted to slap her smug face.

"Cold?" Conner asked, paying special attention to Elantra's erect nipples.

"Yes," Elantra said through chattering teeth. "So are you getting your thrills?"

"Not yet," Conner said with a wicked smile. "Here." She threw Elantra the towel. "Dry yourself off."

Elantra barely caught the towel, and she used it to cover herself. "How?" she asked.

"I thought you'd never ask." Conner took the towel and started to dry Elantra.

"Hey, hey!" Elantra protested.

"I'm just showing you how to do it so next time you can do it yourself." Conner towel dried the girl's head, rubbing her body up against Elantra's in the process. "And now I'm getting that thrill you were asking about earlier," she breathed in Elantra's ear.

"OK, OK!" Elantra grabbed the towel out of Conner's all too willing hands. "I think I have the idea now. I think I can do this myself."

Conner smiled. "It won't be as much fun."

"Maybe not for you," Elantra said hotly. Conner laughed as she left, closing the door behind her. Elantra started drying herself off. It was a lot of work, and McVee was right, it wasn't as much fun.

"Your clothes are on the shelf there. You want me to help you get dressed?"

"I think I can manage on my own. Thanks anyway," she hissed back.

"If you need any help..."

"I won't." She felt of the cloth; it felt good. The pants were made out of some sort of heavy blue cloth, and the bright red blouse was very soft – like Mr. Buttons. She put them on, and they made her feel instantly warm. She liked the way they felt even if she wasn't particularly thrilled by the way they looked. Her hair was still wet. "Conner McVee, my hair is still wet." Conner walked in, opened a drawer manually and pulled out a thing that looked like a weapon. There was a thing hanging off of it with two little prongs on it. Conner pushed the prongs into some holes in the wall and pushed a button on the machine. It made a hideous noise and warm air blew out of it. She handed it to Elantra, who looked into the end of it. When the hot air blew in her face she dropped it. Conner caught it just before it hit the floor.

Conner laughed and turned the machine off.

"You help me only to have an excuse to touch me."

"Yeah... But do you want my help or not?"

"Show me how," Elantra said in an exasperated tone.

Conner grabbed a broad-toothed comb out of the drawer. "This is a comb. I'm going to drag it through your hair to get the tangles out."

Elantra made a face. "Will it hurt?"

"Probably not. It may even feel good." Conner carefully combed the tangles out of Elantra's shoulder length hair, and then she started to blow it dry, enjoying running her fingers through the length of it. When Elantra's hair was dry it fell in soft ringlets all around her face.

Conner looked into Elantra's eyes and felt something she hadn't felt in a long time, something emotional, internal. Something more than the external lust she had been feeling just moments before. It was crazy! She couldn't afford to get attached to anyone, and of all the women in the world certainly not this one. She owed it to Peggy to make sure that Tarent paid, one way or the other. Elantra looked quickly away.

Conner took a deep breath, and put the comb and hair dryer away. "Go on out and wait for me, and don't do anything stupid." The girl nodded and left the bathroom silently.

Damned empathy! The girl had felt something, too. Hammer had felt it with her implant, and she'd seen it in Elantra's eyes. First lust, and then confusion. Conner wasn't particularly surprised; the building brat had probably never been touched that much by human hands in her entire life. It was only natural that she would enjoy it, and only natural that it would confuse her.

Elantra walked into the living room and sat down on the couch. Conner had built a fire and it blazed. Elantra had seen a computer image of a fireplace, and she now realized that was what it was and not a cat potty port. The fire was beautiful and hot. The whole room was getting warm. She was warm, but not from the fire.

When Conner had looked into her eyes she had felt a strange tingling sensation, like a slight electrical charge was running through her body. She had wanted Conner McVee to touch her. She had wanted to touch Conner McVee, not so much on the outside, but inside in her soul. The weird part being that she had never really believed in the whole soul thing.

Elantra had never actually had sex with a person, but she'd had virtual sex dozens of times. What she had felt in the program had been very close to what she had felt when Conner McVee had looked at her, and that just wasn't right.

Conner walked out of the bathroom dressed in much the same way she had been before. She sat down on the couch and pulled some long tubular things onto her feet. She threw some at Elantra. "Better put these on. It's going to be cold out tonight." Elantra watched how Conner put them on, and then she did the same thing. They were warm and soft. She smiled.

"What are these clothes made out of?" she asked.

"Cotton fiber. It's a plant. Beats the hell out of poly and rubber doesn't it?" Conner asked with a smile.

"It's soft." She watched Conner put on her boots. Conner threw her a pair and she pulled them on.

Conner smiled. "You look like one of us now," she said.

"I don't know if that's a good thing," Elantra said pulling a face.

Conner laughed. She stood up and grabbed her leather jacket from the chair where she'd put it. Then she threw on her tool belt. She tossed Elantra a blue cotton jacket, and the girl put it on.

Elantra looked around quickly. "Where's Mr. Buttons?" she asked in a panic. It didn't take a genius to figure out that Conner McVee didn't like the cat.

"I put him outside where cats belong..."

"He's only ever been outside today. He doesn't know how to take care of himself anymore than I do..."

"He's a fucking cat," Conner said.

"He's the only thing I have of my life," Elantra said in a panic. "I'm a billion miles..."

"Oh, at least that..."

"... from everything I know. Mr. Buttons..."

"OK, OK. I'll get the fuckin' cat." Conner went to the door, opened it, and the cat ran in. "If that fucking cat shits in my house again..."

"You use fuck as a slang term to show that you're displeased," Elantra said having a proud moment.

Conner took a deep breath and counted to ten.

They ate dinner in the same restaurant they had eaten lunch. Elantra insisted that she was never eating something that had once had feet, and then ate all of her burger and part of Conner's. The food was just too good, like nothing she had ever eaten. She was beginning to see why people were drawn to a Constructionist lifestyle.

The club was a separate one-story building with bright lights all over it. The signs had writing on them instead of pictures so you couldn't really tell what they said, unless of course you could do that reading thing that all the Constructionists seemed to do. Elantra only hoped it wasn't some perverted sex den like the ones they'd passed in Slum Town.

"Now listen to me," Conner was saying as Elantra was staring at all the lights. Conner took her chin and made her look at her. "By now everyone in Wrench Town knows I'm here. If I didn't show up at Heaven's Gate..."

"Heaven's Gate?"

"That's the name of the club... The point is that they expect me to come in tonight. I don't want anyone, not even my own people, to know who you are. That there is anything at all strange about you being here with me. Here's the story. You're a friend of mine who's thinking of becoming a Constructionist. Do not tell anyone that you are Tarent Powers daughter or that you're here hiding from Mishy. And in case you're contemplating telling someone for whatever reason your sick building brat little brain might have worked out, I have an audio implant which allows me to detect a pin dropping in a crowded subway."

"What's a pin?" Elantra asked.

Conner hit herself in the head. "It's a very small thing, OK? So just be cool. Don't ask a lot of questions, don't answer any, and we'll be all right."

Elantra nodded. For some reason she was all hopped up and full of energy. She said as much to Conner, who laughed.

"It's from eating meat and real sugar. You'll get used to it."

As they walked into the club five women all descended on Conner McVee. They acted as if touching her was the most important thing in their life. One redheaded woman took things a step further; she wrapped her arms around Conner's neck and kissed her full on the mouth without any kind of screen at all for what seemed like probably longer than it actually was. It made Elantra more than a little uncomfortable. It wasn't the sort of thing you could just pretend not to see, and it certainly wasn't something she wanted to watch.

When the woman finally let go of Conner, McVee smiled stupidly and said, "I missed you too, Dedra. Girls, this is my friend Lanny."

"Friend or *friend*?" Dedra asked with a half pout.

"Just a friend," Conner said. Dedra smiled, grabbed Conner by the hand and dragged her onto the dance floor, where they proceeded to rub bodies in a most peculiar way. There were some people in a corner of the club holding strange looking things that made sounds and they were singing. Almost without noticing it she walked closer to look and listen. She hated to admit it, but it did sound better than dygarhythms, and it was fascinating. It was a hell of a lot of work. The people making the music were sweating, and yet they were smiling as if they were having the best time of their lives. Nothing in Elantra's life had ever made her feel that way. Someone tapped her on the shoulder. She turned to face a dark haired man. "Want to dance?" he asked.

"I... I'm," Elantra didn't know what to say. There were almost as many gay couples in the club as there were straights. She'd always felt rather ambiguous sexually, and had tried both male and female virtual lovers. She found neither very stimulating. She wanted to believe she was straight because she knew that was what her father wanted for her. Right now she had no idea whether the part she was playing was supposed to be gay or not, because Conner McVee hadn't bothered to tell her. She opted for an easier out. "I've only ever virtually danced. I don't know how to dance with a partner."

"I could teach you," he said enthusiastically.

"That's nice, but... not just yet." Unwillingly she found herself looking for Conner McVee.

The man smiled a knowing smile. "Oh, I see. Well good luck. Conner hasn't been serious about anyone since Peggy."

"What happened with Peggy?" Elantra asked.

"You don't know? I guess she doesn't like to talk about it. Don't guess anyone would..."

Later on Elantra would wonder if Conner had heard the direction of their conversation, because suddenly she was at Elantra's shoulder seemingly appearing out of thin air. "Come on, I'll teach you to dance."

"I... I don't know..." Conner grabbed her and pulled her into her arms. "Conner McVee, I don't know what you think gives you the right to woman handle me, you might have pulled my arm out of the socket..."

"Ouch," Conner said as Elantra stepped on her foot. "Let me lead."

"I don't know how to dance."

"So I'm teaching you. Here." She took Elantra's arms and wrapped them around her neck. She wrapped her arms around Elantra's waist and pulled her close. "Can you feel where my feet are?"

"I can feel where your *leg* is," Elantra protested.

"That's to help guide you," Conner said with a smile. "Now just kind of let your feet and your body follow mine." Elantra nodded. Conner laughed. "You know for a straight girl you're awfully tense."

"What's that supposed to mean?" Elantra asked hotly.

"It means if you weren't at least a little turned on you'd be able to relax a little bit anyway. You're stiff as a board."

"Well, I hate to poke a hole in your inflated ego, but I'm completely out of my element, doing something I've never done before with somebody I don't like. Excuse me if that makes me a little tense."

"Give it a rest, Lanny, your chest's pressed up against mine, I can feel that your nipples are hard."

"I'm cold... and you're crude!" She tried to push away, and Conner pulled her still closer. Elantra felt like her back was going to break.

"Look at me," Conner said. Elantra refused. "Look at me," she ordered.

Despite herself she looked at Conner McVee. Conner's expression was impossible to read, and she hoped hers was, too, because again she got that weird electrically charged feeling. They were both silent. "What do you want, Conner McVee?" Elantra asked holding her gaze unblinkingly.

Conner moved her head and breathed into her ear, "To see the fire in your eyes."

Elantra felt weak in the knees, almost faint. She lay her head against Conner's chest, trying to stop the sudden wave of disorientation. It was the strange food, that was all. The food, or something in the air. Or she had been drugged. Conner laughed suddenly.

"Guess what kid? You're dancing."

Elantra realized she was, too. She looked into Conner's eye again, and this time Conner looked away.

Dedra looked out at the couple dancing and frowned. "Friend my ass."

All the physical activity had totally wiped Elantra out. When they had gotten back to the cabin she'd all but collapsed on the couch. Conner had covered her up and she'd been out like a light. She awoke to severe muscle aches in places she'd never had aches before. She took a deep breath; the air was heavy with the smell of food. She got up wrapping the cover tightly around her and went to the kitchen. She sat carefully in a chair. Conner McVee was preparing food by hand. Steam rose in the air over the cooking device. Conner set a cup of dark black liquid in front of Elantra. Elantra took an experimental sip.

"Coffee," Conner told her.

Elantra frowned. This she didn't like.

"Try it with some cream and sugar," Conner said, pushing the containers towards her. Elantra spooned sugar into her cup. She picked up the cream container and looked in suspiciously.

"What is this?"

"It's cream. It comes from a cow."

"What part of a cow?" Elantra demanded.

"Its tits," Conner said.

"I'm never drinking anything that came from a cow's breasts," Elantra started. Conner poured the cream into her coffee.

"Try it," Conner demanded.

When Conner turned her back on her to finish breakfast, Elantra took an experimental sip. She immediately poured a more generous helping into her cup. Conner laughed, but didn't turn around. She set breakfast in front of Elantra, who ate it without asking any more questions. "If you keep eating like this you're going to weigh about four hundred pounds," Conner said.

"Not with all the exercise I've been getting." She looked into her plate. "When can I go home?"

"Soon. I can't say exactly when, but soon." Conner said

non-committally.

Elantra didn't know if that was good news or bad news. "I hurt everywhere."

"Your body will adapt..."

"I know that. I'm almost a doctor, you know."

"Did you ever work on a person?"

"Well, no, but..."

"Then you're not almost a doctor," Conner said.

"Why do you go out of your way to make me mad, Conner McVee?" Elantra asked in a voice filled with as much hurt as anger.

"Because I like to watch the little veins stand out in your neck," Conner said with a smile.

"Fuck you!" Elantra shrieked experimentally.

"Ah! See? That's what I like – a girl that begs for it."

Elantra got up and stomped towards the door, where she stopped long enough to remember how to open it. When she got it open, she stomped through and instinctively slammed it hard behind her. She stopped, turned around, opened the door back up and slammed it again. She heard Conner McVee laughing, and she walked into the room again and stared down at Conner. "That, that felt... It felt good. So fulfilling."

"Still think Constructionists are crazy?"

"I think *you're* crazy!" Elantra yelled at her then walked back through the door and slammed it one more time just for good measure.

CHAPTER 6

"Well?" Tarent asked Wayne as he swept into the room.

Wayne shrugged. "This wasn't easy to get. Between her being a cop and a Constructionist there were some serious blocks on any information about her... Computer, call up file Conner McVee," he said. The computer started to spit out a long stream of data.

Wounded June 5, 2250 lower right leg broken and foot shattered. Titanium skeletal implant used to make repair. Dec. 2, 2251 lost right eye to gunfire. Heat sensitive, infrared, five hundred yard scan implanted. July 23, 2251, left ear damaged in explosion. Sonic amplifier implanted. Aug. 12, 2253 skull fractured. Titanium plate with empathic sensitivity amplifier implanted. January 9, 2254. Both lower arm bones broken in left arm, Titanium skeletal replacements. Wrist and hand assembly implanted. Tracer unit implanted with wrist pin.

"Computer repeat last entry," Tarent ordered.

Tracer unit implanted with wrist pin.

"Computer, link me to Brakston Agency, James Rank."

Jason Hunter rubbed at his feet, where huge blisters had welled up. "My feet will never be the same again..."

"Would ya quit whinin'? You had walked maybe a mile when we found ya."

"You ever walk a mile out there, Rank?" Jason hissed back.

"No," Rank said truthfully. One of the Agents walked in looking like he'd been run over. "Well Peterson?" Rank asked, not bothering to look up.

"Mishy's not taking visitors," the man said. The chair anticipated that he wanted to sit down and moved to catch him as he dropped. "No, no, Rank don't worry about me, I feel fine... Any other units call in?"

"They have checked every Constructionist quarter in a four state area, there is no sign of Hammer. Not that the Constructionists are likely to cooperate with any agency save their own. We don' know shit 'bout Hammer's personal life, so there's no way of knowin' jus' where she might go. Hell, she might not even be in the country anymore."

"You knew she was married to Mishy's sister," Jason mumbled. "And you knew she thought Tarent Powers had her killed. You should have given me that job..."

"Shouldah, couldah, wouldah, didn'. It don' matter a fuck. If I'd given you the assignment the girl'd likely as not be dead right now. Hammer's a lot of things, but she ain't no murderer."

"Someone cut my old lady up into that many pieces, I'd be ready to make an exception to my rules," Peterson said.

"Yeah... Well, you ain't Hammer."

Rank was interrupted by Tarent Powers on his main line, "I want you to transfer Conner McVee's tracer code to my computer..."

"McVee doesn' have a tracer implant..."

"Don't try to blow smoke up my ass, Rank. I have on terminal six McVee's medical record. The bitch is nothing but hardware, and one of her spare parts has a tracer unit in it. I want the code transferred. Since she is now working for me, I have the right to have the code."

"Fine, but I got to tell you she's out of tracer range."

"The global positioning system..."

"It doesn' work with GPS. It's low frequency radio waves..."

"How idiotic! I thought she was the Constructionist, not you, Rank."

Rank just shrugged. He hadn't done it at all, his father had. He wouldn't have done it. Nothing he could think of was really worth pissing Hammer McVee off. It was too bad Tarent hadn't known that.

"Well, she has to come back sometime," Tarent observed.

"Actually, she doesn't," Rank said. He smiled at the startled look on Tarent's face as he transferred the data. Apparently the idea that Conner might choose not to return to Freight City at all had never occurred to Tarent. When he had transferred the tracer data he finished his thought. "She's a Constructionist, remember? The bitch could hunker down and keep house in the middle of the woods. There's yer data. Happy huntin'." Rank closed transmission, happy to see Tarent's ugly mug leave his screen. "I hope Hammer knows what she's doin'."

Conner spent most of the day mucking out the cabin and trying to teach Elantra how to exist in a Constructionist house. The girl balked and whined the whole time, but for all her whining, she was a quick study, and surprisingly willing to try to adjust.

Conner had insisted that Elantra walk with her to the store to get supplies, and the girl hadn't stopped bitching since they left the house.

"My everything hurts. I don't see why we can't take the car. It's cold, and it hurts to breathe... I have to go to the bathroom... And about that, the way you do that is just disgusting..."

"Maybe it wouldn't hurt to breathe so much if you'd shut up for a minute," Conner mumbled.

Elantra couldn't hear what Conner said. She was too far behind her, so she ran to catch up.

"Your legs are longer than mine, and I'm taking three steps for every one that you're taking. When I get home I'm going to tell my father how I've been treated, and he'll have your pay cut... he'll..."

"Do you always bitch like this, or is it just for my benefit?" Conner asked with a laugh.

"You go out of your way to be mean to me," Elantra pouted. "My feet really do hurt."

"OK, I'll slow down." Conner slowed her pace. She put an arm around Elantra's shoulders and the girl jerked away.

"I didn't say you could touch me. No one gave you the right to maul me. I'm sure that my father didn't tell you... *Oh, by the way, while you're watching my daughter, touch her where ever and when ever you want.*"

"You said you were cold. I was just trying to help you keep warm," Conner said innocently, although what she'd actually been doing was exactly what the girl was accusing her of.

"Oh," Elantra moved over close to Conner, but Conner didn't put her arm around her again. "You can put your arm around me now."

"No. You hurt my feelings," Conner said with a mock pout.

"Bitch!" Elantra screamed experimentally.

"I would be for you, baby," Conner said sticking out her tongue.

Elantra let out an exasperated sound and charged up ahead

of Conner. Conner followed behind her and enjoyed the view. A car pulled up beside Conner and stopped.

"Hey, Conner, need a ride?" Dedra asked.

"No, I'm taking my bitch for a walk," Conner said loud enough for Elantra to hear. Elantra marched back to Conner.

"I... I hate you." She turned and stomped off again.

"Lovers' quarrel?" Dedra asked.

Elantra turned around and walking backwards screamed. "Most definitely not!" Then she tripped over something and started to fall. She was ready for the impact of her butt on the ground when Conner McVee caught her by her shoulders and stood her back on her feet in one motion. Elantra would rather have fallen and broken every bone in her body than to have had Conner McVee catch her at that moment. She made a fist and hit Conner in the shoulder. When Conner laughed in her face, she kicked her in the shin. Conner stopped laughing. She glared down at Elantra, and Elantra took off running. Conner limped along behind her. "You little bitch, when I catch you I'm gonna kick your ass."

Dedra waved wildly. "Well, you two kids have a good time."

Conner caught Elantra easily; hanging onto her was another story. The girl seemed to have bones of rubber, and she fought to get away for a good five minutes. "You fucking little bitch. Kick me in my good leg. I ought to rip your fucking head off and shit in the hole."

"You let me go or I'll kick you again!" Elantra screamed.

"OK, you ungrateful little bitch." She not only let her go, but she pushed her away from her. "You know I saved your fucking worthless life, and you never even so much as thanked me. I stop you from falling on your ass and you hit me. You're a twisted, screwed-up little brat. You want away from me so bad, get away from me." Conner started limping in the other direction. Elantra stood there for a moment watching her go.

She didn't know where she was, she didn't even know how to get back to the cabin let alone Power's Tower, but... *All I have to do is get to a computer and Daddy will come and get me. But is there a computer around here? I could ask at a store. I could... Did I really not thank her? She saved me from that pit, surely I did.* But she thought about it, and she couldn't remember doing so. She looked down the road at Conner McVee's limping form. She ran after her. "Conner McVee." Conner ignored her. "I'm sorry I hit you, and I'm sorry that I kicked you, and thank you for saving my life."

"You're welcome," Conner said. "I can't believe I have fucking metal all over my body and you kick me someplace that's real. You really are a rotten little cunt."

"I said I'm sorry." Elantra put her arm around Conner's waist. Conner looked down at her. "I'm still cold."

Rank hadn't been lying about the tracer. McVee had taken his daughter out of range, which meant she was several hundred miles away in any given direction. He now knew everything he could pull from the net on Conner "The Hammer" McVee. It wasn't a lot. Constructionists had a special aversion to having anything of a personal nature in the net, and almost like a baptism when they joined the cult they had any personal data washed from it. Police Agency records were hard to get into and even harder to decrypt. But money bought almost everything, and a good programmer had gotten him into Conner's agency files. Unfortunately, they were cold and vague and didn't actually paint a picture of a real flesh and blood person.

It wasn't much to go on, but it was enough if you knew how to read it, and Tarent did.

Conner McVee was a very dangerous person, highly intelligent and motivated to his destruction. If she'd ever been able to get a clean bead on him she would have killed him in a heartbeat, he had no doubt. She didn't believe in playing by the rules, she saw herself as a sort of superhero, saving innocents from the bad guys. For some reason perps with bad rap sheets filled with violent crimes always attacked her or ran and wound up dead. She took down guys most other agents had failed to get close to, but it seemed impossible for her to locate and bring in small-time crooks she had been assigned to arrest. This meant she had connections in the underworld, but then of course she would. She'd been married to Peggy Mishy.

McVee and Mishy. Now there was an uneasy alliance if ever he'd seen one. The most decorated police agent in the city, literally in bed with the Mishy family.

But then, McVee was a creature of contradictions. She kept the law by breaking it. She saved lives by killing people. She was a cyborg and a Constructionist. Not the sort of person it was easy to do a profile on, yet one thing had become crystal clear.

She could blow and strut all she wanted, but now Tarent knew for a near certainty that there was no way that Conner "The Hammer" McVee was going to do anything at all to hurt Elantra.

By now Hammer would have figured out that – as unbelievable as it might have seemed to her at first – Elantra knew nothing at all about his business.

Elantra wasn't part of his world. He never wanted her to be. Tarent had picked out a husband for her, and he was grooming him to take over the business. In this way Elantra would never have to get even the least bit dirty. She'd supply an egg, a male child would be born, and he would eventually take over the business.

Elantra was the only pure thing in his life, and he wanted to keep her that way.

McVee had a doctorate in criminology and a batchelor's degree in political science. She had graduated with honors from the police academy. She wasn't just some dumb cop, so she had to know that Elantra was no less innocent than the people she had worked to protect most of her adult life. Knowing this, there was just no way that the woman whose files he'd just listened to for hours was going to kill Elantra.

McVee had been decorated six times for bravery and had the highest arrest-to-conviction rate of any agent in a three state area. She had killed twenty-seven people in the line of duty, and that was just the ones on record. She didn't know what fear was, so his usual intimidation techniques were not going to work. She certainly wasn't squeamish about killing.

But Conner McVee had one weakness that he could prey on – she was a person of ethics and integrity, a deeply religious woman with a very firm concept of right and wrong.

Elantra had done nothing illegal; she had done nothing wrong. There wasn't an evil bone in her body. The more he'd learned about McVee the safer he'd felt his daughter was.

Tarent was more than capable of killing a perfectly innocent person, he'd done it many times without one moment's guilt. McVee, he now believed, was a different story.

Of course you could never be too sure. Because sometimes when you pushed even the most righteous of people to the edge they went crazy, and crazy people were capable of anything. He wondered if McVee was crazy yet, if one more failed attempt to bring him to justice might be what pushed her over the edge.

He buried his face in his hands. One moment he was sure he had it all figured out, and the next he was plunged back into darkness.

God only knows what she's telling Elantra about me. I think I've got the bitch figured, I don't think she'd harm Elantra, but... If she's not playing with a full deck she might do God only knows what if I push her hand. What choice do I have? I'm not going to turn myself in, and I sure as hell am not going to kill myself. Maybe that shows just how unreasonable she's become. She's hunted me, she knows me; she should have known I wouldn't go for this. Maybe she just needs to give me this chance so she can feel like her hands are clean when she kills Elantra.

He needed to play for time, because his only real chance was to find McVee, kill her and take Elantra back.

Of course, finding her wasn't going to be easy. The woman had contacts in several underground worlds, loyal friends, and her enemies were too afraid to say what they might know.

As if his thoughts had conjured her up, McVee's face filled his screen. As before, the screen behind her was being grounded out. McVee wasn't taking any chances that her location might be discovered.

"Well?" she asked plainly. "I see you aren't dead."

"It's not much of an offer, McVee... What about money? I could give you any amount you could ask for. You could use it to help your Constructionist friends."

Her rage, even through the screen, was almost tangible. "You can't buy people, Tarent. Elantra isn't for sale. Peggy wasn't for sale. You can't buy me off with blood money. I want *justice.* Finally, after all these years, I want *justice.* Not just for Peg, but for everyone who you've killed or ruined. I want it for myself. Your life for Elantra's seems a fair trade. I would have given my life for Peggy's..."

Tarent relaxed then. *She's weighing things out. She wants to make things balance. She knows that killing Elantra will not tip the scales her way. She won't kill Elantra.* He kept the smirk off his face only with an effort. "See, that's the difference between people like you and people like me, McVee. I care about Elantra, but it's more the way one might care about a very nice car. It's pretty, and I don't want it dinged up, but if it got totaled tomorrow it wouldn't be the end of the world, because I could always get another one. I'm not about to give up my life or my freedom to save her. She just isn't that important to me. Unless you're more like me than I think you are, you don't have the stomach to kill her. Oh, you kill people. You kill them all the time, and go to sleep, and never wake from a nightmare seeing their faces. In that way you are just like me. The difference is you haven't ever stepped over the line and killed someone helpless just because you could. I suggest that if you're going to do it you kill her and send me the pieces. Otherwise it's stalemate."

Her face was a mask of black rage as she spat back, "You may have just overplayed your hand, dickwad."

Her face left the screen. The link was broken, although it was hard to know whether this was because she had severed the link or crushed her terminal.

He sighed and leaned back in his chair, hoping that he was right about Conner McVee, and contemplating just what a stalemate meant for him and for his daughter.

CHAPTER 7

Conner quickly terminated the link. Her hands were shaking as she completely dismantled the machine. She wanted to crush it, but hoped that this exercise was going to calm her down. It didn't. When she had finished disabling the machine she put all the pieces back in the case. She took several deep breaths, but it didn't keep her from crying. Damn the bastard! It should have all been very simple. Part of her had known, had always known, that Tarent Powers was not going to give in to her demands.

That same part had told her over and over that if it came down to it she was going to kill the girl and avenge Peggy's death. She stood up and took hold of the handle of her weapon with conviction. She was going to do it, just walk in there and stick a nail in the girl's head. One good, quick, clean shot. Kill her instantly.

Her hand flew from the handle as if scalded, and she flopped back into the chair and started sobbing painful, racking sobs. She lay her forehead on the table, barely resisting the impulse to smash her brains out. Anything to stop the pain. She couldn't do it, and the bastard knew she couldn't, so she had utterly and completely failed.

"I'm sorry, Peg," she breathed. "So sorry."

She took a deep breath, pulled her head off the table and dried her face on her sleeve. Then she opened the case and put the computer back together, once again hoping that the tedious exercise would help to calm her.

"Computer, call Mishy."

Mishy's face came up on the screen. She was glad she'd caught him in his office. "Ah! Hammer McVee, what can uncle Mishy do for you?"

"I might have outsmarted myself, Mishy. Tarent Powers isn't taking my bluff, and I can't kill the girl..." She started crying again in spite of herself.

"Buck up, little camper. You have to do it for Peggy..."

"That's just it, Mishy. Peg would never want an innocent

girl killed to avenge her death. Peggy wasn't like you, Mishy. She wasn't even like me. This girl doesn't know shit. She didn't kill Peggy, and she doesn't even know what kind of scum her father is. She thinks he's some sort of fucking businessman. I don't know what I was thinking. I guess I wasn't, not really. Maybe that just once I wanted to have the upper hand with this bastard, just once I wanted to hold all the cards... Tarent called it a stalemate, and he's right."

Mishy looked thoughtful then he smiled. "You don't have to kill the girl. You're right. Peggy wouldn't want it. No one can find you, Hammer. Tarent is going absolutely nuts. He's got everyone and his brother combing the streets. He's spending thousands of dollars on computer time, and the only thing he's figured out is that you aren't the type of person that kills innocent girls. Keep the girl. Keep her out of Tarent's hands. Call him every once in awhile just to rub his nose in the fact that you have something he wants and he can't have it. Everyone knows. He's tried to keep it hushed up, but I ain't allowed him to. He's losing face, and in this business losing face means losing respect and losing respect means losing money. Maybe it even means that someone else decides to take the bastard out. While he's wasting all his time trying to find you I've been squeezing the hell out of him here. Somewhere in between us, the bastard just might break. One thing's for damn sure. As long as he's spending all his time looking for his daughter he can't run his business. Just don't lose it, Hammer. You owe it to Peggy to ride this thing out."

"Two wrongs don't make a right," Conner said.

"Save your Constructionist crap for someone else. Tarent killed my sister and my wife and my kid. He's got to pay. If you don't got the stomach for it, give the girl back to me."

"Don't give me ultimatums or orders, Mishy. I'm not one of your hired thugs. Watch your back, desperate men do desperate things."

"Yeah, and there isn't a man alive as desperate as I am."

"Terminate link." Conner disassembled the computer again. Only this time she tore it down into so many pieces that you would have to be a high-tech genius to get it back together. While she was, she knew the girl wasn't.

She dried her face again, stood up and headed for the living room. She opened the door and saw Elantra sitting on the couch rubbing her feet. "So can I talk to my dad?"

"I can't figure out what's wrong with the unit. I've got it all in pieces. It may need a new converter relay. I'll work on it again tomorrow."

"I need a doctor," Elantra said. Conner sat down and looked at where the girl pointed.

"It's just a broken blister. Bite your lip and I'll go get a bandage." She got up and went to the bathroom. When she came back, she sat down on the couch and poured some hydrogen peroxide on the busted blister, dried it off and then put some salve and a bandage on it. *Yeah, I'm a real bad ass. Who the hell did I think I was kidding? Gonna kill this girl? Yeah right, gonna play nursemaid to her worthless building-brat ass.*

"I know it's just a blister, but I really ought to see a doctor," Elantra protested. "It really hurts."

Conner laughed. "You're a giant wuss."

"If I knew what that was, I'm sure I'd be insulted," Elantra said. She looked at Conner. She must have noticed the redness in her eye, the drag in her voice. "Are you all right?"

Conner wasn't all right, and the concern in Elantra's voice pushed her over the edge. She got up and walked into the kitchen quickly, but not before Elantra realized that she was crying, and followed her.

"What's wrong?" Elantra demanded.

Conner went to the sink and splashed water in her face. "You wouldn't understand... I wanted to do something for Peggy, but I just realized... it's too late."

"Maybe not," Elantra said helpfully, "Maybe you could work things out, maybe..."

"Elantra," Conner took a deep breath, "Peggy's dead."

"Dead!" Elantra breathed. She had assumed there was some kind of break up, a divorce or something; it had never occurred to her that the woman from Conner's past might be dead.

"That's right. Dead. I had the dangerous job, and Peg wound up dead." Conner leaned over the sink and let the water and tears drip off her face. She couldn't remember the last time she had cried. Probably at Peg's funeral.

"How did she die?"

"See..." Conner laughed, though she obviously wasn't amused. "That's just it. It doesn't really matter how she died. I thought it did, but it doesn't. She's gone, and nothing I do is going to bring her back. Nothing I do is going to make me feel any better about losing her." She took her patch off.

When Elantra saw the patch land on the counter beside Conner, she took a step backwards and steeled herself.

Conner dried her face. She walked to the refrigerator, pulled out a bottle, opened it and took a drink. She felt like an idiot. *Gee! I'm the badass that was going to hold the crime lord's daughter hostage. No wonder he saw right through me, I'm on the verge of a complete emotional breakdown.*

"I'm sorry," she said to Elantra. "Must be PMS." She turned around, and saw Elantra standing there with her fists in tight balls by her sides and her eyes closed tightly shut. Conner looked at her patch on the counter and smiled. "It really isn't all that bad, Lanny."

Elantra opened her eyes carefully. It was pretty fucking creepy. The eye was metal. There was a glowing red dot in the middle of it that swiveled as if watching everything in the room at once. Elantra forced a nervous smile.

"I realize it's somewhat unnerving, but it could be worse." Conner forced a smile. "It might be some half-healed, infected-looking chunk of flesh with what was left of an eye in the middle of it." Conner took a long drink from the bottle of beer in her hand. "Want one?"

"I don't know." Elantra said honestly. "What is it?"

"Beer, a wheat and barley beverage, very low alcohol content." Conner grabbed a beer out of the fridge and walked over to the table. She put her own beer down, twisted the cap off the other one and held the beer out to Elantra. "Try it. If you don't like it, I'll drink it."

Elantra took the beer from Conner and sipped at it experimentally. She liked the taste. She smiled and nodded, then sat down at the table as Conner did. "I'm sorry about kicking you."

Conner shrugged. "You ought to be." She laughed at the expression on Elantra's face. "Don't sweat it. It's obvious from all the metal in my body that I've been hurt worse."

"If you're a Constructionist, why..."

"...all the implants?" Conner finished. Elantra nodded. "The implants are the cause, Constructionism is the effect. I got them when I was young and stupid, and I didn't really give a damn whether I lived or died. I'd say I thought I was bullet proof except that bullets did most of the damage, and it didn't stop me. I would take jobs no one in their right mind would take, and do things no sane person would do, knowing that if I got something shot up, or broke it doing something crazy like jumping off a building, I'd have an excuse to get another implant. To enhance myself, make myself better than mere human. The more implants I had the more valuable I was to the agency. I was good, damn good. I made them a lot of money, so they spent a lot of money on 'upgrading' me. In my quest to become more like God I moved ever further away from the image of God and ever closer to the image of man. The implants made me stronger, less vulnerable, smarter than a normal human. They enhanced my sight, my hearing, and the less I was like a normal human the less I was like God.

"One day I woke up and realized that there was very little of me left. I was more machine than human, and while the implants had made me something more than human, they had also stolen away part of my humanity. The implants enhance my abilities, but they also cause problems that I wouldn't have had with my original equipment. They hurt in the cold, sometimes they leak fluid, and they have to be repaired. They're harder to break, but unlike my real body parts they can't fix themselves.

"Then Brakston Agency put something in me that I didn't ask for, a tracer that allows them to follow my every movement unless I'm fifty miles away from the base. I think that was the moment that opened my eyes. It was real obvious that they saw me not as a human with my own life, but as a rather expensive possession that they couldn't afford to lose. It really pissed me off. I had done it to myself, but they had encouraged me, then they just *marked* me without my permission. They think they own me, but they don't." She looked into Elantra's eyes. "*They* don't own *me*, and your father doesn't own *you*. You can love a person, but you can't own them."

Elantra couldn't argue with what Conner McVee said. It was true; her father thought he owned her. He treated her like a possession. Even now he had thrown her into the protection of this strange woman without bothering to ask Elantra how she felt about it. Elantra was caught up in something she didn't understand, because he'd never bothered to tell her that she was ever in any danger. Or had he? He'd warned her not to leave the building, she'd done it anyway, and now here she was. She took a long swallow of the beer. It fizzed up in her nose and she coughed.

Conner laughed, and said too late, "Watch it, kid, that stuff will bite you on the ass."

Elantra nodded and took another drink, more carefully this time. It was funny, the more of it she drank the better it tasted, and two beers later she was talking easier than she had in her whole life. "...I want to go to college, you know. Not online, a real university, where I could interact with real people, work on real patients, learn from real doctors, but my father won't let me. I bet you could count on your fingers the number of times I've been out of the building, and any time I have been, I've had to take half a dozen security people with me and go to a destination of my father's choosing. Unless of course I snuck out, and then I was always so afraid of getting caught or something really bad happening like... well, what happened, that I didn't really have a good time. The only people I ever see are my father's business associates and his staff, and they all act as if they aren't allowed to talk to me. I have experienced more in the last couple of days than I have experienced in my whole life till now. Computerized school, virtual swimming, virtual dancing, a virtual life. Maybe you guys are right. Maybe it is too much."

"So, you ever have sex?" Conner McVee asked plainly.

"Of course I have," Elantra laughed then came clean. "Well, only with the computer...."

"Virtual sex?" Conner laughed. "What about the real thing?"

"Are you kidding? Nasty!" She made a face. "Besides, Daddy would flip. He's got a husband picked for me. Buddy something. He works real close with my dad. He's all right I guess. Someday we'll get married, they'll hand us a screen and put us in a room together, and that will be it..."

"Gee! You sound excited," Conner said sarcastically.

Elantra shrugged. "It's expected of me. I'll get married. The marriage will make a corporate merger between two strong companies. We'll have the obligatory sex, then they'll put our genetic material together and make a couple of kids. He'll help my father with his business, and I'll be free to practice medicine."

"Your dear father is marrying you off to the son of one of his crime lord cronies, and you don't see anything wrong with that whole picture? I got a better idea, what about you look around till you find someone you actually like. You date them.

If you have any chemistry with them, you screw them. If you fall in love, then you get married and have kids," Conner said.

Elantra laughed. "You guys have some really weird ideas."

Conner laughed and shook her head in disbelief. "Even when you're married you're going to have sex through a screen, and *we* have weird ideas."

"Unlike you who exchange body fluids with just anyone, I don't care to do that. It sounds messy, and…"

"God in a car! You people are fucked!" Conner stood up shaking her head. "You're going to marry someone you don't really even know, because Daddy wants you to, but you're going to fuck through a screen to make damn sure that you don't enjoy it… For God's sake! You're not even *straight*." Conner laughed.

"Am, too," Elantra insisted.

"Tell it to someone else, Lanny. I have a sensitivity implant in my brain, remember? If no one else in the world knows, I do. Do you want to…" Conner looked at the empty bottles on the table, counted six that were hers, and realized she was letting the alcohol talk – so she fell silent.

"Do I want to what!" Elantra demanded standing up with an effort and weaving ever so slightly.

"Nothing," Conner said.

"Do I want to what!" Elantra screamed again.

"Do you want to spend your whole life wondering what it would be like to love someone and to have them love you? To feel another body against yours, to feel the warmth and the passion." She got up and walked over to Elantra. Without warning Conner took Elantra in her arms. Elantra started to look away, and then their eyes met. "Do you want to spend your whole life never knowing what it would have been like if we had kissed, on impulse, without any screen? Without anyone giving us permission. Just two people in the moment, letting passion seize them, right here, right now."

"No," Elantra breathed. She threw her arms around Conner's neck and pulled her head down. Their lips met. It was warm. It was wonderful. Conner pulled back.

"Open your mouth," she breathed. Elantra's lips parted, and Conner's tongue moved to probe the willing void of Elantra's young hungry mouth.

Elantra's whole body came alive. She didn't really know how it happened, but the next thing she knew she was lying on Conner McVee's bed, and Conner was all but ripping her clothes off. Wherever Conner touched her skin it felt hot. Conner took her own shirt off. She lay on top of Elantra so that their bare skin met, and then Conner's lips were soft and warm against her throat. Elantra felt her whole body jerk and then a sensation she had never even come close to feeling. The computer hadn't prepared her for this. Virtual sex wasn't even close to the real thing. This was going to be something explosively different, and she wasn't ready for it.

Terror suddenly gripped every fiber of her being. She couldn't be doing this, not with Conner McVee, and not without a screen. She wrestled herself out from under Conner and out of Conner's grasp. She stood up, pulling her shirt around her. "Don't touch me," she said, close to tears.

Conner flopped back on the bed with instant frustration. "God in a car! Why not? Because you're enjoying it too much? Come on, baby, it's all good. You want me; I want you. I'm not going to hurt you. I'm not going to spoil you in an irreversible way. I'm going to make love to you. I'm going to take you someplace that you've never been before."

Elantra looked at Conner McVee and realized that she had never wanted anything more. Her body was still warm where Conner had touched her and ached for more.

"No, no I can't." She held her hands to her head and ran out of the room. She had expected Conner to follow her, but she didn't. She sat down on the couch, bent over and tried to catch her breath. She was mildly intoxicated, she'd been intoxicated before, she knew what that felt like. Conner had told her there was a small amount of alcohol in the beverage.

That's it. I'm drunk. That's all.

Problem was her thinking didn't seem to be affected.

Her whole body trembled. She turned around and saw Conner still lying on the bed with no shirt. She stood up shakily and walked over to the door. She looked at Conner, who looked unblinkingly back. "Conner, what's wrong with me?" she asked in a pleading tone. She expected some flippant answer, so was surprised to hear Conner speak to her in a calm, even reassuring tone.

"Nothing's wrong with you. You're just afraid; I would be, too, in your position. You're a long way from home tasting the world for the first time in your life. You didn't plan on me, and you sure didn't plan on this." She stood up then and walked over to Elantra. She looked down at her and lifted Elantra's chin with her finger so that Elantra had to look at her. "If it's any consolation, I didn't plan on you, or this, either, and I'm also a little afraid." She kissed Elantra's lips gently then moved away and smiled at her. "That's part of the fun, the not knowing. You can't program people, Elantra, you don't know what I'm going to do, and I don't know what you're going to do. But I've done this before, and I know how good it can be." She bent down and kissed Elantra's throat. "I'm going back to bed, where are you going?"

Conner hadn't slept that well in a long time. She looked at the woman she held in her arms. She was beautiful, she was warm, and she was real. Conner didn't know how or why, but she had feelings for Elantra. Feelings that made no sense. No sense at all considering who the girl was. It was confusing, but it felt good to be alive again. There had been women since Peggy. Women who had satisfied her body, but none that had satisfied her soul, no one had breached the hole that Peggy's loss had left in her heart... till now. Elantra stirred and pulled herself closer to Conner. Conner held her tightly, afraid that in the light of day Elantra would have different feelings about their coupling.

Her fears were not unwarranted.

Elantra pulled herself closer to the warmth that shared the bed with her and snuggled between two breasts. She woke immediately with the realization of where she was, what she had done, and who she had done it with. She shoved quickly away from Conner and jumped out of bed, pulling the sheet around herself and completely uncovering Conner.

"Hey!" Conner protested.

"Conner McVee!" Elantra screamed, backing away from the bed. "You got me drunk and took advantage of me."

Conner laughed. "You've got to be fucking kidding me! You drank two eight ounce six point beers for God's sake," Conner said sitting up on her elbows. "Save it for someone else, baby, no one gets that good without experience unless they've spent a whole hell of a lot of time thinking about it. I'll even bet I could tell you what your favorite virtual program was."

"I... I don't even like you," Elantra stammered out, "and I'm not gay, so what other reason can there be?" Elantra looked around for her clothes. Not finding them, she grabbed Conner's shirt off the floor, put it on under the sheet and then threw the latter at Conner's naked form. "This will never happen again." She pulled the shirt tightly around her body and headed for the door. "I only hope I can wash all the germs off of me before I am infected."

"Damn! You look hot in my shirt. Your beautiful legs, and what I can see of your gorgeous ass," Conner sighed. "It's really a shame." She clicked her tongue. "Yeah, I had me some real plans for that body this morning."

Elantra turned in the door and glared down at Conner, noting that she hadn't even attempted to cover her naked body. "You are an egotistical... bitch!" Elantra spat at the irritating smirk on the woman's face.

"Look me in my infrared scan and tell me it wasn't good."

Elantra started to scream something back and wound up staring silently down at her own feet instead.

"You are an incredible beauty, Elantra, and an incredible lover. It would be a shame to let all that go to waste on some man who could never satisfy you. Someone who could never feel for you what I am feeling. Never want you the way I want you right now."

Elantra crawled back into bed with Conner, and wrapped herself around her. "My father would kill me," she said in a whisper.

Conner laughed. "No. Your father would try to kill me and even that wouldn't keep me away." She picked Elantra's chin up with her fingers and kissed her gently on the lips. "You made me remember something I had forgotten. Sometimes you have to take risks. Some things are worth taking risks for."

CHAPTER 8

Conner McVee told her to stay in the car, so she did. She didn't want to, but Conner insisted in that "I am the law" tone, so Elantra sat and waited not so patiently for Conner's return.

Elantra wasn't such a 'building brat,' that she couldn't figure out what was going on. A crew of workers was building some sort of building; *framing* Conner had called it. They were working with primitive tools, and all the workers wore the same sort of belt that Conner wore. She caught a glimpse of Conner through the "frame" and smiled. She was probably going to get some horrible disease from having unprotected sex, but for some reason she wasn't really worried about that. In fact, all she seemed to be able to think about these days was Conner McVee. She found herself more times than not smiling for no particular reason, and everything that Conner said was suddenly just hysterically funny, or brilliant.

Even now as she watched the builders, the sight of Conner made her heart quicken, and she had to fight the urge to go to her to touch her. She could still feel Conner's touch, smell her, taste her. Sitting in the car thinking about how they had made love that morning she came in her pants. It wasn't a particularly comfortable feeling.

Conner seemed to be looking for someone, or something. Elantra wished she would come back to the car and that they would go home and make love again. She didn't understand what could be so important that they had to leave the house. What could be more important than being alone together?

Conner crawled up the ladder. She walked across the roof and sat down beside a big, burly-looking man with a full beard. She took the shingles he handed her and a fist full of nails from the sack he set between them, and using her hand-held hammer she started to help him shingle the house. They worked for several minutes, and then the man set his hammer down, and Conner set hers down so that the handles of their hammers made an X. No one knew how or why, but this had become a tradition, so they did it and didn't worry too much about the logic behind it.

"So, Hammer, I was wondering when I was going to get to see you. What can I do for you?" he asked.

"Great Contractor... I've got a problem," she said.

"So I see," he said with a laugh waving at the girl in Hammer's car. The girl gave him a confused look then waved back, and he turned to smile at Conner. "She's very pretty."

"Yes she is, and very young. I need to know something that only you can tell me."

"I'm sure that's not true, but ask anyway."

"If you love someone, truly love them and they die, can you love someone else?"

The Contractor laughed and adjusted the blue hard hat that showed him to be a member of the clergy. "If you are asking the question, you already know the answer... Hammer, the heart can love as much as the brain will let it."

"But, if I truly loved Peggy... How can I love..." She pointed at Elantra in the car and snarled almost hatefully. "How can I love that girl? She is *nothing* like Peggy, nothing at all. She's weak where Peggy was strong, and strong where Peggy was weak..."

"And you are a different person now than you were when you loved Peggy. Peggy's death has made you a different person. You needed Peggy then, and maybe you need... What's her name?"

"Elantra."

"Maybe Elantra is what you need now. Just because you love this woman now doesn't mean that you loved Peggy any less then. Peggy wouldn't have wanted you to go through life unloved or unloving..."

"It's not that simple, Contractor." Conner took in a deep breath. "Elantra is... Well, she's Tarent Powers' only child."

By the look on The Contractor's face, he realized the implications, so Conner continued without waiting for his reply. She told him everything that had happened. "...and I kidnapped her from Mishy because I thought I could play Tarent's game better than Mishy could. I think maybe part of me just wanted to stop Mishy from doing something that would make him the same as Tarent, and part of me just wanted to have something, *anything*, that I could use to get Tarent to stick his head out of his glass and steel tower so that I could get a clean shot. I don't really know what I was thinking. None of it seems to make any sense to me now. I told Tarent I was going to kill her unless he killed himself or turned himself in. I told myself I would, too, but even Tarent knew I was bluffing. Mishy isn't too pleased with me. I get the feeling that he's probably looking for me just as hard as Tarent is now." She sighed and ran her fingers through her hair. "I've got a damn tracer implant built into the components of my left arm. It's got a fifty-mile radius, and I'm well out of that, for now. But it's only a matter of time before they start traveling with the base, if they're not already. Eventually they'll find me, either Mishy or Tarent. Mishy will be hell bent on killing Elantra, and Tarent will be hell bent on killing me and dragging her back into a life that she doesn't deserve. There is too much life in her for her to be trapped in a building."

"We can protect you here, Hammer. You're one of us, we have a code..."

"I appreciate it, but I wouldn't bring this trouble down on anyone else's head. Not for the sake of saving my own ass, or even Elantra's. I need Doc Pherson. I need the tracer removed before they have a chance to find me, but as I'm sure you know, he's up at the lake."

"I'll see what I can do about getting him back here."

"Thanks."

"She's not a Constructionist is she?"

"No."

"A mixed coupling..."

"With all due respect, Contractor, right now I'm not even sure I can keep us both alive long enough to enjoy a serious commitment. If I do, it's only a matter of time till Elantra finds out what I've done..."

"You mean... she doesn't know that you kidnapped her?"

Hammer shook her head sadly. "I told her some cock and bull story about how her father hired me to keep her out of town till Mishy cools off. When she finds out... I don't think she's going to take it well."

"Maybe you should just tell her and get it over with. Explain to her how you feel..."

Conner laughed and patted him on the back. "You don't know Elantra. Nothing I can say... Why can't anything be simple?"

It was the Contractor's turn to laugh. "If it was simple, it wouldn't be life, and it most assuredly wouldn't be love. Will Elantra convert?"

"You're awfully worried about that, seeing as we probably have no future together," Conner laughed.

The Contractor looked from the woman in the car to Conner, and seemed to concentrate for a moment. He looked into Conner's eye and held her gaze. "I see a future for you together. I see it in the way she is watching you and in the way you can only go a few moments without looking at her. Feelings like these don't go away, and they can outlive almost anything. So is there a chance that she will convert?"

Conner smiled stupidly. "She likes sex too much not to."

The Contractor smiled then. He picked up Conner's hammer and handed it to her. Then he picked his up. "In that case, go with my blessing, Hammer McVee, and a blessing on your lover as well. Bring her to see me when things cool down and we'll start the conversion process."

"I will, if things go my way."

"You are a Constructionist, Hammer, *make* it go your way. Work for what you want, and you will have it."

"Thank you." Conner stood up. "A blessing on you, on your tools and on your house."

"A blessing on you, and on your tools, and on your house. May the things that you build bring you closer to God, and may God be in all that you build."

"So, why did you go there, and who was that guy you were talking to?" Elantra asked before Conner had started the car.

"This is the Building Site. The Building Site is the holiest place in town. It is where creation is taking place. The man I was talking to is the General Contractor; we sometimes call him the Great Contractor or just the Contractor. He is the spiritual leader of Wrench Town. I came here because I needed spiritual guidance." She started the car and started driving.

"Why did you need spiritual guidance?" Elantra asked.

"Why do you think?" Conner hissed back.

Elantra smiled broadly. "Because of me."

"Yes." Conner shook her head in disbelief. Elantra hadn't been out in the real world long enough to know when to keep her mouth shut, and she went on to prove the point.

"So what was it about me that caused a spiritual dilemma?"

Elantra asked, thinking that she had every right to know.

"If I had wanted to talk to you about it, why would I have made a special trip to see the Great Contractor?" Conner all but yelled back.

"Are you mad at me?" Elantra asked.

"What do you think?"

"I don't know," Elantra answered truthfully. "I can't think of a single logical reason why you would be angry. If you were a reasonable person, I would have to assume that you aren't. Since you are anything but a reasonable person, you most probably are."

Conner took a deep breath, and counted to twelve. She realized she was driving out of town and kept going. She wasn't really mad at Elantra. They had spent the last week trying to screw each other to death, talking and arguing about everything and nothing, eating and sleeping and not much else. At that moment there was very little the stupid little shit could have done that would have made Conner really angry, which was of course what was really pissing her off.

She was mad at herself and the situation, and if she didn't love Elantra there wouldn't be a situation for her to be mad at herself about.

Conner had been in love before. She knew what it felt like. She didn't know how Elantra felt, lust was not the same as love, but her sensitivity implant read them the same way. Elantra might not be emotionally old enough to fall in love, and even if she was, she might not fall in love with a walking hunk of hardware like herself.

"Conner McVee!" Elantra screamed. "Have you heard a word I said to you? Are you listening to me at all?" she demanded.

Conner smiled broadly. "I heard you say that I wasn't a reasonable person..."

"I was talking for a good five minutes after that," Elantra said sitting back in her seat crossing her arms over her chest and staring out the window.

Conner smiled. There was no way it had been anywhere near five minutes. "I was so hurt by what you said that I didn't hear anything else."

"Yeah right," Elantra shot back. She looked over at Conner, saw the smile on her face, and any trace of animosity was washed out of her. "So where are we going?"

"You ask too many questions, Lanny." She pulled the car onto the shoulder and stopped. From the wear on the area around the shoulder it was obvious that she wasn't the first person to do so. Conner got out of the car.

Elantra opened the door and got out, marveling at how it no longer seemed like work. How normal it was now to do things that had before seemed impossible. She got out, and looked up at the huge trees in front of them. She took a deep breath; the air smelled good.

"Come on." Conner grabbed hold of her hand and started pulling her along down a path through the trees. She started to protest, and instead just stopped walking, causing Conner to stumble.

"What kind of trees are those?"

"Redwoods. Big, huh?" Conner continued, dragging Elantra along.

"What's that smell?"

"The trees, the flowers, the dirt, the air. It's what the world outside town, even a Constructionist town, smells like. We create buildings, things, but God creates this. God is the ultimate Constructionist."

"It's beautiful," Elantra said then. "Conner McVee, my feet hurt. You drag me around like I'm some old doll. Would you please slow down?"

Conner laughed and slowed down. She put her arm around Elantra and pulled her close. "Do you have to say my whole name whenever you talk to me? I mean... we're lovers for God's sake."

"I like saying your name," Elantra said in an embarrassed whisper.

"Why?" Conner asked with a laugh.

"I don't know. I just do." She put her arm around Conner's waist. Suddenly they walked out of the trees. Elantra took in a deep breath and took a step backwards. "My God," she breathed. "I've seen hologram pictures, but... So much water. It's so..."

"It's hard to put into words, isn't it?" Conner pulled her closer and started walking again. She was glad it was a warm day.

"It's so big, so loud. It looks like it doesn't end or begin. The sky and the water just seem to run together."

Conner was a little taken aback by her perception. "There

is an old Constructionist story that says that spot where the water runs into the sky is the place where heaven meets earth. Theoretically, if you could somehow bring that line from there to here you could communicate with God."

"Is that something you'd want to do?" Elantra asked curiously.

"That's a good question." Conner shrugged. "I don't think so. I mean, I believe in God, most Construc-tionists do, but I don't really believe that God could relate to a human like that, or we to God. I'm not sure I'd want hard, cold proof that there really is a God. I believe God is like a contractor who builds a house then sells it and goes away. It's up to the person who buys the house to maintain it. Not the contractor."

Conner let go of Elantra and sat down on the sand.

"What are you doing?" Elantra asked.

"I'm taking my shoes off so I can walk in the water. You ought to go in with me, it will be good for those blisters..."

The blisters were just about healed now. "It will burn a little at first, but the salt water should be therapeutic," Elantra said thoughtfully. She sat down on the sand next to Conner not without an effort, she still wasn't accustomed to getting all the way down to ground level without something anticipating her action and popping up to catch her. She realized Conner was staring at her, and after a moment's thought, she also realized why. "I may not have worked on real people, but I still know medicine." She ran her fingers through the sand and smiled. It felt good; it was warm. She took her shoes and socks off.

Conner jumped up in one effortless motion, and then reached down and took Elantra's hand to help her up. Their eyes met for a second, then Conner pulled her close and they kissed. Their lips parted.

"Let's make love," Elantra breathed.

Conner laughed and pushed her gently away.

"You've got to be kidding. Honey, we would have sand in places sand should never be. We can save that for when we get home. There are lots of ways to make love." She took Elantra's hand again and they walked towards the ocean.

"What do you mean?" Elantra asked.

"Hopefully, you'll answer that question yourself in time," Conner said.

"That's not an answer to my question, Conner McVee."

Elantra protested.

"Yes it was." Conner laughed then. "You know why you're so horney all the time, don't you?"

"I don't even know what the word means."

"Why you want to have sex all the time," Conner explained.

"Because I like it." Elantra said with a smile.

Conner laughed. "All right, I'll give you that, it's a good reason... In the cities they put chemicals in the water that lower a person's sex drive, strips them of most of their sexual desire. They think this makes them better, less animal, but there's nothing wrong with being a little animal, is there?"

"I don't think any chemical could stop me from wanting you, not now," Elantra said, looking up at Conner with a smile. She watched in amused amazement as Conner's cheeks turned red. Then Conner dropped her hand and ran towards the water.

They started out wading. Then Conner splashed Elantra a little. Elantra splashed Conner a lot, and Conner chased her down and tackled her in the water so that they both wound up soaked. Being wet on the drive home, they were a little chilled. Conner had let Elantra use the shower first. Elantra hollered and Conner came running in. "You OK?"

Elantra opened the shower door and gave Conner a mock pout. "I'm lonely."

"Horney is a little closer to the truth." Conner had already started stripping her wet clothes off. She finished undressing and got into the shower with Elantra, who immediately pounced on her, kissing her over and over again til she got the response she wanted.

Elantra drank it all in – the feel of the water, the warmth of it, the warmth of her lover, the passion. Conner's touch seemed to burn into her flesh.

She had never felt so alive. So vital. The whole world had been opened to her. A real world, where food tasted like food. Air smelled like air. Trees, water, sand and a thousand other things could be seen, touched, and experienced.

She had stopped asking to talk to her father, because she didn't want him to tell her it was time for her to come home. She never wanted to go home. She wanted to stay here with Conner McVee.

Conner lay beside her asleep. Elantra was exhausted, but she had too much on her mind to sleep. She wrapped herself tightly around Conner and Conner stirred and pulled her close. "Conner McVee?"

"Uh," Conner said, sucking the drool off her lip.

"I don't want to leave. I don't want to go back there."

Conner woke up and looked into Elantra's eyes. "Then you won't go back," Conner assured her. She started to tell her how she felt, but stopped. If she told Elantra she loved her that would put pressure on her to reciprocate, and if Elantra felt that way she would have said so. That's the way Elantra was. Still, just because Elantra didn't *know* she loved her didn't mean that she didn't. It just meant that she was too green to recognize it.

"My father will make me go back, Conner McVee," Elantra said trembling.

"Your father can't make me do anything I don't want to do, and I don't want to give you back..."

"Why not?" Elantra asked.

"Why do you think?" Conner asked.

"Conner McVee, must you always answer in riddles? Can't you give me a straight answer?"

"I'm not straight..."

"You know what I mean," Elantra said with a frustrated sigh.

"I like you," Conner answered.

"You like me, or you like having sex with me?" Elantra asked bluntly.

"Can't I have it both ways?" Conner asked with a smile. Elantra smiled back and nodded.

"Won't you get in trouble with your agency?"

Conner shrugged. She wasn't ready to explain that she already was or why.

"I'm scared," Elantra said quietly.

"I won't let anyone hurt you if I can stop them," Conner assured her. "Ever."

"I'm not afraid of that," Elantra said.

"Then what?"

"I don't know exactly. It's like I'm... like I'm becoming a different person."

"It's called growth, Elantra, and it's nothing to be afraid of.

It's what happens to everyone when they are exposed to the real world."

Elantra laughed then. "You think *this* is the real world, and my father thinks *that's* the real world."

"It only matters which one *you* think is real. Which one makes you feel alive," Conner said.

"I like it here, with you," Elantra said quietly. "What about you?"

"What about me?" Conner asked, confused by the question.

Elantra rolled away from Conner. "Nothing," she said.

"What?" Conner demanded, going after Elantra and pulling her against her. "What do you want to know?" she asked, then kissed her ear.

"Do you ever... Do you wish I was Peggy? Was that what you were talking to the Contractor about?"

Conner let out a long throaty growl. She had thought that their trip to the building site had already been discussed and forgotten. She pulled Elantra still closer and said into her ear. "I don't want you to be anyone else. I don't wish you were Peggy. I loved Peggy, but she's dead. I'm not trying to turn you into Peggy if that's what you think. I couldn't even if I wanted to. You are too stubborn and pig headed to change in any way that you don't want to. Besides," she tried to remember what the contractor had told her that morning. He was after all a hell of a lot better with words than she was. "I'm a different person than I was when I loved Peg. I needed Peg then, and maybe I need you now..." She realized she had said more than she intended when Elantra turned quickly in her arms to face her.

"What did you say?" Elantra asked in a shocked tone of voice.

"Nothing... I'm not trying to make you into Peg, that's all." Conner said quickly, nervously looking away from Elantra, unable to look her in the eyes.

"You said you needed me. What does that mean, Conner McVee?"

Mr. Buttons picked that moment to jump right in the big middle of the bed. "Stupid fucking cat," Conner grabbed him and hurled him across the room.

Elantra jumped out of bed and went to check on her disgruntled pet. "You might have hurt him!" Elantra accused.

"No such luck," Conner mumbled. In the fight that ensued

over the cat, their previous discussion was completely forgotten – for which Conner was very grateful.

CHAPTER 9

Mishy sat at his desk contemplating the numbers on the screen. Business was good, Tarent was losing ground, and for once it seemed Mishy had the upper hand. However this did not satisfy Mishy's burning lust for revenge.

It wasn't enough to throttle Tarent Powers financially, not when Tarent had killed everything that Mishy cared about.

The debt Tarent owed Mishy couldn't be paid in credits on the computer screen, it could only be truly paid in blood.

Powers blood.

He had called all of his most trusted men in, they had regarded him silently for several minutes, and now as the silence became unbearable, Jumpy spoke up nervously.

"You ah... you wanted to see us, boss?"

"Yeah," Mishy said looking up from the screen. "I got a problem."

"What problem, boss?" Jumpy said with a smile. "Business is back up. With Tarent wasting all his time, money, and man power looking for his kid and the Hammer he doesn't have time to fuck with us or his business."

"Jumpy," Mishy looked up at the man, "I don't care about business. How can I care about business when the blood of my family remains unavenged?"

"As long as Hammer's got the girl..." Tank started.

"What?" Mishy pounded his fist into his desk, and when he looked up at them his eyes were all but glowing. "As long as Hammer has the girl what? It's messing with Tarent's head. You don't understand my sister's widow, but Tarent Powers does. Oh, Hammer's been on both sides of the law. Sometimes at the same time. But she's basically one of the good guys. Hammer McVee is probably one of the most honest, decent people I've ever known. In short, she makes me want to puke. She took the girl as much to protect her from me as she did to get even with Powers. She thought she could force Tarent into giving himself up, or killing himself. That was a fool's game. Tarent cares for no one as much as he cares for himself.

Hammer didn't count on him figuring out what I knew all along – Hammer McVee isn't going to kill that girl. She isn't even going to hurt her, because Tarent did the one thing that he could have done to protect her from people like Hammer, he kept her innocent. Hammer can't bring herself to kill the girl, even to avenge the blood of my sister because the girl is innocent of any crime and it goes against that horrid code of ethics of hers...."

"But as long as Tarent doesn't have his girl..."

"Let me finish, Jumpy!" Mishy screamed, standing up. "Don't anyone else interrupt me until I'm finished. I just learned from one of our sources in Powers' employ that Hammer McVee has a tracer implant in her arm and Tarent Powers has been given the codes. Now she's apparently out of scanner range, for the time being, but eventually he's going to find her, if he doesn't just get tired of looking and go back to business as usual. I want the girl killed before either of those things can happen. I want her killed while it still matters to the selfish fucker. I want him to feel a little bit of my pain. We've got to find McVee before Tarent does."

"How, boss?" Tank asked.

"I know more about Hammer McVee than damn near anyone, because she was married to my sister. Hammer is a big hero amongst these Constructionist weirdoes. As such she and Peg had several cabins in different Constructionist towns. Peg never told me exactly where, but she had a strange hobby. Peg liked to take old-fashioned still photos, and Hammer is too sensitive to have thrown anything of Peg's away. I want you to go to Hammer Town, break into McVee's house, and get the pictures. We'll feed them into the computer and *Voilá!* it will start popping out locations, and I'm betting that one of those locations is where McVee is."

"Boss I hate to point this out but... I'd rather screw with Powers than McVee. The bitch is crazy, and she's wired..."

"I don't want to hear any of your whinin' chicken shit crap, Jumpy. As my sister used to say. *If ya can't take the heat ya get out of the kitchen.*"

None of them really knew what that meant, but they knew what Mishy meant. Do what you were told or leave the organization – which wasn't really an option, because people who left Mishy's employment wound up mysteriously dead.

Each passing day brought warmer weather. They were eating a breakfast of cold cereal with cow juice. It tasted pretty good. Elantra looked across the table at Hammer. "It's a beautiful day, could we maybe go to the beach?" Hammer was silent as if she hadn't heard Elantra at all – which wasn't possible. "What's wrong?"

Conner thought about lying, but then thought better of it. There were enough lies between them. "I have to have some work done on my arm... I want... No. I need to have the tracer unit removed. There is only one doctor in the entire Constructionist community that has the necessary expertise to do it. He lives here, which is part of the reason I came here, but he's out of town and they're having trouble finding him."

"I know quite a bit about implants. Maybe I could fix it." It was obvious by the tone in her voice that not only did she not feel ready to do surgery, but that even if she had she wouldn't have wanted Conner to be her first patient unless there was no option.

"I'm afraid that this is beyond your expertise. You see my entire left hand now has a metal skeleton. My wrist is metal, so are my elbow and my lower arm bones. The tracer unit is in the wrist pin. Screw it up and my whole arm doesn't work. They knew what they were doing. They didn't mean for it to be easily removed. Hell, I'm lucky they didn't use GPS technology. We wouldn't have been able to get away in the first place."

"But... I don't understand," Elantra started, confusion etched into her features. "If the codes belong to your agency... Why would they come looking for you? They know you're working for father. Surely they wouldn't give the base codes to Mishy."

Oh, good job, Hammer. You just smacked into your own lies. Why not just tell her that the person you're really running from is her loving father the hood? Why not tell her the truth the whole truth once and for all and have it over with?

Because, she doesn't believe Tarent's dirty and even if she did, how do I explain what I've done and make her understand? But... I can't keep lying. Lies beget lies. Eventually I'll have to tell her the truth and deal with the consequences.

She looked at Elantra's beautiful face, streaked with the morning sun and eagerly awaiting Conner's answer and decided it wasn't going to be today.

"The agency wouldn't give Mishy the codes, but he could get them. A good hacker can get into any system, and I ought to know – I used to be a hell of a hacker."

"You... but you're a cop." She pointed to Conner's agency tattoo, which was visible because Conner wasn't wearing a shirt.

Conner smiled. "Don't look so shocked. I wasn't born a cop, you know. Why do you think I'm so damn good? I know how the criminal mind thinks, because I used to be a criminal." Elantra started to ask another question, and Conner reached across the table and took her hand. "We're running out of time. Staying put we're making it way too easy for them to find us. Doc Pherson is the only one I know who can do the surgery, and unless I have it... We'll never be able to get away from them. We'll spend our whole lives running."

Elantra smiled. "There are an awful lot of *we's* in that statement, Conner McVee."

Conner looked nervous. "Yes... well, we're sort of in this together, aren't we?"

"Yes," Elantra moved to sit in Conner's lap, "We are." She let go of Conner's hand and wrapped her arms around her neck.

Conner laughed in spite of herself. "Damn it, Elantra, I'm trying to have a serious conversation with you."

"You can have it with me in your lap." Elantra leaned her head on Conner's shoulder. "I'm listening."

"I'm going to go to the Contractor again, make him understand how important it is that we find Pherson right away. See if maybe there's something they haven't tried yet. But first," she stood up with Elantra in her arms, "there's something I've wanted to do every since I got out of bed."

"What's that?" Elantra asked with a laugh.

"Get back in."

They walked out of the house and started down the road. Elantra stopped suddenly and made Conner stop short to keep from hitting her.

"Listen," Elantra said. There was not a sound except the wind in the trees and bird song. It was as if the whole world was sleeping. No car sounds, none of the tool sounds she had begin to associate with Wrench town. "What's wrong?" she asked of the silence in a whisper.

Conner laughed, grabbed Elantra's hand and started walking again dragging Elantra along behind her. "It's Saturday. In six days God created the heavens and the earth, and on the seventh day he rested from the acts of creation and created rest. So, too, Constructionists create on six days but make rest on the seventh. Sometimes you walk to the Building Site and admire creation and talk about construction. The General Contractor will sometimes tell a story, and relate it to building. Everything ethical can be explained and better understood through building. That's where we're going, to the site, to see the Contractor."

The building site was full and surrounded by people sitting in folding lawn chairs that they had obviously brought with them. Some were standing, while others had found a pile of lumber or saw horses and sat down.

The General Contractor was standing on the mostly – finished porch behind a workbench, talking to the "congregation" which were all decked out in their best work bibs and adorned with their best tools. They were an odd-looking lot, and Elantra had to work at not laughing. She and Conner sat on the fence in back of the crowd. Elantra wondered what they did when it rained.

"They stay home and screw mostly," Conner whispered in her ear.

"Can you see everything I think?" Elantra asked in an angry whisper.

"Of course not. The longer you're with someone the more you know how they think. Don't you know what I'm thinking?"

Elantra smiled and whispered in her ear. "Sometimes."

Conner put her arm around Elantra and whispered back. "Be quiet, the Contractor is reading from the *Book of Creation*."

"So God did create the whole world and all the planets. It created animals and plants, water and air, and then It created people to finish creation, but people became lazy and created machines to do their work and turned away from God saying, if there is God where is It, and why can't we see It? And the machines and the computers did take over and populate the earth and became most numerous, so that they could not be counted, and all of the things which they created made people more lazy and less involved with each other. Machines were created to take the place of mothers and fathers of brothers and of sisters. Machines created people in their image and did blur them. All of that which God had created for us the machines and the computers did take away, and of all the things they took away the worst thing was our purpose, our drive to create and to interact with one another. To depend upon each other for companionship.

"God makes forever a distinction between those who do Its work and those who do not, and It blesses those who follow It with sky and earth and water, so that they never lack for beauty to look upon, smell and taste. It blesses them with the ability to touch each other, to give love and to receive it.

"But as for those who do not do God's work and who live in a computerized, mechanized world, this shall be their lot. They will neither see nor smell nor taste God's goodness. They will be locked away from each other, so that they cannot touch one another. They will neither truly love nor receive love. Loneliness shall be their portion.

"They are like a pot which is thrown and never filled, a chair which is built but never sat upon.

"The computer was meant to be a tool. A tool to be used by man to build things. But man did use the computer not as a hammer to create, but as a wrecking bar to tear down. The computer built walls between the people, so that they did not have to interact on a personal level, until the arts of reading and conversation were lost. Touch became as a thing to be feared, screens were created by machines, through which one could feel but never truly touch. Or be touched. Relationships were delegated by business and convenience not by love. Children raised by drones have trouble embracing their fellow man. From whom have they learned compassion?"

Elantra couldn't deny anything he said. She had lived in both worlds now, and every word the man said rang absolutely true. She lay her head on Conner's shoulder then, glad to be feeling and to be felt.

The Contractor seemed to see them then and he smiled broadly.

"I see that today Hammer McVee is with us, so we are truly blessed. For the children who do not know that this day they stand, or sit, with one of the great heroes of our people, I will tell the story of the Cleaning of the Cabinet Shop."

Hammer stood up and started to pull on Elantra's arm. "Come on let's go, I can talk to him later," she insisted.

"No. I don't want to go," Elantra said holding her ground atop the rail fence only with an effort. "I want to hear his story."

"Hammer!" the Contractor bellowed. "You must stay, and be an inspiration to our children."

Hammer sat down and looked at her feet. Just once she would like to go to a service where the Contractor doing the service didn't feel compelled to tell the story of the cleaning of the cabinet shop. She didn't want to be held up as an icon to the community. It was just too damn much responsibility, and right now she didn't feel she deserved to be honored.

She wanted to scream out. *Hey! How honorable is this? I kidnapped this girl and was going to kill her, but instead I'm just having sex with her about four times a day.*

The Contractor started. "In those days the community in Freight City was very new, yet it still had in its midst the holy of holies, the Cabinet Shop in which much work was done, and the finest of cabinets were made by hand as God had intended. The Contractor there did gather the people every Saturday and do worship. But the owner of the shop wanted to move, and so he did sell the shop to a man he believed to be one of our own. But this man was not a Constructionist. He was in fact only a front for a huge corporation, which proceeded to lay off the employees of the cabinet shop, and they did mechanize the shop with every sort of evil furniture making machine, and the noise from the place was a curse to all that heard it. What had once been the holy of holies in the community had been turned into a blemish in the town.

"There was at this time a young proselyte who took it upon herself to do battle with the evil city Board to bring them to justice for their crimes against our people, but they hid behind their positions of power, cowered behind their machines and would not make the corporate raiders sell back to us what was ours. So the proselyte did use her security clearance to get into the shop and did find there an illegal VR disk ring, and she did bring them to justice. Then the proselyte with a sledgehammer did run all the non-believers from the Cabinet shop, and then did she lift the great hammer and destroy all of the abominations. The cabinet shop was then sold back to the people of God, the tools of our faith were put back into place, and the Cabinet Shop once again became a center of work and worship. That is why the name of the place is called

Hammer Town to this day, and the name of the Proselyte was Hammer McVee. The same Hammer McVee who stands among us today."

"Hammer Town is named after you?" Elantra asked, looking at her in disbelief. "You're a Constructionist folk hero!"

Hammer just shrugged. "He tells it a lot prettier than it really was. I obtained the security clearance illegally, I planted the VR disks, and I was shit-faced drunk when I sledged all that equipment," Hammer said in a whisper.

Elantra sat there a little overwhelmed, as it seemed like everyone in the entire community had to come up and embrace Conner. No wonder everyone knew her here, no wonder they seemed to bend over backwards for her. She was a living legend to these people. No doubt written into their records to remain a hero for all generations. Someone grabbed Elantra's arm, and she looked up into the soft gentle eyes of the Contractor.

He smiled at her. "Come with me."

Reluctantly she followed him a little ways from the enthusiastic crowd. "I take it Hammer didn't tell you about her star status here." Elantra shook her head. "We've been trying very hard to find Doc Pherson. This morning I decided that we just needed more man power. There are thousands of acres of timberland up there. I sent three teams of six people out this morning to comb the lake region. The only problem with a community like ours is that it's very hard to find someone if they don't want to be found. Ironically Hammer probably wouldn't have any problem finding him. But she can't leave you alone."

"I could go with her..."

He laughed a little. "You only think you're roughing it now. Maybe in another couple of months, but right now..." He shook his head. "You'd never be able to keep up. It's rough terrain."

"What will they do to her if they catch her?" Elantra asked.

The Contractor was a little taken aback. "Shouldn't you be asking what they'll do to you..?"

"I know Mishy wants to kill me... What will he do to Conner McVee?"

"The worst thing he could do to Hammer would be to kill you."

"Do all of you Constructionists talk in riddles?" Elantra asked.

The Contractor laughed again. "I'm sure everything will be OK. You and Hammer are in for some rocky times. I want you to remember this, remember it always and hang onto it when everything looks its worst. There is nothing in this world as important as love, nothing as strong and absolutely nothing as worthy of putting up a fight for." He reached into his pocket and pulled out a tool. He handed it to her, closed her hand around it, and held it there. "A blessing on you, and on your tools, and on your house. May the things that you build bring you closer to God, and may God be in all that you build."

"Ah... thanks," Elantra said nervously.

He smiled at her and walked away.

Elantra looked from the man's back to the tool in her hand and back again, trying to make some sense of anything he'd said. A few minutes later Conner broke free of the crowd and found her way back to Elantra. "Come on." She took Elantra by the hand and started dragging her towards home.

"One of these days you're going to pull one of my arms right out of the socket, Conner McVee," Elantra complained, pulling on Conner's arm till she slowed down. "Why didn't you tell me you were some sort of hero?"

"Well, it would have sounded sort of egotistical if I did, wouldn't it?" Conner answered hotly.

"So... that didn't stop you telling me how good in bed you were or a hundred other really egotistical things," Elantra said, laughing at the look that came across Conner's face.

Conner mumbled something inaudible then asked. "In all the confusion I didn't get to talk to the Contractor, what did he want from you?"

"I'm not really sure. He talks in riddles like you. He told me they sent more men to look for the doctor, and he gave me this." She held out the tool for Hammer to see. Hammer stopped in her tracks and stared at the object. "Well, don't just stand there. Tell me what it is, and more importantly why he gave it to me."

"It's a screwdriver. It's a very versatile tool, but mostly it's for putting in and taking out screws."

"So, why did he give it to me?"

"Did he give you a blessing?" Hammer asked, although she was sure she knew the answer.

"Yeah. He said 'A blessing on you, and on your tools, and on your house.' Then he said something about may everything

I build be something and another..."

"He had to give you a tool to give you a blessing." Conner ran her hands down her face. "Blessings only come to those who have tools."

"Is that bad?" Elantra asked.

"That rather depends on how you look at it. On the one hand, it can never hurt to have a blessing." Conner took a deep breath. "On the other, you're not one of us, and yet he gave you a blessing. He must have thought you needed it."

"Anybody living with you would," Elantra laughed, trying to break the sudden tension of the moment.

Conner wasn't laughing. "He must have seen something," Conner mumbled.

"What does that mean, oh cryptic one?" Elantra asked.

"A Contractor works on other people's problems. Because of this he becomes like a computer that has been fed a certain type of data. They can assemble all the data that is fed to them, and sometimes they see pieces of what might be." She walked away and Elantra followed, still not clear on why Conner had suddenly become so sullen.

Elantra replayed in her head the entirety of the conversation she had just had with Conner, and then she went back over what the Contractor had said. She looked at Conner's back and replayed what the Contractor had told her once again. Finally she had a startling revelation of her own.

"Conner McVee, do you love me?" she asked Conner's slowly disappearing back. Conner stopped and turned to face her, almost falling in the simple process.

"What did you say?" Conner asked in that way that let you know that she had heard you, but was sure you couldn't have said what she thought she heard.

Elantra walked right up to her and looked in her eye. "It's a simple question. Do you love me?"

"Did the Contractor tell you that I did?" Conner asked accusingly.

"No. He spit out a bunch of psycho-babble which you would need a major computer to figure out, but he kept saying love this and love that, and I want to know. Do you love me, Conner McVee?"

"So what if I do?" Conner spat out angrily, then turned on her heel and walked three times her normal pace. Elantra had to run to catch up with her.

"Does that mean yes or no? It's a simple question, do you love me?" Elantra asked as she hurried to keep up.

Conner stopped abruptly and turned so quickly that Elantra almost ran into her.

Conner looked down at Elantra, an air of total contempt etched on her features. "Yes!" Conner screamed angrily. "Yes I do. I love you. In fact I'm fucking crazy about you. Does that answer your stupid question?"

Elantra smiled smugly. "I don't know why you're so mad about it."

Well you wouldn't, would you, you little shit. I'm standing here with my guts spilt all over the ground, waiting. Waiting to see if you're going to reciprocate – say that you love me, too, or if I'm going to be engulfed in an awful chasm of silence, where you hold all the cards and my heart and I'm left holding hope and air.

Elantra threw her arms around Conner's neck and kissed her gently on the lips. "I think I love you, too."

Conner felt her guts clinching. *I almost wish you'd said nothing. You don't know how you feel. You* think, *as in you* think *you might, maybe love me. What did I expect? She's young. I'm the only partner outside a machine she's ever had.*

"What's wrong?" Elantra asked.

Conner hugged her tight and forced a smile. "Nothing, come on let's get home. I'm getting hungry."

"Hungry or *hungry*," Elantra asked with a sly smile.

Conner laughed. "Are you trying to see if you can wear it out?"

Peggy had obviously really enjoyed her hobby. There were pictures everywhere, thousands of the damn things. Mishy had been feeding the pictures through the computer for days. It took the computer hours to identify a location, when it could do it at all. He had learned that his best luck came when he found pictures with plant life, rock formations and birds or animals in them. Then it started honing in on locations. This sort of animal, bird, or plant lived in these areas... these areas were close to these Constructionist colonies. It was unbelievably tedious. So far they had only locked on three possible locations, and if Hammer McVee had been in any of those locations the Constructionists were more clever than he had given them credit for.

The only up side to this monotonous task was that Tarent Powers wasn't having any better luck finding Hammer, and subsequently his precious daughter. From his sources Mishy had learned that when you moved the base around just about anything would set it off. Tarent had spent weeks now running after one bogus signal or another, and while his attention was turned to finding Hammer, his attentions were turned away from his business. There were even rumors of infighting among the members of his syndicate.

Mishy's people thought he ought to be happy with this. That he should discontinue his own search and concentrate on taking advantage of Tarent's weakness, before it was a thing of the past. Some even suggested that this was much better than just killing the girl. "If she was dead, he'd grieve, get over it, and get back to business. Right now it's a matter of pride that he get her back," Jumpy had suggested.

It wasn't enough. Not for Mishy. He'd let Tarent get away with killing Peggy, and as a result he'd killed Mishy's wife and his son. While he hadn't really given one good damn about his wife, his son had been his world, and Peggy... Peggy had been the only good part of Mishy, and when she'd been murdered so had his conscience.

His computer terminal buzzed, and then Tarent Powers was staring at him. He smiled broadly and then snarled. "What do you think I'm going to tell you, Tarent?"

"If you don't tell me where Hammer McVee is..."

Mishy didn't let him finish making his threat before he started laughing. "Tarent, we have been through this all before. You haven't left me with anything, so any threat you make is empty and we both know it. Right now in fact I think I'm more in a position to threaten you."

"Damn it, Mishy! Elantra's not part of this..."

Mishy laughed still harder. "You made her part of it, Tarent. You made her part of it when you killed my family. When you killed my sister and my son. The children have to pay for the sins of their fathers, isn't that what you told me, Tarent? Well, now your girl is doing the paying."

"Mishy... Do you know where Hammer McVee is?"

"I've got a better question for you, Tarent. If I did, do you really think I would tell you? Computer, terminate transmission."

The computer hummed again, and this time it showed him

a picture of his sister sitting against a tree trunk. In the background you could see a cliff that jetted out over the ocean. He smiled. "Ah, Peg, I miss you. You understood me in a way no one else does." He sighed. "I'm sorry, Peg. Sorry because if I wasn't who I am, you'd be alive right now, and it wouldn't matter where your big, dumb, cop, mate is. Where the fuck is she, Peg? She couldn't just disappear. You know where she went. Where did she go?"

The computer hummed. "The picture was taken on the California coast, in Big Sur," the computer said. "The closest Constructionist town is Wrench Town."

Mishy smiled. "Thanks, Peg."

Tarent fumed as he looked at the swirling colors on his screen.

"Maybe it's time to give it a rest, Dad," Buddy said from his seat across the desk from Tarent.

Tarent spun on the young man and glared at him. "Did it ever occur to you that without Elantra, there will be no marriage? Without a marriage there will be no merger, and that you can stop calling me *Dad*."

From the look on Buddy's handsome face, it hadn't. "But all these years... You've groomed me to run the business, to..."

"Because you were going to marry my daughter, be the father of my grandchildren." Tarent stared at his desk. "All my plans laid in the dust by some technology-hating cyborg with a nail gun."

"There's no reason for our business deal to end," Buddy said. "In fact, I'm pretty sure my father is going to make sure that you don't back out of our deal."

Tarent stood up behind his desk and glared down at the young man. "Buddy, your family is a very little fish in my rather large pond, so I want to make damn sure that you didn't just threaten me. You didn't, did you?"

Buddy swallowed hard. Tarent was the one who'd taught him to be ambitious and ruthless. Of course he wasn't supposed to use those talents against Tarent. "No, sir... I just... I like working with you. I have plans, too."

"Good...Because I would hate it if you were to suddenly become so distraught about the loss of my daughter that you would throw yourself from the top of Powers Towers," Tarent said.

Buddy's lip curled into a snarl, but he was silent.

Perhaps your energy would be better expended helping to look for my daughter, your *fiancé*," Tarent said. "Computer, send Wayne in here." In mere seconds Wayne was there.

"Need something, boss?" Wayne asked.

"Yeah... Poor Buddy is just sick with worry over Elantra's abduction, and he wants to help find her. I thought maybe you could outfit him and take him with you when you go down to Slum Town to shake up the locals and find out what you can about this McVee character. Our man at Brakston said she had connections down there. Find out who, and find out why."

"Yeah, sure thing, boss."

Buddy looked at Tarent, a look of defiant terror on his face. "I... I can't go to Slum town, Tarent. I won't."

"Don't be so modest. I'm sure you'll do just fine," Tarent said, and the tone in his voice, if not the murderous look on his face, said that he would not be denied. He waved his arm dismissively in the air. "Wayne."

"Right away, boss," Wayne took hold of Buddy's arm and escorted him from Tarent's office.

Buddy looked up at Wayne. "How dangerous is Slum Town?"

"Don't be a wuss, it's not like you aren't going to be wearing a bullet-proof vest and carrying a gun," Wayne said.

"My... my father isn't going to like this."

Wayne laughed. "Maybe not, but he ain't gonna say shit unless he's a whole lot dumber than you are."

When they'd walked into the club, some woman had laid a big, wet kiss on Conner. They sat at the table in the corner, where they usually sat. Elantra glared daggers at Conner, but said nothing.

"What?" Conner asked.

"What! We're together. Aren't we together?" Elantra asked hotly. Slinging her hand back and forth between them.

"If you want us to be," Conner said, smiling at the waitress as she set her drink on the table.

"I want us to be," Elantra said. "If you stop doing that."

"Doing what?" Conner asked with a laugh.

"You didn't have to smile at that waitress..."

"I was being friendly..."

"What about the woman at the door?" Elantra asked hotly.

"She kissed me!" Conner defended.

"Yes... Well, you didn't have to enjoy it," Elantra spat.

"OK. I won't," Conner said.

"I don't want it to happen again," she said in an angry whisper. "I don't want other women to kiss you, and I sure don't want you to kiss them. It's bad enough I share germs with you. I don't want to share their germs as well."

Conner laughed. "That's cute."

"What?"

"You're jealous. That's so cute."

"I'm glad you're amused," Elantra bit off. She started to get up and leave, but Conner grabbed her arm and pulled her back into her chair. "Would you please stop woman handling me? How would you like it if I just went around letting strangers kiss me?"

"I wouldn't," Conner said honestly.

"Well, I don't like it, either. So quit it."

"If someone touched you, I'd tell them to quit. If they didn't, I'd beat them senseless. If you don't want people to touch me, I suggest you tell them so."

"*You* tell them," Elantra insisted.

"Why? I don't care if they touch me," Conner said smiling wickedly.

"That's it! I'm going home. I knew this was a bad idea." She started to get up again, and again Conner grabbed her and pulled her back into her seat. "Conner McVee, if you don't..."

"Dance with me." She got up and pulled Elantra behind her to the dance floor. Elantra fell into her arms. She was mumbling about having her arms pulled out of there sockets and being treated like an old sock. "Lanny?"

"Yes."

Conner kissed her lips gently. "Shut up."

Elantra smiled at Conner in spite of herself. "I would call you really bad names if I knew any. You really are mean to me."

"No I'm not." Conner swung Elantra around, and she laughed.

When the song ended they went back to their table. Elantra took a drink of her beer. It tasted especially good tonight, and the band was good, too. She asked Conner to explain the different instruments, which she did happily. She was enjoying herself, but she'd almost rather be home alone with Conner than to have to share her with everyone else, and when people weren't coming by every few minutes to chat, several women were making no bones at all about the fact that they were drooling over Conner McVee. Dedra entered the bar and headed their way. Elantra's distress must have shown on her face because Conner smiled. "Don't let her kiss you," Elantra ordered in an angry whisper.

"Tell her," Conner said, smiling wickedly.

Dedra was there then, and she leaned over to kiss Conner.

Elantra stuck her hand between the two of them. "Please don't do that," Elantra said forcefully.

"Wow! I feel a chill." Dedra straightened and looked at Conner with raised eyebrows.

"We're together," Conner said to Dedra.

"Damn! Well, I knew the way you were fighting it was only a matter of time." Dedra snapped her fingers. She pulled up a chair and sat down looking at Elantra. "We could share her," Dedra suggested.

"No, we couldn't," Elantra said, making a face.

Dedra slapped Elantra on the shoulder. "Loosen up, kid, I was only teasin' you."

Dedra's words did anything but put her at ease. Dedra was treating her like a child. Using her lack of knowledge about the world outside the building against her, and she didn't care what the woman said, her body language was doing the real talking and she, at least in her mind, was all over Conner McVee.

Dedra struck up a conversation about closet making, about which Conner apparently knew a great deal, Dedra knew very little, and Elantra knew absolutely nothing.

Elantra was loath to leave the table with Dedra there, but she'd had to pee for ten minutes, and she couldn't put it off any longer.

Dedra waited till Elantra was a safe distance away. "Isn't the building brat a little young and way too green for you, Hammer?"

"Lay off Elantra, Dedra... Now, you're bugging the hell out of her, so why don't you not be here when she gets back?" Conner suggested.

Dedra laughed. "Are you in love with this girl, Hammer?"

"It just so happens that I am, so why don't you bugger off?" Hammer said, not without good humor.

Dedra stood up. "Never let it be said that I don't know when I'm licked."

"Or when you're not, as the case may be," Conner said with a smile. Dedra laughed and left. Elantra came back to the table, still zipping up her fly. She hadn't wasted any time. She was glad to see that Dedra was gone.

"I'd like to dance again," Elantra said, liking the tune that was being played. Conner nodded and followed her out to the floor. "She really..."

"Pisses you off," Conner finished for her.

Elantra laughed, falling into Conner's arms. "Yeah, I think so. Did you ever... were you ever... you know... with Dedra?"

"Yes. It was a long time ago, and it wasn't very good," Conner said.

"Well, apparently that's not what she thought." Elantra looked across the room at where Dedra was chatting up some woman and snarled at her. She didn't want to think about Hammer being with anyone but her, but that wasn't really realistic. After all, Conner had been married to Peggy.

"Conner... what happened to Peggy?"

"She died," Conner said. "I told you before, it doesn't really matter how."

Someone tapped Elantra on the shoulder. She decided that if she turned around and saw Dedra there she was going to punch her, if she could figure out how. It was the Contractor. He smiled at them both, and putting his arms across their shoulders led them back to their table. How he knew which table they had been sitting at was a question she never got to ask. They sat down and he smiled broadly. "I've got good news. We've found Doc Pherson, and he's on his way now. He should be here by morning."

Conner sighed with relief. "A blessing on you, and on your tools, and on your children," Conner said.

He smiled and stood up. "You'd better get some sleep. A blessing on you, and on your tools, and on your house." He started to walk away, but stopped and walked back over to the table and leaned down. "This time, Conner," he looked at Elantra and smiled. "This time start a family. Yours is too rich a tradition to have it end with you." He walked away, and Elantra tried to absorb what he had just said.

"Did he just..."

"Yes, I think he did," Conner said with a laugh.

"I don't even want to know how you people go about procreating..."

"We carry our own young."

Elantra covered her ears. "I said I didn't want to hear. I'm not doing that. Do you hear me, Conner McVee? No way, that is just too prehistoric."

Elantra didn't know why, but right after sex she always wanted to talk. Conner mostly wanted to cuddle and then go to sleep. Of course, Elantra most felt like talking at the moment that it looked like Conner was almost asleep.

"Conner McVee?"

Conner jerked. "Damn it, Elantra! I was almost asleep... again."

"How dangerous is the operation?"

"It's not life threatening if that's what you mean, but if my luck holds true it won't be a walk in the park, either. I won't really know till I see Doc Pherson tomorrow, and he runs some x-rays to find out just where the device is."

"X-rays! That's a little primitive, don't you think?"

"It's adequate for the procedure."

"If you say so." Elantra shook her head in disbelief. "When it's done... When it's done then we don't have to worry anymore, do we? We can stay here together, no one can find us."

"I hope so, but I wouldn't hold my breath, baby."

"I want to tell my dad about us..."

Conner laughed. "Are you crazy? He'll have me killed for sure."

"I know you think my father is some horrid gangster, but he's not..."

"I don't want to get into this right now, Elantra..."

"Well I do. You haven't even tried to put the computer back together."

Conner smiled wickedly. "You've been keeping me pretty busy, baby."

"Don't try to change the subject, Conner McVee. My father must be worried sick by now. I want him to know that I'm OK. I want him to know about us..."

"Elantra, think about that for a minute. Your father has a husband picked out for you. A very nice little marriage of convenience, which should breed wonderful little petri-dish babies. I'm a woman, a Constructionist, and I'm a police agent. Somehow I don't think Daddy's going to be very pleased about our union."

Elantra wasn't listening any more. She was running her hand down Conner's arm, liking the contrast in color between her skin and Conner's. She liked all the things that were different about Conner and all the things that were the same. She didn't really care what her father thought, and right then she didn't care whether her father was worried or not. She was hot again. She rubbed her body against Conner's expectantly.

Conner laughed, "You are the horniest bitch who ever lived."

"Is that a bad thing?" Elantra breathed.

"No."

Elantra was appalled by the primitive medical equipment all around her. She knew what the instruments were, but not from any classes she had taken in practical medicine. She recognized them from her medical history class.

Doc Pherson was a middle-aged man of average size and looks with loads of unruly white-gray hair. He presented himself in jeans and a flannel shirt with a white cotton doctor's smock thrown over the top.

He clicked his tongue as he looked at the x-rays, and Elantra walked over to look over his shoulder.

"Well?" Conner asked impatiently.

"The transmitter isn't located in the wrist pin, it basically *is* the wrist pin. You won't be able to knock it out with a laser probe without welding the wrist piece solid. The pin is going to have to be replaced," Elantra answered.

Doc Pherson stared at the young woman with squinted eyes. "Do you mind?"

"Sorry," she said with a shrug.

"Well?" Conner asked Doc Pherson.

"The building brat is right," he said.

"How complicated is that?"

"If I had a replacement pin lying around we could fix it today. But it is invasive. About a two inch incision. Pull the muscles out of the way, remove the old pin and subsequently the transmitter, replace the new pin, put it back together. It'd take about an hour, an hour and a half if we run into any complications. Recovery time... Well, once the pin's back in place, the wrist is as good as new, so all you'll really have to deal with is the incision and the pain from the incision. Two, three days healing time, and you should be as good as new."

"How long is it going to take you to get a pin?"

"A week if we're lucky," Doc Pherson said.

"I'm running out of time, Doc. Couldn't you substitute a piece of nail or something..."

"Do you want to risk infection, Conner McVee?" Elantra protested.

Doc Pherson walked over closer to Conner. "She a med student?"

"Uh huh."

"She your partner?"

"Yep."

"Then why does she call you Conner McVee?"

"She says she likes the way it sounds," Conner shrugged.

Elantra stiffened, she was pretty sure that they were making fun of her. "Surely you're not thinking of putting just any ole hunk of metal in her arm," Elantra said.

"Well, duh!" Doc Pherson said. He turned to face Elantra. "I'm a Constructionist, not a quack." He focused his attention back on Conner. "We have an excellent jeweler here in town. He may be able to build what we need, but it won't be titanium, it will have to be stainless which means the arm is not going to be able to take the sort of abuse it is now."

"It will still be stronger than bone. Sounds good to me," Conner said. It didn't sound good to Elantra, and she said so loud and long on the walk back to the house.

Conner mostly ignored her. She was busy looking around seeing if anyone or anything looked out of place. The fact that they hadn't been found by Tarent, Mishy, or Brakston Agency by now was nothing short of a miracle, and it would be just her rotten luck to get caught this close to getting away free and clear.

When the arm was fixed she was going to take Elantra and move on. She had a cabin in Axe Town; they could live there. They could be happy there, and Elantra would never have to know that she had kidnapped her, that Conner had taken her to use in her battle against Tarent. She'd get a job as an agent in Axe Town, and they'd live happily ever after.

"Have you heard a word I said to you, Conner McVee?" Elantra screamed right in her ear.

Conner put an arm around Elantra and pulled her close. "No," she answered truthfully.

Elantra squirmed and pushed away from her. "You are the most infuriating, antagonistic person I have ever known. Go ahead, get gangrene, see if I care." She tripled her pace to walk in front of Conner.

Conner smiled at Elantra's departing form. Elantra had passed her easily and without even breathing heavy. She was young, and she had gotten in shape quickly and without even being aware of it. Elantra was wonderful, full of life and full of passion, and she made Conner feel alive again.

Conner frowned. If Elantra found out what she had done, she could lose her forever. Conner couldn't deal with the prospect; she shook her head to clear her thoughts. The jeweler would make the pin. They would remove the transmitter, and she and Elantra and the damned cat would get out of there. They'd start a life far away from Freight City, the agency, Mishy and Tarent. Maybe someday when they were old and gray and had spent a lifetime together she'd tell Elantra the truth, and maybe she never would.

Elantra had almost reached the house. Conner ran to catch up with her, grabbed her and wouldn't let her go.

"Conner McVee," Elantra struggled half-heartedly against Conner's arms. "Let me go. I'm mad at you. I'm..."

Conner kissed the back of Elantra's neck, and Elantra shivered and stopped struggling.

"That is really unfair," Elantra said. Conner's arms loosened, and Elantra turned to face her lover, wrapping her arms around her neck. "I'm trying to be mad at you."

"I love you, Lanny. Don't forget that, never forget that."

"I don't usually forget something unless I want to," Elantra breathed back. "I don't want you to take risks. I want you to have the operation done right..."

"Lanny, it'll be done right. Doc Pherson wouldn't do anything experimental. I trust him, and you have to trust me."

"I do trust you, Conner McVee."

Mishy threw the binoculars down. "Is that how she avenges my sister's death!" He all but screamed. "By screwing around with Tarent Powers' daughter. Is this how she remembers Peggy? I'll fucking kill her *and* the girl. I'll make her watch while I kill the girl and then I'll kill her."

"We gonna kill 'em now and go home?" Tank asked. He'd never been out of the city before, and all this nature was creeping him out. They were perched on a dirt road about two hundred feet up a hill from Conner's cabin.

"Are you kidding, you giant cockroach? Conner McVee is a walking arsenal. If we get any damn closer she's going to see, hear, or feel us. We intercepted some audio signals. Conner is having some sort of surgery on one of her implants soon. After the surgery she'll be dopey, drugged out. We'll make our move then."

Mishy didn't like the woods any more than his men, but he wanted to be in on the kill, and unlike this walking bag of muscle and bone, Mishy knew just what Hammer was capable of. There was no sense taking chances, not when Hammer herself was giving them the perfect window of opportunity.

Tarent's screen buzzed to life, and Little Jimmy stared back.

"Well, don't just sit there like an idiot!" Tarent screamed. "Do you have something or not?"

"We followed Mishy and his boys to a Constructionist colony called Wrench Town. About forty-five miles out of town the transmitter started to buzz. Mishy is staking out a house here. According to the tracer she's there."

"Can you see Hammer McVee? Is Elantra with her?"

Little Jimmy looked over at Big Bobby. Big Bobby was looking through the binoculars trying to see through all the nature. He saw them and he pulled the binoculars quickly away from his eyes as if he'd been burned. "Christ almighty!" he screamed.

"What's with him?" Tarent ordered.

"Miss Elantra's there all right," Big Bobby choked out. "She's in bed with Hammer McVee."

"What!" Tarent screamed. "Maybe they're just sharing a bed."

Big Bobby looked back through the binoculars. He looked over at Little Jimmy, grinned broadly and shook his head no, then put the binoculars back to his eyes.

"Well?" Tarent screamed. Big Bobby didn't answer.

"Well?" Little Jimmy asked, slapping Bobby.

Bobby lowered the binoculars reluctantly. He smiled at Jimmy. "Well, they ain't sleepin'."

"Are they at least using a screen?" Tarent demanded.

"Oh, hell no," Bobby said excitedly.

"Damn it to hell!" Tarent screamed. "Kill her. Kill Conner McVee and bring my daughter back here. We'll have Elantra reprogrammed. You kill Conner McVee and get my daughter back before she can be corrupted any further by those stinking religious fanatics."

"How?" Little Jimmy asked.

"I don't know how, just do it!" Tarent ordered. "Close transmission." He was gone. Big Bobby put the binoculars back to his eyes, but Little Jimmy slapped him and took them away. He looked through them.

"It looks to me like the boss's little girl is pretty much into pussy." He laughed.

"Re-program my ass," Big Bobby snorted. "So... how we going to take the bitch out and bring the boss's little dyke home?"

"Mishy ain't movin' in for the kill, which means he's waiting for something. I say we find out what. Let Mishy's goons get Hammer busy, and then we'll grab Elantra."

"If we wait for Mishy to make his move, the girl might get killed."

"So, we tell the boss we did everything we could. Everything we've learned about McVee over the last few weeks... I'd rather deal with the boss than the cyborg."

CHAPTER 10

The phone rang as Conner was towel drying her hair.

"Hello," she said, raising the receiver to her mouth.

"Conner, the pin is finished, do you want to wait till morning?"

"Is there any reason you can't do it now?" Conner asked. Elantra came in wearing a towel and draped herself on Conner, resting her head on Conner's chest. "If you're too tired or something I understand, but the sooner I can get this over with the better. I need to leave town like yesterday."

"I don't have any help right now, my nurse and my partner are both home sick with some sort of bug, but if your woman can help me..."

"She can," Conner said quickly. "We'll be there in ten."

"I'll get the surgery ready," Dr. Pherson said.

"He's ready to do the surgery?" Elantra asked.

"Uh huh," Conner said pushing her gently away. "Come on, get dressed."

Conner started towards the bedroom and Elantra grabbed her hand. Conner turned to look at her. "Conner McVee, I... I love you."

Conner smiled bent down and kissed her on her forehead. "I'm not going to die, Elantra."

"I know that. I just... it's just I... Just now, in the shower. I knew. I knew I loved you."

Conner kissed her gently on the lips. "And I love you, so quit stalling. Get dressed so we can get this damn thing out of my arm, then all our problems will be solved."

They started to get in the car, but Conner suddenly whipped the patch off her eye and did a scan.

"What's wrong?" Elantra asked.

"Shssh!" Conner ordered. She listened, but she didn't see or hear anything that shouldn't have been there, still she felt something. "Damn sensitivity implant, useless piece of crap! I never know how much of what I'm feeling is my own intuition and paranoia and how much is the machine. Come on, let's get this over with."

They got in the car. Conner put her patch in her pocket instead of putting it on, and Elantra knew her fears were not completely gone. "We'll leave town in the morning as soon as I've slept off the dope."

"You shouldn't drive…"

"We're leaving in the morning, Elantra." Conner told her.

"But I like it here, I…"

"We can't stay. We'll come back. I promise."

Elantra nodded silently.

Doc Pherson was waiting for them. He looked at Elantra. "Scrub in," he ordered.

"But I've never worked on a real human, only virtual patients…"

Pherson looked at Conner impatiently. "Not only did you not ask her, you didn't even bother to tell her. I swear, McVee, I don't know how you always manage to have such beautiful, intelligent women around you."

"I give great head," Conner said with a smile.

Elantra slapped at her shoulder. "You're rude and arrogant."

"That was sort of my point," Pherson said with a laugh, then added on a more serious note. "I need you to scrub in and assist me. Can you do that?"

Elantra looked at Conner. "I can't."

"Yes you can," Conner said gently.

She looked at Pherson and said again. "But I've never worked on a person before."

"Well, there's a first time for everything. Don't worry, you'll just be assisting, and I'll walk you through it."

"But I know very little about your primitive implements."

"Then now is a good time to learn. After all, we're only replacing a wrist pin not doing brain surgery."

Elantra nodded and scrubbed in the way he told her. "This is not a sterile environment…" she started to protest.

"Sterile enough, my girl. No environment is completely sterile, I don't care what they say."

Elantra looked at Conner, a look of pure panic on her face.

"It'll be fine, Elantra. You will be wonderful. If it helps, pretend like it's not your favorite hand," Conner said with a wicked grin.

"It's not funny, Conner," Elantra said hotly.

"It's just my arm, Lanny, I won't even be out."

"Oh yes, yes you will," Doc Pherson said. He nodded, and an anaesthetist walked into the room. Conner looked at him and shook her head no. The man looked at Pherson, who nodded his head yes, and the man started to put a mask over Conner's face. She protested and waved it away.

"A local..." Conner started.

"No way, Hammer. People do weird shit when you're cutting on them. I need you perfectly still. And to be quite honest, with all the hardware you've got in you, I'm afraid if you freak out you might accidentally rip my arm off. This is a very delicate operation, I need your ass gassed."

"But..."

"No buts, Hammer. It's my way or the highway. Don't worry. The Contractor made sure you'd be safe."

The mask went on, and Conner went out.

"Now?" Tank asked Mishy as they watched the clinic.

"No," Mishy said looking through the binoculars.

"But, boss... during surgery..."

Mishy interrupted him, pushing the binoculars into his hand. "Have a look." Tank lifted the binoculars to his eyes. "See all those people just hanging around down there?"

"Yeah," Tank answered.

"See anything funny about them?" Mishy asked.

Tank looked close, then answered in a shocked tone. "They're all packing heat."

"Yeah." Mishy took the binoculars and thumped Tank on the back of his head with his fist. "I told you. McVee is like a hero to these Constructionist dorks. She's not stupid. She knows she's in trouble, and she's got them protecting her while she's at her most vulnerable. We'll just have to wait."

The operation only took forty-five minutes from start to finish, but Elantra learned more about medicine in those few minutes than she had learned in six years of virtual school. She was surprised by the man's knowledge, his skill, and his patience with her. She hardly breathed until the incision was closed, glued, and dressed. She collapsed onto the nearest chair, and Doc Pherson laughed at her.

"You did OK for a building brat," he said.

"Thanks. I think. Is she going to be all right?"

"She'll be fine. She'll wake up in a little while. We'll give her a couple of pain killers and ship her ass home." He paused, throwing his latex gloves in the trash. "So are you going to become one of us?" he asked curiously.

"A Constructionist?"

"Yeah."

"I don't know. I don't know what I want anymore. These last few weeks... Well, let's just say they have been rather enlightening. I know I love Conner McVee. I know I want to spend the rest of my life with her. If I have to become a Constructionist to do that, I guess I can handle that, too. I mean – if I can get used to the sort of bathrooms you people use, I guess I can handle just about anything else you can throw at me."

"Good, then we'll do a little ovum splicing and make an heir for Hammer McVee."

"Then again I could be wrong," Elantra said pulling a face. "Conner told me you people carry your own young. That's barbaric! I'm not having any infant attaching itself to my insides and pushing my body out of shape until it's ready to claw it's way out of me. Let Conner do that if that's what she wants."

"She can't," Pherson said. "Too many implants. Bones give, but metal doesn't."

"Wait a minute... Ovum splicing is unnatural, high tech. I thought you people were dead set against our evil technology."

"We are only against technology when it stifles creation. Using technology to allow Hammer McVee to reproduce would bring blessings upon me. Each couple should have at least two children, to replace them when they are gone. One person to replace another, if at all possible. No more and no less." He finished cleaning up. "Knowledge is a tool, Elantra. No tool is evil. Technology is only bad because people misuse and overuse it."

"Why is everyone so hot for Conner McVee to procreate?"

Doc Pherson laughed. "Because she is the only living hero of our history. If she leaves with no heir, who will replace her? Could any but her own child be as brave or daring as she? So... Now you answer a question for me. Why is it that Conner had to have this implant out so badly? The Contractor wouldn't tell me."

Elantra could think of no good reason not to tell him. "There is this gangster... Mishy, he's trying to kill me and Conner McVee."

"Mishy's trying to kill Hammer McVee? That doesn't make any sense. Why is he trying to kill you?"

"He thinks my father killed his family."

Pherson looked visibly shaken then. "You're Tarent Powers' daughter." It wasn't a question, it was a statement of fact.

"Yes. He hired Conner to protect me," Elantra said.

"Hammer McVee is working for Tarent Powers!" he exclaimed, seeming completely confused.

Elantra would have liked to know why the man seemed so incredibly uncomfortable about who she was. She didn't get to find out because Conner picked that moment to start coming out of the anaesthesia. Elantra moved to stand beside her.

"How'd it go?" Conner asked.

"Very well," Elantra said.

"Lanny I... I have to tell you something. I..." Conner looked up into her dark eyes and froze.

"What?"

"I'm tired. I want to go home," Conner said.

"I'll get someone to drive you," Doc Pherson offered.

Conner didn't want to eat. She didn't want anything to drink. The man who had driven them home helped Conner into the bedroom where she took a pill, took off her shirt and her boots, lay down and went to sleep. Elantra usually wore nothing to bed, but tonight it was a little chilly and there was no chance she was going to get any. She put on a blue sweat suit, and turned the CD player on low. She saw the screwdriver the Contractor had given her lying on top of the dresser. She grabbed it and stuck it in her pocket for no better reason than she liked having pockets and sticking stuff into them. She walked over to the bed and lay down beside Conner.

She liked Constructionist music. She liked this particular CD above all the others because it's the one that had been playing the first time she and Conner had made love, and just as Conner had said, listening to it reminded her of that time. Filling her momentarily with that wonderful mixture of fear and confusion and need. Reminding her of how quickly Conner had quieted her fears, and satisfied both her curiosity and her longing. Dygarhythms never did that. They were pretty noise at best.

Mr. Buttons jumped on the bed, and this time it was Elantra that kicked him off. The last thing they needed was cat germs around Conner's wound. She chased the cat out of the room and shut the door.

"What was that?" Conner asked, more asleep than awake.

"The cat. I threw him and his germs out. Go back to sleep."

"Hold me." Conner whined. Elantra lay down and curled herself around Conner, who smiled.

"You're kind of cute when you're pathetic," Elantra said.

Conner was asleep again. Elantra was almost asleep when she heard a noise. She sat up in bed, and before she had time to react in any other way the bedroom door burst open and three big men with huge guns jumped in the room.

"God damn you, Hammer!" the one in the middle screamed. "Is this how you remember my sister, by fucking Tarent Powers' daughter?"

Now Conner had been fast asleep, so Elantra was a little shocked when Conner rolled over, grabbed her, and rolled to the floor just as a bullet went into the pillow where Conner's head had been.

"Damn it, Mishy!" Hammer screamed as she grabbed her nail gun from under the bed. "Don't make me kill you."

"Fuck you, McVee, and your little black bitch, too." Before Mishy could squeeze off another round Conner started firing wildly. Across the room the window broke out, and two men Elantra recognized as men who worked for her father jumped in, firing at the other three men.

Conner reached under the bed, grabbed her tool belt and slung the strap over her shoulder. She grabbed Elantra, who was still lying underneath her, in her free hand and literally pulled her under the exchanging gunfire and out of the room. She stood, up dragging Elantra to her feet, and they ran out of the house as the room behind them disintegrated in gunfire.

They made a run for the car.

Elantra turned around to see if anyone was following them. What she saw was her cat. "Mr. Buttons!" She jerked out of Conner's grasp. Conner tried to grab her, but groggy and with her one good arm full of nail gun she just flat missed.

"Elantra, no!" Conner screamed. Elantra didn't stop. Hammer started after Elantra and realized that someone was running through the house. "Elantra, come back." She wasn't going to make it in time. She hadn't lived through all she'd lived through without learning one hard and fast rule. Desperate times called for desperate measures.

Conner aimed and fired. The cat spun across the living room floor to land quietly against the far wall. He never knew what hit him.

Elantra stopped in her tracks, screaming in shock, and Conner caught hold of her and started dragging her back towards the car. They jumped in and Conner roared off just as two men ran from the house firing at her.

Conner tore off down the driveway and onto the main road. She drove with her knees for a second and threw her belt in the back seat. She put her gun between the seats.

"Poor Mr. Buttons," Elantra cried, "and I was mean to him, too. God damn it, Conner! You killed my cat." She slapped Conner in the shoulder, and Conner flinched. "Why did you do that? Why did you kill Mr. Buttons?"

"Elantra... You were going to go back into a house filled with warring crime lords to save a fucking cat!"

"But why'd you have to kill him? Why? Why?" Elantra cried.

"Damn it, Elantra, I only have one good arm right now. I'm drugged completely out. I'm not really thinking straight. First Mishy and his thugs jump in the room screaming and then Tarent's goon squad. I'm trying to get us out of there in one piece, and you start to go back for the cat. I could only hold onto you and the gun if you weren't jerking away from me. I couldn't catch you. I knew if I killed the cat you'd stop. So I shot the fucking cat, all right!" Conner screamed. "It was you or the cat. The cat lost. I'm sorry. Right now I've got bigger things to worry about. Either Tarent's men or Mishy is right on our tail, and I've got to tell you the truth – everything's a blur to me."

Conner headed out of town, or at least she thought she was. The last thing she wanted was a firefight in the middle of a bunch of civilians. "Radio on," Conner ordered.

"Radio on," it responded. Elantra looked at her.

"Hey, I can be religious, but I still have to be practical," Conner defended. A shot bounced off the car and she flinched. "Wrench Town police agency."

"This is Wrench Town agency. We read you, Hammer."

"I'm being pursued. I need help."

"Have heard shots and am responding. Cars have been sent to your residence, and we're putting a bead on the car following you now."

Conner heard the anti tank gun go off. When she looked

in her rearview mirror the car that had been chasing her was nothing but flames. "Thanks, guys."

"Our pleasure," they replied.

"Radio off," Conner ordered. Elantra was still crying. Conner drove out of town and headed in the direction of Axe Town. It was normally a two-day drive, but in her condition it was probably going to take three. She looked down at her wrist. She didn't know whether she had ripped it open or not, but the wound was bleeding. There was blood on her left shoulder as well. Something had knocked a nice little hole in her flesh. It was nothing to be worried about. It was mostly just annoying. Like not having a shirt. Her head was pounding, and her vision was blurred. "I'm really sorry I killed your cat, Lanny. I really am...." Elantra only cried louder and turned her shoulder to Conner.

Mishy got up from the floor and dusted himself off. Luckily he was wearing a good bulletproof suit. Tank and Jumpy hadn't fared so well. They were both shot all to hell. There was a sixteen penny nail between Jumpy's eyes.

"Fucking McVee! She doesn't even have to be awake or even *try* and she kills people."

He'd heard Tarent's men roar off, and then a few minutes later he'd heard them blown up. The Constructionists took care of their own, and if he didn't want to end up the same way he had better get the hell out of Wrench Town. He stumbled out of the house and then stumbled up the hillside to his car. He had just reached it when four cars pulled in around the cabin. He got in his car and waited for all the cops to go inside. "Car, drive me back to Freight City as fast as you can." The car drove off without being noticed. "Seat recline." It did, and he lay down. Now he'd have to go through the task of finding Hammer all over again, but he'd done it once, and he'd do it again. And this time he'd be damn sure he hadn't picked up a tail.

Tarent knew when he couldn't get through that Hammer had killed Little Jimmy and Big Bobby. He took a deep breath and let it out slowly, trying to think. Elantra could be dead, too. There was no way of knowing. Mishy had been there, and who knew what Hammer might do if they had pinned her down. Any of them could have killed her.

No. Elantra must still be alive. Mishy or Hammer would have called gloating by now if she were dead. Unless of course they were dead as well. He was going to have to wait for his answers, and Tarent didn't like to wait.

An hour down the road Elantra was still crying about the cat. Conner had learned the hard way that saying things like, it was only a cat, I'll get you another cat, or even, I'm sorry, were not helpful.

"You never did like him," Elantra cried loudly. "You always hated him. You wanted to kill him. You enjoyed it."

"Lanny, I said I'm sorry. I can't take it back now. I wish I could. I'm very, very, grovelingly sorry. Now please stop crying. You're tears are more punishment than I deserve."

Elantra sniffled and dried her eyes and nose on her sleeve. "Why, Conner McVee, that was almost poetic." She sniffled again. She thought maybe she was done crying, so she settled back into her seat. "I don't understand why my father's friends were trying to kill us..." She remembered the horrible moment when the night had been splintered by intruders, the words the man had said, and who Hammer had said he was. Somewhere in Elantra's brain it all started to click. "That man... he was Mishy... Peggy was Mishy's sister... My father's men weren't here to kill them, they came here to save me, from you." She hauled off and hit Hammer in the shoulder as hard as she could. Hammer swerved and pulled the car over and stopped. It was a good thing she did. Elantra started pounding on her everywhere she could reach. Conner held up her good arm to protect herself. "You... You never rescued me. You kidnapped me. That's why you wouldn't let me talk to my father. You made me love you. God damn you, Conner McVee!" She hit Conner again. "Do you care about me at all?"

"Yes, I love you. I never lied about that," Conner answered. Now she really wished she had a shirt. This was not the kind of discussion she wanted to have bare chested, especially if Elantra was going to keep hitting her, and it didn't look like she was going to quit any time soon. "Mishy kidnapped you first, he would have killed you..."

"Has anything you've told me... Has any of it been the truth?" Elantra started to cry again.

"The way I feel about you, almost everything I've told you, only the part about me working for your father was a lie,"

Conner said weakly.

"Peggy was murdered, wasn't she?"

"Elantra... it doesn't matter."

"Was she?" Elantra demanded.

"Yes!" Conner screamed back, crying herself now. "Yes! Gang raped, killed and mutilated by your father's men, at his command. All captured on DVD except of course for faces. So that we know exactly who did it, but it isn't enough evidence for a conviction."

"I'm... I'm sorry that happened to her, but it doesn't excuse the fact that you kidnapped me to get back at my father. Because you believe he killed Peggy..."

"Damn it, Elantra, wake up! I'm not trying to excuse what I did, but Tarent did kill Peggy," Conner defended.

Elantra quit hitting her then, and just started sobbing. "You made love to me. You said you loved me."

"I do, Elantra. I love you more than anything, more than life. I'd never do anything to hurt you."

"You kidnapped me! You killed my cat!" Elantra screamed, in angry disbelief. "So what was the deal? What was the ransom?"

"Lanny, I didn't know you when I kidnapped you. I couldn't have known that I was going to fall in love with you..."

"What was the ransom?" Elantra demanded.

"I Told Tarent I would kill you if he didn't kill himself or turn himself in. I loved her, too, Elantra, and I wanted him to pay for what he did to her. What he's done to a thousand people like her. What he did to me..."

"Were you planning to kill me before or after we'd had sex..."

"I couldn't kill you, Lanny. I never could have. I had decided that I couldn't even before I realized that I was in love with you."

"How very nice of you," Elantra hissed through her tears.

"I could never hurt you, Lanny. Don't you see? That's why Mishy came after us. Because I wasn't giving him the revenge he wanted..."

"But you were still getting revenge, weren't you, Conner McVee? By sleeping with me, turning me into a Constructionist, a lesbian, making me all the things my father hates. Making sure that I couldn't return to building life."

"If that were true, why wouldn't I say so, Elantra? Why

would I care one bit about how you feel now? If that were true, why wouldn't I have encouraged you to call your father and tell him?"

"Because the computer doesn't work," Elantra said.

Conner looked down at her hands silently. Elantra knew what the silence meant.

"It's not broken, is it?" Elantra screamed.

"I took it apart so that you couldn't use it."

"Another lie!" Elantra screamed. "How can I believe anything you say, Conner McVee? You kidnapped me and held me prisoner..."

"Oh, come on, Elantra. You were the happiest damn prisoner I have ever seen," Conner said with an exasperated sigh. "I knew this was going to be hard, but I didn't think that even you would be hardheaded enough to make it impossible."

"Were you ever going to tell me the truth?" Elantra demanded.

"I don't know," Conner said honestly. "I wanted to. I started to a dozen times, but I didn't want this. I didn't know how to tell you so that there wouldn't be this. I knew it would hurt you, and I never want to hurt you."

"Let me guess, you couldn't find the words for, 'I kidnapped you and I was going to kill you to get back at your father but I fell in love with you'... It's lame, Conner. To put it in terms you'll understand. 'It sounds like bull shit.' You're using me to get back at Daddy for something that I know he didn't do, but you don't have the guts to kill me, so you're just going to fuck me instead." She cried harder. Conner reached over and dried a tear off Elantra's cheek. Elantra pulled away from her.

"I do love you, Elantra. What do I have to do to prove that to you?" Conner said.

"Take me home," Elantra ordered.

"Elantra, your father is a criminal. He's kept you a prisoner your whole life, do you really want to go back to that? Back to the corporate crime groom? I love you, we got away from them, and we're free now. All we have to do is keep driving and start our life someplace new."

"Why?!" Elantra screamed accusingly at Conner. "Because you love me, or because you aren't finished punishing my father yet. If you care about me at all, you'll take me home."

Conner took in a deep breath. The trust between them had been shattered, if not forever, at least temporarily. She quickly ran all possibilities through her brain. *Elantra isn't ready to forgive me, not even ready to try. She may never forgive me. This may be something that we can't overcome. Tarent isn't going to hurt her, at least not physically, and going back there just might prove to her how much she no longer wants to be there. Tarent will have no doubt beefed up security to the point that Mishy shouldn't be able to get at her. One thing's for sure, she can't be out here on her own. Of course Tarent's probably never going to let her back out either, at least not willingly. I could force her to go with me. It would be safer for both of us, but if I do, then she's always going to resent me. This is always going to be between us and we'll never get back to where we were.*

She didn't really have a choice, not if she wanted to save the relationship. Not if she were going to have any chance of regaining Elantra's trust. And without Elantra, she didn't really care what happened to her.

Conner had a change of clothes in the car for just such occasions, and although she would have liked to take a few minutes to get them, there was something suddenly comforting about the discomfort caused by her shoeless feet and shirtless body. She started the car, turned it around, and headed back towards Freight City. "All right. I'll take you home then," she mumbled. Tears stung at her good eye. Luckily her implant was starting to function normally, so that she was able to see. She took a deep breath and tried to speak calmly and without the choke of tears in her voice, it didn't work. "I'll take you back to that steel and glass hell, because that's what you say you want." Unable to stop herself she added sarcastically. "Well, this really worked out well for me, didn't it? Tarent's got a price on my head, and now Mishy wants me dead. You hate my guts, and Peggy's death remains unavenged."

"Just take me home!" Elantra cried.

"I'm taking you home!" Hammer's pain eroded into anger. "I'm putting my very life on the line to do it. You're as big a liar as I am, Elantra, because you said you loved me and now you're making me do this," Conner said. "You're just walking away from me."

"Don't you dare!" Elantra screamed back. "Don't you even *try* to act righteously indignant. You did this to me."

Hammer swallowed her own anger. Elantra was right. *If the tables were turned, I wouldn't believe one word she said.*

She doesn't believe her father is a crook, much less a killer. Why would she believe that? She's probably never seen him do anything more horrible than sit at his desk. Except...

"I'm sorry, you're right. Why should you trust me? If you ever had any feelings for me at all, make me one promise."

Elantra sniffled. "What's that?"

"Don't trust your father. Your mother did, and now she's dead," Hammer said.

"My father didn't kill my mother. Damn it, Conner McVee! You are completely obsessed with the thought that my father is this evil monster. Haven't you hurt me enough?" Elantra said through angry tears.

Hammer sighed. Everything she said seemed to make things worse, so she fell silent.

The drive was longer even than Elantra remembered. At one point Conner pulled off the road. "Why are we stopping?" Elantra demanded.

"Elantra, I know you no longer remember a few hours ago when you used to care for me, so I'll refresh your memory. I just had surgery, then I had to save us from Mishy and Tarent's hired thugs. You no longer want anything to do with me, and now I've been driving for hours. I'm emotionally and physically spent. Since you apparently don't love me anymore anyway, and I'm expected to continue my life without you, I have to take care of myself. I need some sleep, I need to dress my wounds, and I need a shirt. I have a first aid kit and a change of clothes in the trunk."

"Are you hurt then?" Elantra asked, concern suddenly entering her voice.

"Don't pretend to care. I'll slap a couple of bandages on, put on a shirt, catch a couple of hours sleep, and then I'll take you straight home as promised."

Elantra nodded silently.

Conner drove up the dirt road till she was out of sight of the main highway and killed the engine. She stepped out of the car right into a mud puddle, looked down at her wet stockinged foot and said through gritted teeth, "Oh, this night just *keeps* getting better and better."

She walked around to the trunk and opened it, pulling out the first aid kit. Elantra walked over to her.

"Let me help," Elantra said quietly, and Conner nodded. It

was a dark night, and the only light she had was the trunk light. She did the best she could. Elantra found some hydrogen peroxide and boiled out both the cut on Conner's shoulder and her wrist. Upon removing the dressing on Conner's wrist she found that the wound had opened slightly, so after having cleaned it she found a butterfly bandage and pulled the wound closed again. "You'd better watch that."

"Uh-huh," Conner said woodenly. Elantra dressed both wounds and then Conner pulled her shirt on and buttoned it up. She noticed that Elantra was watching, and a little glimmer of hope flickered inside of her. "It's not too late to go back, Elantra," she said quietly.

"I can't be with you right now, Conner." Elantra started to cry again. "I just can't. There is so much confusion in my head. Please, don't try to make this harder than it is. I need to think, and I can't do that around you."

Conner nodded silently. She grabbed a flashlight, a pair of boots, and a dry pair of socks, then she closed the trunk. She sat down in the driver's seat, pulled her wet socks off and then put the dry ones on. She pushed Elantra's seat back and then her own and lay down. Elantra got in the car and lay down on her seat.

It was so dark that Elantra literaly couldn't see Conner. She closed her eyes to try and get some sleep. She lay there sleeplessly for several minutes, tossing and turning trying to get comfortable. Her socks were wet, and she was way too cold. She wondered how someone could be prepared enough to have a change of clothes and a first aid kit in the trunk, but not a blanket.

She had grown accustomed to sleeping in Conner's arms, feeling her body pressed against hers. Conner was not a cold-blooded killer; she knew that. Conner could never have killed her, even to avenge Peggy's death, but Conner was more than capable of using her to get back at her father if it didn't include doing Elantra physical harm.

She wanted to believe that Conner McVee loved her, that it hadn't all been just an elaborate lie. But how could she ever be sure? Conner had told her one lie after another. Maybe she was proving how she felt by taking Elantra back to Tarent, or maybe this was how she was exacting her ultimate punishment on him, by returning a daughter who could no longer be happy to live in polite building society.

Confusion was eating away at the corners of her brain, and all she really wanted to do was find some soft spot on Conner's chest and lay her head down. Feel her warmth and listen to her heart and believe as she had just a few hours earlier that it was beating only for her.

All she really knew for sure was that the world had just opened up to her, and if she went back to her father the world would be locked outside the building again. It was also true that while she had never known such pleasure in building life, she had also never known such pain.

"Conner McVee?"

"Yeah," Conner said in that voice that said she had been almost asleep.

"Are you cold?" Elantra asked.

"Yeah," Conner said. She sat up then and turned on the flashlight. "I just remembered." She got in the glove box and pulled out a small packet. "Solar blanket." She held the flashlight in her mouth, opened the package and opened the blanket out. She made a face. "It isn't very big, it looked bigger on the display. You can use it."

"If we moved to the back seat, we could both use it, and we could keep each other warm." Elantra said.

Neither wanted to risk getting her feet wet – or wetter as in Elantra's case – by getting out of the car again, so they shifted and scooched until they were in the back seat. Conner lay with her back to the seat, and Elantra curled into the space in front of her, and when she touched Conner she sighed. Conner covered them both with the blanket as best she could and then turned the flashlight off. She put her arm around Elantra and drew her closer, and Elantra didn't fight her. In fact, she moved to lace her fingers with Conner's.

"I will miss you," Elantra said.

"Then don't leave me," Conner begged in a whisper. "I know what I did was wrong, but if I hadn't done it I never would have met you, and we never would have had this, so I can't say I'm sorry I did it. I'm only sorry that I hurt you."

"I have to go back, Conner. I have to see my father and ease his mind. I have to get away from you and see if my feelings for you are real, or if it's just a case of me buying into your lie. I trusted you, and now I can't, and if I can't trust you, how can I ever trust me?"

Conner pulled up in front of Power's Tower and stopped the car. "Are you sure this is what you want?"

Elantra nodded silently and reached for the handle.

"Please, Lanny..." Conner grabbed her shoulder. Elantra glared at her and she removed her hand. "I do love you. When you're tired of punishing me, call me. I'll leave my computer on. I'll get you out, or die trying."

"I don't know if I can ever trust you again." Elantra dried a tear from her eye. "I have to think, Conner McVee, and you... when I'm around you I don't want to think. I just want to believe you. I know you think, no *believe*, that my father is evil incarnate, but you're wrong. If I want to leave he won't like it, but he'll let me go." She turned and kissed Conner gently. Conner grabbed her and they exchanged a passionate kiss. Elantra pushed away, and she smiled sadly. "That's what I mean." She got out of the car at the same time Conner did. She realized Conner was checking to make sure things were safe. Then she noticed Conner's bandage was bloody. "Conner your hand..." She started to come around the car, and Conner held up her hand.

"I'm not your problem anymore. I'll take care of it myself. Hurry and get in the building. You're a sitting duck out here. I'll cover you."

Elantra nodded and made a dash for the building. At the door she turned to look one last time at Conner McVee. Conner wouldn't meet her gaze, and as the door opened for her and she walked through, Conner drove away. Her entire body seemed to suddenly be hollow, and she immediately regretted her decision. She started to cry.

CHAPTER 11

Conner drove to her home in Hammer Town to find it in ruins. They had turned everything upside down, and what they hadn't poured out or ripped apart they had purposely broken. They had taken all the pictures, every one of them. Conner immediately knew why, and exactly how Mishy had found her. Tarent's boys had no doubt had a bug on Mishy's car and followed him at a distance. All the worrying she had done over the transmitter, and Conner only now realized that wasn't how they found her.

It was a good thing she had brought Elantra back to her father. She had been stupid to think she could hide from Tarent and Mishy. At least for the time being Elantra was safer with Tarent.

She sat down at what was left of her kitchen table and put her computer back together. It took awhile because even though she was really good with computers, she had really done a thorough job taking it apart.

When she was finally done, she called up the Brakston Agency. James Rank glared back at her; obviously he still had his panties in a knot.

"Tarent Powers jus' called me, Hammer." Rank said hotly. "He told me ya killed two of his men fore he got his daughter back. He's talkin' about bringin' kidnappin' charges against ya. He's threatenin' to sue the agency less we fire ya..."

"He isn't going to do shit, Rank. He's just blowing smoke out his ass. He can't prove anything. I'll just say he's pissed because I slept with his daughter."

"Ya did what!" Rank screamed angrily.

"I've been screwing his daughter. It's no big deal. We're in love. As soon as she gets over being pissed at me because I kidnapped her we'll be together again," Conner said confidently.

"Do ya have any idea how stupid ya sound?" Rank screamed.

"This from a man who took speech lessons so that he could learn to talk like an Okie." Conner smiled at the brand new look of rage on Rank's face. "Since when does Tarent Powers call the shots at Brakston Agency?"

"Since one of our agents stupidly kidnapped and apparently molested his daughter. Ya had ta run this game all the way out, didn' ya, Hammer? I'm sorry, but ya've become a liability to the agency. I'm terminatin' yer employment with us effective immediately. I've petitioned to have your permit revoked and your security clearance knocked down…"

"You can't do that!" Hammer said hotly. "You want to fire my ass, that's great, but you've got a hell of a nerve trying to revoke my permit. As for knocking down my clearance… I got bigger and better connections in this town than you have ever even thought about having, and I can guarantee you that's not gonna happen."

"Watch me," Rank hissed. "Yer a loose cannon, Hammer. Ya don' give a loose cannon with the kind ah hardware yer' carryin' an open license to kill. Ya made me the laughing stock of the agencies. It will take a long time to build up the reputation of Brakston again. It will never happen as long as yer on the payroll…"

"Oh bull shit! Bull shit!" Hammer yelled. "I haven't hurt the agency's reputation with this whole thing. I've improved it. I got to Tarent Powers. I got to him in a way that no one else ever has, and I did it leaving no evidence that I have broken one single solitary law."

"I've been livin' in the tidal wave of shit you left in yer wake, Hammer!" Rank bellowed back, "Don' tell me what's been happenin' here. You don' have ah clue."

"You owe me…"

"I could ah denied yer whole little workin' fer Tarent story. I didn', way I see it the debt has been paid."

"You pompous, impotent little fuck! You have no idea who you are screwing with."

"A has-been. Ya ruined yourself in this town, Hammer. Terminate transmission."

The screen went dead. Hammer almost picked up her computer and tossed it into the wall, but reminded herself how hard she'd just worked to put it back together. She went to the bathroom, cleaned up her hand and redressed it. The butterfly Elantra had put on had come loose, and the wound was gaping, by now it was no doubt too late to close it up again, and she really didn't give a shit, that was basically the worst thing that could happen to it. She slapped some salve and a clean dressing on it and hoped for the best. Then she sat and looked at her hand for a minute. It wasn't really hers, and at times like this she was all too aware of the fact. That wasn't bone in there, it was metal. The doctor had to go through her flesh to get to the pin, but it wasn't like it had to heal. Take the old pin out, put a new one in. The flesh could pull apart at the incision area, but it wasn't like her hand was going to fall off. Right now, only hours after the surgery, even with a weaker pin, she could put on a bullet shielded glove and punch a hole in a brick wall with no problem.

It would have been real easy to fall into a pool of self-pity and just wallow there, but she couldn't afford the luxury, not if she was going to get Elantra back, and not if she was going to stay alive. And getting Elantra back was the only reason to stay alive.

Tarent Powers had his daughter back safely, so now he'd want to regain face. The only way for him to do that would be to take Hammer out. Then there was Mishy. It was only a matter of time till he realized she was back in town, and when he learned that she had returned Tarent's daughter to him – if not completely unmolested, still very much alive – he was going to want her dead even more than he already did.

She gathered up some clothes, tools, and her computer, and drove over to the local Contractor's house. He let her stay without asking why. He showed her to a spare room. She showered, brushed her teeth, and went to bed. She was beat, physically, emotionally and spiritually spent. She lay there for thirty minutes, missing the feel of Elantra beside her before she finally went to sleep.

Elantra had stepped on the moving sidewalk, and with a simple voice command she was in her father's office without lifting her foot. Oddly enough the feeling of homecoming she had expected felt more like dread.

Her father was busy at the computer console. "Tell me what you want and get out. I'm busy."

When she heard his voice, her dread went away. He was not the monster Conner McVee said he was, he was her father, and hearing his voice she just knew he couldn't have done any of the horrible things Conner said that he had.

"Daddy." She ran up to him and threw her arms around

him, without really thinking about it. It had seemed like the most natural thing in the world, and it wasn't until he quickly pushed her to arm's length that she remembered that hugging was something "normal," people didn't do. She fell to her knees at his feet and buried her face in her hands.

"Elantra... Thank God you're safe." He patted at her back, without ever actually making contact.

"Daddy, oh Daddy." She couldn't say anything else, she just cried.

"Are you all right? I mean physically." Elantra nodded her head yes. "She didn't hurt you?"

She shook her head no.

Tarent didn't ask any more questions. Elantra was home, and given time she would revert to her old ways.

Doors opened for her. A drone came bearing her food on a little tray and announced that her supper was ready. When she finished eating the drone came and retrieved the little tray and it was disposed of, to be recycled into something else. From the taste, or lack thereof, probably more food.

Chairs anticipated that she wanted to sit down and rose to meet her. Her clothes were picked out by computer and she was washed, dried and shampooed without ever feeling wet. That night she lay down in her bed, and when it moved around her to make her comfortable, it all just became too much. She realized only now that what it was imitating was the comfort and security you got from being held in someone's arms. It was a substitute for warmth, and like the food it just didn't stack up to the real thing.

She tried to ignore it and go to sleep, but she couldn't. It gave her the creeps. She finally got out of bed and lay on the floor. She longed for a pillow and a cover, but made do with the sweat suit she had worn that day, the suit she had been wearing when she had arrived that her father had wanted thrown out and which she had saved just short of the recycling machine without anyone noticing. The suit was soft and reminded her of the first time she had worn cotton clothes. There was the faint smell of Conner's perfume on one of the cuffs, probably left over from Conner holding her last night. She held it up to her nose and smelled it. She wiped the tear from her eye.

It was hard to believe that Conner McVee had never loved

her. That's what her father had told her over and over again when she had tried to explain to him how she felt about Conner. He said Conner had only used her and it was time to get on with her life. That Elantra wasn't really gay, that it was just some brainwashing technique Conner had used.

Elantra might be confused, but if she knew one thing, she knew she hadn't been brainwashed. For one thing she had fantasized about having sex with a women long before Conner McVee had stepped into the picture. Hell, if he had bothered to check he would have found dozens of lesbian virtual sex programs in her terminal.

Her father had started talking about Buddy. Saying how if he, Tarent, had insisted they marry sooner this wouldn't have happened. Apparently being married to Buddy would have stopped her being kidnapped by Mishy. Somehow Elantra was sure that wasn't what he'd meant, but it had put a smile on her face at least momentarily.

He had looked at her, frowned, and then completely lost his cool. "What's so damn funny? This isn't some joke, Elantra. If you were going to screw this automated, fanatic, dyke you might have at least protected yourself with a screen."

Elantra had almost laughed then. "But Dad... Remember, I was brainwashed. I had no idea what I was doing."

"Don't mock me." For a moment the look on his face had been so dark and so angry that she almost begun to believe that maybe what Conner and the others had said about him had been true. Then he had taken a deep breath and let it out and his features softened. "I'm sorry, you've been through quite an ordeal, you can't be held responsible for what you did."

What a horrible ordeal. To be held by a human instead of a bed. To eat food that you could actually taste. To smell air that actually had scent. And orgasm, how awful was that?

There was this horrible empty feeling in her chest. A longing in her body and her soul which taunted her saying, *This was your choice.*

Maybe it didn't really matter how Conner felt, or what her motives were. Maybe the only thing that was important was that she couldn't stand to be away from her. That she needed to be with Conner McVee. Problem was that she doubted seriously that she was going to convince her father that it was in her best interest to go live with a person who was the epitome of all that he hated.

The bed was too weird, and the floor was too hard, and she was lonely. She'd made her bed and now she had to lie in it.

On a whim, Tarent physically went in to check on his daughter instead of running a computer scan of her room. He wanted to see for himself that she was all right. At first glance he didn't see her, and he started to panic. When he saw that she was sleeping in the floor, he was outraged.

He went back to his office, flopped down behind his desk and started mumbling to himself. "That fucking dyke has done unspeakable things to my daughter. She took an innocent girl who had been sheltered from all the cruelties of the outside world and exposed her to every sort of disease and danger, but worse than all of that she has changed Elantra into a filthy Constructionist."

He let his rage reach an appropriate level before he screamed, "Dacker, Squat! Come to my office immediately."

Seconds later the two men, looking disheveled and wearing bathrobes, were standing in his office.

He looked slowly up from his desktop. "I want a hit put on Mishy. I am tired of dicking with him."

"You sure, boss?" Squat started uncertainly. "Some of the other syndicates... they ain't gonna like that too much."

The veins stood out in Tarent's neck as he screamed. "I'm the biggest fish in this barrel! I'm going to remind all these pencil-dicked morons just who runs Freight City. If any of them dare balk, they'll be next on Mr. Tarent's hit parade. But even more important than Mishy's death is the death of that walking piece of hardware, Hammer McVee. I want her found, and I want her killed. Tell all of our associates; get the word out on the street. I will give five hundred thousand dollars to the man who brings me Mishy's head, but I will give a million dollars to the man who brings me the head of Conner "The Hammer" McVee."

"With an offer like that it shouldn't take long, sir," Squat assured him.

"It had better not. You imbeciles failed dreadfully in finding and retrieving my daughter. First they have to follow Mishy to find her. Then they let Hammer get away..."

"They was dead, boss." Dacker reminded. Tarent glared at

him, he cringed and quickly looked down at his feet.

"If it wasn't for that freak goody-goody bringing Elantra home because she wanted to come home... Well, I begin to believe that all of the idiots in my employ wouldn't have been able to track her down, let alone bring her in. Now, I want the head of Conner McVee, and I want it yesterday. So I suggest you get out of your jammies and get to work. Because if Hammer isn't dead and dead soon, I'm going to become very angry. And you know what happens when I get angry, boys, heads roll. You hear me!" He slammed his hand into his desk to show his displeasure. "No one in this organization is inexpendable. No one beyond punishment. If I don't get what I want and soon... do I have to get vulgar?"

"No, boss." They started to leave, almost running into each other in their haste.

"Oh, and one more thing..."

They both had to jump off the moving walkway to keep from being carried out of the room.

"Yes sir?" Squat asked, panting from all the exertion.

"As of this moment Power's Tower is a closed building. No one gets in without a screening, and no one leaves without one. All of Elantra's pass codes are to be erased from the memory banks, and under no circumstances is she to leave this building. Do I make myself clear?"

"Yes, boss," they answered.

"If there is a breach in security, no matter how small, I am going to hold you two personally responsible."

They waited to make sure he was done this time.

"God damn it! I told you ass holes! Get to work!"

They bumped into each other again as they raced to get on the walkway. Once out of the office they looked at each other.

"The computers run the security in this building, and he tells the computer what to do, but it's going to be our fault if something goes wrong. That don't make a damn bit of sense," Dacker said.

"So, why didn't you tell him that?" Squat asked.

"Are you out of your tiny fucking mind? That man is a killer, I never want to make him mad."

"So here's another question for ya," Squat swallowed hard. "What's scarier? Going up against Hammer McVee or disappointing the boss?"

"I don't know, man," Dacker said shrugging. "I think either

way we're fucking hosed."

CHAPTER 12

Conner got up early the next morning, took a shower, got dressed, and wrote the Contractor a note of thanks. Then she walked out of his house onto his porch and looked out at Hammer Town. The air was already filled with the sounds of people working, and Conner breathed deeply of the creation. She could drive to one of her many cabins in a Constructionist town, get a job either in construction or law enforcement, find a new woman – one who was neither the sister nor the daughter of a crime boss – settle down and live a simple life.

Except that wasn't who she was. She was a Constructionist and proud of it, but that didn't just mean you lived a simple life. It also meant you worked towards the things you truly wanted, truly desired. She loved Elantra, and she wanted a life with her. That meant she was going to have to work for it.

She walked to her car, got in and headed straight for Power's Tower.

Anything worth having was worth working for. She would become exactly what God had made her to be and use all that man had made her. She would win absolutely and have what she wanted, or she would die. Either way she would have fulfilled her destiny.

She knew Tarent better than she wanted to. She for sure knew him a hell of a lot better than Elantra did.

She had defiled Tarent's daughter and made him the laughing-stock of the underworld. These things could not and would not go unpunished by him. He would put a price on her head, and every goon in town would be trying to cash in. So she would go to the one place he and his goon squad might be afraid to touch her, which happened to be the only place she wanted to be at the moment. She pulled into the parking garage of the building across from Power's Tower, and parked in a spot on the third tier that gave her a perfect view of most of the west side of the building.

She leaned back in her seat and pulled off her eye patch. Then she dug in her jacket pocket until she found an old half eaten candy bar left over from a stakeout she'd done six months earlier. She looked at it and then ate it. It was hard and crumbly and stuck to her teeth, and she wished she had taken the time to get some breakfast in Hammer Town. She washed the candy down with some cold coffee left over from the night before, and wondered why everything in life had to be so damn hard.

She looked up Power's Tower to the room that she knew was Elantra's. She smiled. With her eye implant, she could just make out Elantra's form. She watched Elantra walk across the bedroom, and then she frowned. If she could see Elantra – with the right equipment – so could Mishy's thugs.

Conner opened the lid on her computer, and keyed in. "Computer, call Tarent Powers."

Tarent's angry features appeared, then glared back at her. "Hammer! You've got one hell of a nerve."

"Yeah, when they was fixin' me up, I had them add a pair of huge brass nuts." Hammer wasn't afraid of Tarent Powers, and she wasn't going to mince words with him. "You should be a happy little megalomaniac about now. You got your daughter back, if not untouched, at least uninjured, and you're still free and alive. Yeah, you must be feeling pretty fucking smug." Her glare turned to a slow sardonic smile. "But wait, you don't have everything you want, do you? Because I'm still alive, and Mishy's still alive, and he's one pissed off mother fucker, and I don't think you're ever going to be able to convince Elantra that she actually likes it in there now that she has been out here. So maybe it's not quite your day after all."

"You and your friend Mishy are as good as dead…"

"I have no intention of letting anyone kill me till you're a rotting corpse and your daughter is back in my bed. As for Mishy, until he's dead you'd best not count him out. Mishy's no fool. He outsmarted you before, and it was Mishy who found me, not you. So I'd say he's one up on you at this stage of the game."

"What do you want, McVee?" Tarent asked hotly.

"Aren't you listening, Tarent? I told you, you dead, and Elantra back…"

Tarent laughed. "You're pathetic, McVee. You and your kind make me sick, with your pathetic code of ethics. I knew you didn't have the stomach to kill her, but I didn't think that even you would be so putridly good that you would deliver her back into my hands simply because she wanted to go..."

"The difference between you and me Tarent is that I actually love Elantra..."

Tarent laughed. "And I suppose you're foolish enough to believe that she loves you, but she doesn't, McVee, she couldn't. She was frightened, she was out of her element and vulnerable, you took advantage of that and she reached out to the only person available to her."

This time Conner laughed. "Think what you like. After all, denial is one of your strong suits. I didn't call to chat. I can see Elantra in her room, and if I can, with the right binoculars so can Mishy's boys. I guarantee you they're watching Power's Tower. Mishy's got nothing to lose, he wants Elantra dead, and he wants me dead. I'm watching my back, and I'm trusting you to watch Elantra's."

"I don't need your hack advice on security, Hammer. The windows are bullet proof."

"What about rocket proof, bomb proof, airplane proof? Mishy is a desperate man, and about now he'd do just about anything to see you suffer. Basically I brought her home because until Mishy can be defused you can protect her better than I can. If you'll do it."

"You're a dead bitch."

"Is that any way to talk to your future daughter-in-law? I'm trying to help you, and you're cursing me." She clicked her tongue.

"You won't look so smug when your head's on a fucking platter on my desk," Tarent said through tightly clenched teeth.

"Actually, I probably would, I've worn this smug look so long it's probably permanent. Enjoy your delusions, Tarent. I'm a hard mother fucker to kill, and better men than you have tried." She laughed. "By now you know as much about me as I know about you. You know I'm connected out the ass, and that I could go to Hammer Town and just disappear."

"Then do it and leave my daughter alone!" Tarent screamed. "She was innocent, and you spread your filth all over her."

"And she spread her filth all over me. It was wonderful." Her tone changed – got more serious. "I'll never leave her alone, Tarent. She needs me, she needs me to save her from you, whether she knows it or not. Now do something with the windows, or better yet move her to an interior room."

"I can take care of my own daughter thank you, McVee."

"Then do it. Computer off."

She was gone as she had come – without warning.

Tarent felt the veins throbbing at his temples. He was so upset that it took him several minutes to realize the true implications of Hammer's words.

"Computer. Hammer McVee can see Elantra in her room through her window. Where is Hammer McVee?"

"Third story of parking garage across street." It showed a picture of Hammer sitting in her car with her feet hanging out the window. She waved at him. No doubt her hearing implant had heard the camera moving, and she had focused in on it. She raised her weapon, and the next instant the screen was black, she had taken out the surveillance camera.

"Think you've outsmarted me. Well, we'll see about that. *Squat!*"

The man ran in.

"Squat, see that?" He pointed at the blank computer screen, and Squat nodded more than a little confused. "That's Hammer McVee. She's hanging out in the parking garage across the street. She thinks I won't go after her there because it's too close to us. Send some men over there and show her just how wrong she is."

"Boss... I mean... that's gonna bring the agencies right to our door," Squat said guardedly.

"I don't care! I want her dead. If I have to get into a war with the police agencies to do it, then so be it. Maybe it's time they learned their true place in this city."

"Yes sir, boss." Squat nodded and headed out the door.

Hammer waited until she heard them coming. Then, gun in hand, she got out of the car, shouldered her weapon on its strap, jumped up onto the roof of her car, and then jumped up and grabbed hold of a beam. She wrestled herself onto the top of it and waited.

She watched the car drive up to her car, and watched as its doors opened. Four men jumped out and started looking around.

"Where the fuck did she go?" one asked. About that time another one looked up. The look on his face said that he knew he was about to be the first to die. He got one wild shot off before the nail went through his eye and exploded out the back of his head. She sprayed the area, popping the other three before they could even react.

She reloaded, then jumped off the beam as a second car approached. She opened fire on the second car, then jumped on top of another car and started running across the parked cars as the men in the second car returned her fire. She dove quickly between two cars, then popped up like a demented jack in the box, took careful aim and fired. The nail went in the open window on the driver's side and into the man's skull. The car stopped abruptly. As the other three men rushed to exit the stopped vehicle, Conner shot a nail into the alcohol tank. She sprayed the area with nails, and the men fell. She took a flare out of her pocket, lit it, and lobbed it onto the alcohol spill. She ran back to her car, got in and roared off just as the tank exploded. Not as spectacular as the old gas tanks, but still damn impressive.

Conner drove a few blocks away and parked. She got on the computer. "Computer, call Mayor Finkel's office."

Mayor Finkel had been eating breakfast. He looked up at Hammer McVee and cringed. "I figured you were going to call that favor up, McVee," he said.

"All I want is for you to keep them from revoking my permit."

"That's it?" he asked in disbelief.

"I also want to keep my tenth level security clearance..."

"McVee, they're saying you're crazy. That you are dangerous..."

"What, are you quoting James Rank now? It's real simple, Mayor. When we busted that illegal whorehouse I could have brought you in. It was all on my computer. We made a deal, and now I'm calling it in."

"Ya can fuck a hundred prostitutes without a screen, but fuck one sheep, and you're branded a pervert for life," the Mayor mumbled. "OK, Hammer, but how do you suggest I convince the members of the council? If it was up to me I'd do it for you, no questions asked. But you're getting a lot of bad press right now, and..."

"Tell them that I'm about fifteen minutes from bringing Tarent Powers in on charges that will stick."

"What charges?"

"Bribing a police agency, Brakston Agency as a matter of fact..."

"You're kidding."

"I wish I was. Ask yourself why all of the sudden James Rank has brought these charges against me. I'm his most decorated agent. I was protecting Powers' daughter from Mishy, and that's when I found out that Tarent was paying Rank to lose important evidence and look the other way at just the right moment, if you know what I mean. Look at my record and then ask yourself if you really believe this cock and bull story Rank and Tarent are telling about me kidnapping Tarent's daughter. Ask them where the evidence is. Question the girl, see what she says."

The Mayor nodded his head. "It does seem a little far-fetched, and it certainly would be a feather in my cap if you could bring Tarent in. OK, I'll see what I can do, and then we're even, all right?"

"Debt paid in full."

"What should I tell them your status is?"

"Tell them I'm working as a free agent, and I expect to be paid very handsomely when I bring Tarent in. Close transmission." She smiled broadly. "That will teach Rank to bugger out on me."

Conner got slowly out of the car. She scanned the area, and then she put the patch on her eye. She locked the car and slammed the door. The streets were silent. It was morning, and anyone who worked any further away than their building had already gone to work. No one parked on the streets. They parked in buildings so that they could call their cars to them. They sure as hell never walked.

This part of Freight City was not her usual haunt, but it certainly wasn't new to her.

"I was born here," she mumbled to herself looking down the street at the row of high-rises, "and if I'm not careful I'll die here. I don't know whether that is poetic or ironic."

She took a deep breath and let it all just soak in for a minute.

After the great plague of 2050, the world had forever changed. She'd never known that world, but she'd read about it. Technology had flourished, the computer age was in full swing and making new advances every day. The world was badly overpopulated because it seemed that some people thought it was God's own will that they spit out as many children as possible. As had been predicted, a deadly flu was born, one that no medicine could fight. The pandemic swept the poorer nations and areas of the heaviest populations. Two thirds of the world's population died.

That changed everything. In the wake of so much death, the mega corporations – which already owned most of the world – managed to grab everything they didn't already have. Humanity conveniently forgot the problems of over-population, misuse of the land, and over-extending resources, blaming human contact for the plague instead. The population embraced technology and used it to keep each other and the world at bay. Since there had been no major epidemic since that time, they assumed their calculations were correct. It never dawned on them that over-population and the subsequent pollution of waterways and food products had caused the plague. That there had been no plague since because with only minimal human contact and the complexity of how babies were now conceived, born, and cared for, there was no chance of over-population.

The Building District where she now stood was a product of the environment of fear of a returning plague and mechanical achievement. Simply put, in the minds of the survivors, human contact and world travel had caused the plague. With the new strides in computer technology and robotics there was no need to travel or to have anything more than minimal human contact. Follow that thinking a hundred years down the road, and you came to Freight City's Building District population – complete shut-ins who never walked in direct sunlight or breathed anything but filtered air. The most exercise they got was when they stepped off their moving walk way into the parking garage and called for their car. Many of them, maybe even most, never even got that far. They worked, ate, slept and lived – if you could call it that – without ever leaving their floor, much less the building.

Corporations ran everything including city governments and police agencies. Everything now centered on the all-mighty dollar. Rich districts could afford the best police agencies and plenty of patrols. Their crime rate was almost nonexistent these days, if you didn't include all the illegal VR. Of course this was where all the crime lords made their homes. They conducted their sordid business from here, and it was here that they lived to escape the kind of corruption and depravity their "business" created.

Drugs and hookers were still big in Slum Town, and the crime lords – who were connected to yet another corporation – dealt in that. But they made most of their real money selling illegal virtual reality programs, which miraculously appeared in the "crime free" building district. Programs that could screw up your brain every bit as bad and a hell of a lot faster than drugs. If Hammer had a dime for every time she'd pulled a VR helmet off some overindulgent building brat, she'd be rich instead of just comfortable. Their blank eyes would stare up at her, their drooling mouths gaping at some horror or ecstasy that had wrenched their soul from their body. They had never really lived, never touched or been touched by anything but damn machines. They were conceived in them, born in them, lived in them and died in them.

The majority of people were miserable, and they didn't even know why. The programs the pushers sold them for ridiculous prices helped them for a while to escape from the bounds of the walls they'd built all around themselves. It was easy to get addicted, and the younger they were the easier it was. They used it more and more and more until they couldn't stop, their brain overloaded, and they died.

Hammer knew what the programs did to you first hand. Hammer had been a building brat, raised in a building not far from where she stood now. She'd been created in a tank and confined to one of these prisons of convenience. She had parents she never talked to, and was raised by machines, with no warmth. The programs had given her something that life and her parents hadn't, and she found herself doing more and more programs. One program didn't last long before it crashed, and then you wanted a bigger and better program. That's how they sucked you in, by making sure that you got just enough that you had to have more. She hocked everything she owned. She hocked her parents' stuff. They punished her by locking her out of the computer and deleting her access codes, but they didn't talk to her, they didn't pay attention to her, and they didn't include her in a life that they shared together – apart.

She went into withdrawal, and she needed a program, so she left the building for the first time in her life. She had heard over the net that you could buy programs in Slum Town, so she called for a car, charged it to her parents' account and headed for Slum Town with her VR unit in a pack on her back.

The car had been programmed not to go into Slum Town, and it left her on the outskirts. It was a big, dirty place where none of the machines seemed to work right, and Conner fell in love with it immediately. She had been walking in Slum Town less than ten minutes when her legs started to cramp. When she sat down to rub her legs, someone jumped her, beat her up, and stole her pack off her back, leaving her with no money and no VR machine.

It was the greatest thing that had ever happened in her sixteen years of life. The programs had made her an excitement junkie, and virtual excitement couldn't hold a candle to the real thing. She never looked back.

Life outside the building – life in Slum Town was rough, and it was gritty, rich, and intoxicating – a much stronger drug than any program.

Conner never saw her parents again. She heard – years later – that they'd had another baby created, a boy. Conner felt no link to him, no desire to find him or to have contact with her parents. If they had any desire to find her, they hadn't been successful, and she didn't know anything about it. Maybe they were dead – even this thought didn't stir any feelings within her. They had been incapable of forming any kind of emotional attachment to her, and so she was incapable of feeling anything for them now. They had given her their DNA, that was all.

People walked the streets in Slum Town. There were moving sidewalks, but they only worked half the time, and most of the people who lived there didn't make enough money to buy a car. Public transit was iffy at best, and so when you lived in Slum Town, you learned to walk. You also learned to fight, or you died.

Since Slum Town was so impoverished, it couldn't afford to pay for the services of any of the better police agencies. The only time cops came to Slum Town was when they were looking for leads in a case that had taken place in more affluent neighborhoods. Because of the lack of good jobs and the lack of adequate police protection, Slum Town had become a haven for Freight City's ever-growing criminal element. If nothing else flourished in Slum Town, crime did. The more adventurous population from the buildings would sneak in and engage in all the debauchery they shunned in their sterile little Building lives.

All of the program dealing that took place in Freight City went through Slum Town, although most of the real addicts lived in the buildings. The hackers were hidden in dens all over Slum Town. The people in the buildings would find a pusher on the net; it wasn't very hard. They would slip an outrageous amount of virtual cash into a specified account, and then they would receive a program. The new program would satisfy their habit for a while. In Slum Town, small – time program dealers were everywhere, and they'd let you sample their wares for free, so you always knew what you were getting into.

Conner took a lot of free samples, but after she got to Slum Town she never bought another program. For one thing she never had the money to replace her VR unit, much less buy a new program. Besides, after she started living in Slum Town she never had the need to program. Her addiction ended where real life began, on the streets of Slum Town.

She wound up working for a Fagen named Willie Street. He taught "his" kids how to read computer language and how to use an instrument called a keyboard. It resembled its historical prototype only in that there were keys that one pressed. It was smaller, more compact, and the vid screen folded down over the board to make a tight seal. With several ports for input and output, it was a very versatile tool. Using this tool, Willie taught them how to hack into any system. He would take them up town and they would spread out. If they could find any computer feed wire in a building, they would wire the keyboard in, and in a matter of minutes they could hack their way into the personal bank accounts of any tenant in that building. Once there, they would transfer small amounts of money – never more than twenty dollars – directly into one of Willie Street's many secret accounts. A good hacker could easily bring in anywhere from two hundred to five hundred dollars a day, and to be a good hacker you had to learn to read.

Years later she realized that they had made Willie Street a very wealthy little criminal mastermind, while they had cost him practically nothing to keep. At the time he had seemed to her to be the family she had never had. He kept all the money, but he at least acted like he cared about them. He spent time with them, which was more than any of their parents had ever done. He gave them a clean place to live, and the computer spit out three square meals a day for anywhere from six to eight kids, from ages twelve to twenty. That and the fact that he never tried to molest any of them, and protected them from the rougher elements in the city was enough to buy both their loyalty and their devotion.

When Conner got older and it became obvious that she liked girls, Willie introduced her to one of his sidelines. He pimped her out to some very high-classed, older building broads, who had lots of money to spend and had become bored with virtual sex, older mates, or using screens. Homosexuality, while it was largely accepted in modern society, and even embraced by some cultures, was still considered an abnormality among the building people. In their sterilized civilization those kinds of urges were best kept in the closet, and since the desire was more than an urge, Conner never missed a meal for lack of a trick.

Willie let Conner keep half of what she made. It was a good job for a horney teenage girl to have. In fact, at the time Conner had thought it was really no job at all.

One day police agents came and took Willie and locked his ass up. At the time Conner had been outraged. Willie had been more like a parent to her and those other kids than their own parents had. Now they were on their own, and Slum Town was a harsh place for young people to be on their own. They had stuck together for a long time, finding that there was safety in numbers, but eventually they had all gone their separate ways. They all still kept in touch through a fellow named Pinky who had helped them from time to time with absolutely no strings attached. There was still a bond between them, and a loyalty that had made Conner as a police agent look the other way, and warn them away from certain places at certain times more than once. Of course in turn they had helped her out occasionally as well. For one thing they had kept her very well connected in Slum Town.

It wasn't long after Willie went down that Conner was busted for illegal prostitution – the only legal prostitution was run by one of the corporations – and they threw her in jail. She was locked in a small cell with nothing, not even a computer. It was harsh and bleak, and it made Conner's skin crawl.

Different police agencies came through the prison on a

regular basis looking for non-violent criminals to train as undercover police agents. Criminals were much more likely to trust someone they had seen involved in criminal activities in the past.

The deal was simple, the agency trained you, housed you, fed you, and you belonged to them for two years. For two years they kept all the money you earned. You lived in barracks and got three meals a day. Conner was only supposed to spend a year in jail, and even Willie had let her keep part of her money, so the first time they offered her the deal she spit in their faces and told them to shove it. But after six weeks of staring at bricks and steel, she was ready to climb the walls, so when they came through recruiting again, she grabbed them and begged them to put her into their program.

By that time it had been three years since she'd last been cooped up in a building, and she was freaking out. She was used to touching other people and being touched by them. She was used to getting rained on and having the wind in her face, she couldn't live surrounded by walls again. Not unless they were going to supply her with the illegal programs which had sent her into the streets in the first place.

Conner stopped walking and looked up at Powers Towers. Elantra couldn't stay in prison, either. Not now that she had been on the outside. It was only a matter of time till Elantra came out of the building, and when she did Conner would be waiting.

Conner walked across the street and leaned against a lamppost, just watching the building. She was so close that she could hear the machines cleaning up the mess she had made in the parking garage. She looked up the building at the window that she knew looked into Elantra's room. She lifted her patch and looked. She couldn't see through it now. They must have ordered the computer to black it out; she was relieved and disappointed at the same time.

She felt more than saw something, and she turned in time to see someone duck into the shadow of the parking garage. She caught just enough of his face to recognize him as one of Mishy's boys, and she knew from experience that he wasn't alone. Conner harbored no doubt that Mishy wanted her as dead as Tarent did. However she doubted these men were here for her. By now Mishy would have heard that Elantra was now safe at home with Daddy. He'd also know that Tarent had more than probably taken off the kid gloves and had a hit put on him.

Likewise Mishy had raised the bar. No doubt he was no longer going to be happy to simply kill Elantra and make Tarent suffer. Now he wanted Tarent dead. He had his goons watching Tarent's place looking for chinks in Tarent's armor. He had gotten to him once and knew that if he watched closely enough he could figure out a way to get at him again. This time he wouldn't be taking any prisoners.

Conner being here where they could shoot her was just a happy little bonus for them.

At least that was what they thought. Conner put her patch back down and pretended to relax against the post. The guy she had spotted was waiting, too, his actions confirming her belief that Mishy wanted her dead. Conner supposed that in his position she might have wanted to kill her, too.

If it was a choice between Mishy and Elantra, or even saving her own skin, Conner had no doubt that she would kill Mishy. But if she could save herself and Elantra without killing Mishy, she would.

Peggy had loved her brother. They had been close in a way that had been completely alien to Conner. There had been a bond between them that had seemed almost tangible. Peggy and Mishy looked nothing alike, yet when they were in a room with each other you knew they were family. Till now Mishy had always treated Hammer like part of that family, in spite of the fact that she was a cop and he was a criminal. For her part Conner had covered evidence against him more times than she cared to count. Mishy was scum, there was no doubt, but he was at least the scum that rose to the top.

When she met Peggy Mishy, Conner had already been employed by Brakston Agency for six years and had all her implants. She had also already converted to Constructionism and had become a legend among them as well. In fact she was already living in the newly named Hammer Town.

She thought she had everything she wanted and needed until she saw Peggy Mishy.

Conner'd been cruising a popular Slum Town club called Whips, trying to talk a set of identical clones into an incredibly kinky sex act when Mishy walked in with a bunch of his usual thugs and the most beautiful woman Conner had ever seen.

She immediately lost interest in the clones, who seemed more than a little upset when she became less than attentive and told them to bugger off.

She already knew Mishy on sight. Mishy was the lesser of two evils, and the agencies left him alone for the most part to balance out Tarent Powers' operations. Mishy was a thorn in Tarent's side, and since the agencies seemed incapable of affecting Tarent at all, Mishy was considered a necessary evil. Mishy knew this, and tried to hold up his end of the bargain by being very careful not to cross over the line. Which meant he didn't hustle the more dangerous programs – drugs, illegal hookers, gambling, and fairly benign programs, but nothing lethal.

Conner stared at Peggy for an hour trying to figure out how to approach her. In the end she didn't have to. Peggy walked right up to her and asked, "Why are you staring at me?"

Conner answered truthfully, if unromantically. "Because you're turning my guts inside out."

Peggy had laughed. "So is that good or bad?"

"I haven't decided yet," Conner said.

"Homosexual?" Peg asked, never one to beat around the bush.

"Very."

"Want to go to my place?"

"Ah... what about Mishy?"

"My brother. I'm Peggy Mishy," Peg explained. "I don't tell him not to cheat on his wife, and he doesn't tell me who to sleep with, it's kind of an agreement we have."

"I think I should tell you I'm a cop," Conner told her.

Peggy had laughed. "I'm not blind. I can see your agency tattoo. So... you game or not?"

"Oh, I'm game... With or without a screen?" Conner asked.

"Without... I'm a Constructionist."

Conner smiled stupidly. "Me, too! I'm Hammer McVee." Conner knew in that instant that they were meant to be together; she knew then that she was in love.

Peggy would later tell Conner that she had thought Conner was pulling her leg about being a Constructionist, much less THE Hammer McVee. That hadn't stopped Peggy from bringing Conner home with her. They'd made love on a chair, the floor, the couch and the kitchen table that night. They got married a week later, and they were together every day from the first time they met until Tarent Powers had cut Peggy's life short and her body into twenty different pieces.

Conner glared at the building. Tarent had taken Peggy away, and now he was keeping Elantra away.

There was really only one way out of the mess she'd gotten herself into. She had to kill Tarent Powers. With Tarent dead there would be no reason for Mishy to kill her or Elantra. Of course if he were easy to kill she would have done it years ago, and none of this crap would have happened. The real problem was that the bastard had never stuck so much as his finger out of that building in going on twenty years. Try as she might, she'd never been able to crack the bastard's codes.

Conner had a sudden need to hit someone, and remembered the man who had run into the parking garage. She moved away from the lamppost and started strolling leisurely along as if she had not a care in the world. She walked into the parking garage unzipping her pants, and started walking in the direction of a bathroom. She heard a gun cock, turned in an instant and fired. Six nails penetrated the man's jacket and pinned his gun arm to the concrete wall behind him. She swung around quickly and just shot the other one in the head; he dropped like a rock. Conner swung back around to face the one she had pinned. She easily kicked his gun from his trapped hand.

As his gun fell to the floor, he looked at Conner in terror. Conner put her nail gun back in to its holster, reached down and scooped the man's gun up off the floor, and stuck it in her belt, then zipped her fly closed. "One of Mishy's men or one of Tarent's?" Conner asked plainly, although she knew the answer. She wanted him, and subsequently Mishy, to know that Tarent really did want her dead, too. Maybe this would give Mishy the idea that by killing Hammer he would be doing Tarent a favor.

"Mishy's," the man croaked, trying to pull his sleeve away from the wall.

"Tell Mishy," Conner started removing the nails one at a time with her hand, "I said I have to get on with my life. I'm really sorry, I didn't plan it, but I love this woman. I'd die for her. More important for Mishy to remember, I'd *kill* for her. Mishy can do whatever he likes to Tarent. I'm going to kill the bastard myself if I get a chance. But if he comes after Elantra or me, he's fair game. For Peggy's memory, I don't want to kill him, but I will if he pushes me." She pulled out the last nail, and the man rubbed his arm where some of the nails had grazed him. Then she hit the man in the chin with a good right cross, and he hit the floor. He looked up at her with half dazed eyes. "You tell him." The man nodded, got shakily to his feet, and ran off calling for his car.

Conner reached into her pocket and patted the CD case. She looked at the impenetrable fortress that was Power's Tower, and smiled. He couldn't keep her out, not if she wanted in. She looked at the computer terminal standing next to the elevator. She had a keyboard, and she still had the knack.

Elantra sat in her room glaring at her screen. She wasn't interested in her studies, so she was barely listening and only half watching. Real doctors worked on real people. Her father was never going to let her be a doctor. He was never going to let her do anything that meant she had to leave the building. If things had been tight before, she'd found them to be doubly so now.

She never should have come back here. She should have run off with Conner McVee and never looked back. She missed reality, she missed real food, and baths in water, and most of all she missed Conner.

She was about to tell the program to close when the screen went blank and the computer droned out, "Bank transaction in progress." When her screen came back on she was looking at Conner.

"Conner McVee!" Elantra said. She tried to rub the ecstatic look from her face. Forgetting all her previous thoughts, she quickly reminded herself that this was the woman who had so badly used her and shot her cat. "Conner McVee, I have nothing to say to you," she said coldly.

"That will be the day," Conner said with a laugh. "I miss you, brat. How long are you going to do this to us? Hasn't this gone on long enough?"

"It hasn't even been twenty-four hours yet, Conner McVee," Elantra scoffed.

"Any time is too long for me to be separated from you," Conner said. "Come on, baby. Don't you miss me a little?"

Elantra fought her tears and avoided Conner's question. "Conner McVee, how did you get through here? I'm sure Daddy had you locked out."

Conner smiled. "You didn't answer my question."

"I'm not talking to you, Conner McVee. Your kidnapping me has caused me to get weeks behind in my studies and I have to catch up..."

"Fuck that!" Conner totally lost her cool. "You really think your father is going to let you down from your steel and glass prison to practice medicine?"

No, she really didn't, which made it all the harder for her to say, "You don't know my father..."

"I know your father is trying to have me fucking killed! He sent two car loads of thugs after me..."

Elantra took in a shocked breath. "Conner McVee! Is there no end to the lengths you will go to get what you want?" She was really mad now, this was an out and out lie, and it flew in the face of everything Elantra wanted to believe about her relationship with Conner. "My father would never have anyone killed. You are delusional. You're the one who's a killer..."

Conner rolled her eyes and asked again apparently ignoring Elantra's outburst, "Do you miss me?"

Elantra hesitated only a moment before her mouth betrayed her, "Yes, but..."

"Fuck that. Come out. I'll get you past Mishy's boys, and we'll blow this popsicle stand."

"What is that supposed to even mean?" Elantra asked.

Conner thought about it for a minute. She didn't really know, but she knew what she wanted it to mean. "It means let's get the hell out of here. Let them kill each other off..."

"I'm canceling this program now," Elantra said angrily, "Because I don't want to talk to you. You're a liar and a user."

"Wait, wait! I want to send you something," Conner said.

"What?" Elantra asked.

"It's a sound byte," she waited for Elantra to cancel the program, which she didn't do. "I thought you were going to close out on me."

"It's hard." Elantra started to cry. "I wish I'd never met you. Close transmission!" Elantra screamed before she could change her mind.

It wasn't true of course, and five seconds after she had said it and closed the transmission she wished she hadn't.

She damned her own weakness. The awful truth was that she was glad that she had met Conner. She wanted to do what Conner asked, but Conner's new lies proved she had ulterior motives. Proved that her father was most probably right about Conner.

She stared back at her studies mindlessly. Finally she could stand it no longer. "Computer, program off. Play information sent by Conner McVee." Music started to fill the room. Not dygarhythms, but real music with voices and words. Elantra smiled. It was her favorite CD.

She started to lean back in her chair. It anticipated that she wanted to do so and moved. This made her so mad she couldn't think straight. In fact she couldn't remember being so mad in her entire life. She got up and went to the door. She thought that slamming the door fourteen or fifteen times might make her feel better. Of course the cursed door anticipated that she wanted to go through and opened.

Elantra went ballistic.

Tarent heard all the noise and came running. Elantra had locked her door in a half open position and was beating it with her chair, which was falling apart in her hands. "You stupid fucking son of a bitch!" she screamed. "Slam, slam, fucking slam! How do you like that, you stupid motherfuckers? Open for me, I'll show you, you stupid prick! Open now you stupid son of a bitch!" The door made a horrible grinding noise, and Elantra laughed gleefully. "Die you bastard die!" She threw down what was left of the chair and stood there trying to catch her breath. She was shaking with rage. She looked at the faces of her father and his staff. "What the fuck is wrong with you? Didn't you ever want to do that? Just once didn't the fucker make you so mad you just wanted to tear it to shreds?"

"Not really," her father said coolly. "Droids! Clean up the mess in Elantra's room, and repair damages... Elantra, where did you learn to talk like that?"

"The same place I learned everything I know that's worth knowing, from Conner fucking Hammer McVee." A little round cleanup droid arrived, and Elantra kicked it over. She glared over it at her father as it struggled like a turtle on its back trying desperately to try and right itself. "You were never going to let me out of here, were you? You never had any intention of letting me actually practice medicine, or have a life, did you? I'm a fucking prisoner here..."

"Elantra, quit talking like that. Conner McVee has brain washed you against me. Of course you're going to be a doctor. You're not a prisoner here."

"Good then I'm going," Elantra started walking, purposely avoiding the moving walk way.

"Elantra, Mishy's men..."

"Conner will protect me from Mishy's men. Am I a prisoner here or not?"

"I can't let you leave, Elantra," Tarent said.

"Then the answer is yes, I am a prisoner here!" Elantra screamed.

"Elantra, this is your home. We all love you here. This is not a prison. You have everything you need..."

"This is a prison. You don't love me, you think you own me, and I guarantee you that what I need is not here."

The droid struggled up on to its little rollers, and Elantra kicked it over again. "See that thing? That's what I was, a robot. I did just what you wanted me to do. I didn't feel anything, and I didn't want anything. Now I do, and I'm damned if anyone is going to stop me from having what I want."

In that moment Elantra was decided. She didn't care about Conner's lying, she didn't even care about her abducting her. She needed Conner McVee, and whether Conner knew it or not, she needed Elantra, too. She was leaving this man-made hell, and nothing her father could say was going to stop her. He couldn't make her stay if she didn't want to.

She wasn't even allowed to leave the floor. Two of her father's men stood at the doors to the elevator, blocking her path. Her head spun, and then the world went black.

Tarent stared at the screen. Conner McVee was still standing there, right in front of the building like a raptor waiting for its prey. It was pouring rain, and still she stood there staring up at the building, a living testament to how far she would go to exact her revenge on him, and his inability to control her.

When Elantra had awakened from her drug-induced sleep, she was anything but happy. She had refused to talk to him, and three days later she still wasn't talking. She sat in her room and played some Constructionist song over and over again. Whenever he attempted to talk to her she told him to go fuck himself.

She was no longer Daddy's little girl.

He wondered how long Hammer was going to stand out there in the rain. He called Squat into his office. "Squat, raise the price on Hammer McVee's head to two million dollars."

"Sir, she just stands out there. Everyone who tries to get close..."

"Winds up dead. Yes, I am aware of that, but out there somewhere is someone who can kill Hammer McVee, and she's not out there all the time. Eventually she'll give up; she'll let her guard down, and then..." He slapped his fist into his hand, and Elantra walked into the room. She glared at her father across the desk, and he knew from the expression on her face that she had heard their conversation.

Her rage was tangible. "She was telling the truth! *All this time.* All this time she was telling the truth about you, and I didn't believe her. I'm here in this fucking hell because I didn't believe her, and yet you are *exactly* who she said you were. You're trying to have her killed? You know how I feel about her, and you're trying to have her killed?" Her attention shifted to the screen. "Is that Conner McVee?" Elantra demanded.

"Yes it is. She wants to kill you, Elantra..." Tarent defended.

"No she doesn't, that's a lie just like every other lie you have ever told me. My whole life, all of this," she waved her arms around. "Bought with blood money. You're nothing but a common hood." Elantra walked over and stroked the screen. "It may be true that Conner wants to use me to get back at you, but if she wanted to kill me she could have done so about a thousand times, even in here. You know that. Call the hit off, Daddy, and I'll stay here. I'll do whatever you tell me, but call off the hit."

Tarent smiled. He hadn't thought of this angle, but it certainly worked for him. "OK, Lanny, if that's what you want."

"I'll stay here. I'll do what you want. I'll marry who you tell me to marry, only promise me that you won't let anyone hurt Conner," Elantra begged.

"Consider it done," Tarent said

Elantra turned and left the room.

Tarent smiled. He closed his door and leaned back in his chair.

"Squat?"

"Yes sir?"

"Raise the price on Hammer McVee's head to two million dollars."

"But, sir, you just told Elantra..."

"She can only know what we allow her to know. By the time she figures out that Hammer is dead, she will be safely back in the fold. Sometimes you *can* have your cake and eat it, too."

Usually Conner didn't mind the rain. In fact, she thought getting rained on was kind of cool – most of the time. Today it just sucked like everything else.

She had never been a very patient person, and she was getting tired of waiting. When she had tried to talk to Elantra earlier in the day she had been completely blocked out. Attempts to reach Tarent hadn't gone any better, even when she pulled all her best tricks out of her hat.

Tarent wasn't going to let Elantra go without a fight, and neither, unfortunately, was Mishy. His men were watching Tarent's building – if not as openly as she was, definately with the same diligence. Occasionally fights between Mishy's men and Tarent's broke out, which was nice because it took the heat off her for a while.

She hated stakeouts and their usual boring monotony. Of course this stakeout was a little different. Long periods of staring at concrete were broken up by the need to fight for her life. The would-be assassins didn't seem to care whether she was standing in broad daylight in front of Power's Tower, or walking down an alley way. It didn't even seem to matter to them how many of the fuckers she killed. She didn't know how much money Tarent had put on her head, but it had to be a hell of a lot to bring the crawling scum out of their buildings and into the streets to take on a cop with the reputation and the clearance that she had.

The bodies were stacking up, and she'd already been questioned by police agents five times. She told them the truth – well, more or less anyway – their drones disposed of the bodies, and they went on their way. They all knew who Hammer McVee was, and they either trusted her integrity or they were afraid to tangle with her.

They all knew Tarent was dirty, it was just a given. So far all of the bodies belonged to men and women with records and/or ties to organized crime. The shootings seemed to be righteous. In short, until Hammer killed someone they didn't think deserved killing, they weren't going to risk their lives to stop her from doing whatever the hell she was doing.

Conner had taken her patch off and left it off a day ago. She might have looked to the rest of the world like she was completely relaxed, but she wasn't. Her every muscle was tense, and her every sense alert. This wasn't a game, at least not to her. Too much was at stake. She was wearing a hat, and the water dripped off the brim and ran down her jacket. She checked her nail gun to make sure that it was fully charged and loaded. It didn't mind getting rained on. She was thinking about packing it in for the day when she heard a car. She pulled her gun and waited. The car pulled up in front of her and stopped, and even through the rain and his tinted windows she recognized Jason Hunter. Conner relaxed a bit. Hunter told his car door to open and it did. Water almost dripped on him, and he jumped back as if afraid the water would melt him.

"Oh how the mighty have fallen," he said with a laugh.

"I'm wet, but I'm still on my feet," Conner said, forcing a smile.

"You'll never work at Brakston Agency again after the little stunt you pulled with the mayor," Jason hissed. "The city council is currently holding us in suspension pending a meeting to decide the status of our charter..."

"If the city directors decide to revoke Brakston's charter, I don't guess anyone will be working there," Conner said, and this time she didn't have to work on the smile.

"They're not going to revoke our charter. We didn't do anything wrong, and so there is no evidence to prove that we did."

Conner laughed, then glared at him. "Now I wouldn't bet on that. So, did Rank send you here to taunt me? Or did you just decide to do it on your own."

Jason glared at her. "Maybe I was just in the neighborhood and decided to drop by."

She didn't see the gun until it was fired. She felt herself being thrown back with the force of the impact. The wind was knocked out of her as she hit the wall of the parking garage. Even as she was flying backward, she fired wildly in Jason's direction. She heard his car roar off as she staggered to her feet and fired after him. All around her she heard the sound of shuffling feet. Jason had run off, and now they were all coming in for the kill. She looked up at the Powers building.

"God damn you, Tarent!" she screamed. She felt blood running down her side. Whatever Jason had hit her with had gone through her "bullet proof" vest. Someone else fired at her, and she took off running for her car. Running was hard. She was losing a lot of blood, and she felt weak.

Her vision blurred as she struggled with the handle of the car door. As she jumped in and roared off she could see blood on her pants. There was no blood on her shirt. Apparently it was running under her vest and down her leg. There was a pain in her ribs, but she wasn't having trouble breathing, and there wasn't blood coming out her nose, so he hadn't hit her lung. "Computer, call Brakston Agency." James Rank stared back at her. "Rank, you tell Jason to pray to his god that I die, because if I don't I'm going to kill him in a really painful way."

"What the hell are you talking about, McVee?" James spat back.

"Oh, that's good... Well, you better pray to your god that you really didn't have anything to do with Jason shooting me, because if I find out you did... when I get done with him I'm going to nail you, too. Transmission out."

The pain was intense. Outside the rain seemed to have gotten harder just to confound her vision. She couldn't make it to Hammer Town, and in her current position that left her only one option.

Damn it! She had dropped her guard for a minute, and now it was going to cost her everything. The sensitivity implant had picked up hostility from Jason, but it couldn't detect that he was there to shoot her, and her own knowledge of Jason wouldn't have thought him capable of such treachery. She'd known he was an ass hole, but had no idea that he was in bed with Tarent Powers, because up till then Jason had played it very cool. "It must be one hell of a lot of money."

Tarent looked across the dinner table at his daughter. He couldn't stand one more silent meal with her. "Elantra... are you ever going to talk to me again?"

"No," Elantra said plainly.

"Why not?"

"Why? We never really talk. We never really exchange views or opinions. You tell me what you expect of me, what I'm going to do with my life. I pretend to listen, and every once in a while when I can't stand it any more I speak up, and you pretend to listen, and then you decide what I'm going to do with my life. I have lived my life in virtual reality, being entertained, taught, and nurtured by machines. Now I'm back here... I have no life. *You* have my life, and the computers will take care of me... You don't care how I feel. I'm a possession."

"Elantra, this is all just part of the brain washing. In time you'll be happy here again..."

"Again! I was *never* happy here!" Elantra yelled. She pushed her tray of food away. "You want to talk? Let's talk... So are you a business man or a crime lord?"

"Elantra, honey..."

"Are you a business man or a crime lord? It's a simple question, Dad."

"I'm a business man..."

"A legitimate business man?"

Tarent was silent.

"That's what I thought." Elantra shook her head. "Conner McVee tried to tell me what you were. I wouldn't believe her. I defended you. So you tell me who played me for a bigger fool, you or Conner McVee."

"Honey, business is business. They've never proved that I'm anything but a legitimate business man..."

"Save it, Dad. I know what you do. So... did my mother kill herself, or did you do that, too?"

"Elantra, this is really unfair! You're not giving me a chance to defend myself..."

"Did you kill my mother?"

"No. She killed herself," he said. *Why tell her anything else now. Nothing can be proved.*

"Why?" Elantra had never asked before.

"She was unhappy, she was unstable. I told you that..."

"You know damn good and well that's not the answer I want. Why was she unhappy? Why was she unstable?"

Tarent sat there silently for a long time. "Your mother didn't understand my business. She wanted to leave me and take you with her. I couldn't let her do that. I love you, Elantra, you're the only thing I care about..."

"You held her prisoner here." Elantra got up, her chair helped her and she shoved it over. "You held her prisoner here just like you're holding me now, and she finally killed herself. So you *did* kill her. Just like you're killing me now."

"Don't say that!" Tarent ordered. "I'm doing all of this for you. It will all be yours one day..."

"I don't want it!" Elantra yelled in a disbelieving tone. "I don't want a crime empire. I want to be a *doctor* who works on *real patients*. I want to feel the water on my skin and the wind in my face and my lover's body pressed against mine. I don't want your fucking blood money."

"It's not blood money, it's..."

"Father..." Elantra was pacing back and forth like a caged animal, and then she stopped and riveted her eyes on Tarent's. "Did you kill Conner McVee's partner? Did you kill Peggy Mishy?"

Apparently she had spent the last few days thinking about all this. He chose his words carefully. "Elantra, I don't kill people, that's your friend Hammer McVee..."

"Let me rephrase the question." Elantra took a deep breath, stopped her pacing and turned to glare at him. "Did you have Peggy Mishy killed?"

Tarent took a deep breath, no sense sugar coating it anymore. Maybe it was time that she understood her true place. What she really was. He looked back at her unblinkingly.

"Mishy stepped into my territory, and I had his sister killed to teach him a lesson. That's the way the business goes. You have to be tough; you have to be hard. You don't want to admit it, Elantra, but you've got what it takes to run the business, and some day you and Buddy will..."

"I'm not like you!" Elantra screamed, shaking her head. "Do you have any idea how many lives you have destroyed? Do you even *care*? You say you had Peggy Mishy killed as if you were saying you had the droid clean up a mess. The woman was gang raped, killed and mutilated. Conner McVee..."

"Conner McVee is a police agent, Elantra. She is our enemy!"

"No." Elantra shook her head emphatically. "She is *your* enemy. She is *my* lover, and I'd be with her now if it wasn't for you." She turned on her heel and stomped from the dining room. She stopped in the doorway and turned to confront Tarent. "I suggest that if you want an heir to take over your filthy crime empire you build another one, because it isn't going to be me." She stomped out of the room, kicking the door that was opening for her.

Tarent watched as the door closed behind her. "No, Elantra, you will be my heir. Computer on." It came on. "Computer.

Call Doctor Peterson." Dr. Peterson came on line.

"What can I do for you, Tarent?" he asked, seeming less than happy to see the crime lord.

"Smile, Peterson, after this you won't owe me."

"Well, I suppose that's a good thing. So what do you need?"

"I want you to do a brain erase on my daughter."

"How thorough?" the Doctor asked.

"Only the last few weeks."

"That should be easy. When do you want it done?"

"Sooner the better. Tomorrow morning here..."

"My equipment and staff..."

"Bring it here tomorrow. Be here by ten."

The doctor seemed even less pleased. "That's an awful inconvenience."

"And killing your partner was inconvenient for me. Don't make me get vulgar, Dr. Peterson."

Peterson nodded his head. "I'll be there. But this is it. After this we're even."

"That was the deal," Tarent said. "Transmission close." He laughed and leaned back in his chair. "After tomorrow she won't even know who Hammer McVee is. My life can go back to normal."

Tarent got up and went to his office. As he sat down, Squat appeared on the screen. "Boss, Jason Hunter's at the front door."

"Send him right up." Tarent leaned back in his chair farther. A few short minutes later Jason walked in with Squat. "So?"

"Check your surveillance tapes," Jason said cockily. "About two this afternoon."

Tarent did, and he smiled. "But she's not dead," he said.

"She was probably wearing a vest, but I was using armor piercing loads, and it's pretty obvious by the way she's running that she's hit bad. And there," he pointed at the screen, "you can see where the blood is running down her leg. It may not kill her, but now that she's wounded... it's only a matter of time till someone brings her down, and I want part of the action."

"Get out there and finish the job and you can have it all," Tarent said. "The price is for a dead McVee not a wounded one."

"But..."

"We've done business a long time, Jason. You know how I

work."

"Tarent, no one but me even got close to her…"

"Finish it, Jason…"

Jason left in a huff, and Tarent relaxed for the first time in weeks. Everything was going his way.

Everyone in Power's Tower was asleep except Elantra and the droids. No need for human sentries, they were inefficient. They could fall asleep or miss motion. They might see danger where there was none, or miss danger where it was very real and present. Not so a machine. It could look everywhere at once, detect the slightest movement, and determine whether the moving form carried any threat or any weapons. A machine asks itself very simple questions – What was that noise? What moved? Who is that person? Are they supposed to be here? Are they an intruder? Are they dangerous?

It would never occur to the building dwellers that perhaps it would be easier to trick a simple machine than it would be to trick a human.

It had, however, occurred to Elantra.

She crept into her father's office, and the door closed behind her. The machine saw only that she was not an intruder, and that she was one of the people who was allowed to enter Tarent's office.

"Computer, exterior monitors on," Elantra ordered. The computer knew that Elantra wasn't allowed to leave the building, but it hadn't been programmed to keep her out of this room. It had certainly never been programmed to deny her access to anything but the security systems and the secret files which only Tarent himself was privy to. The screens came to life.

Conner was nowhere in sight. "Computer, can you find Conner McVee?"

"She is not currently in our vision," the computer answered.

Elantra sighed. She desperately wanted to see Conner. To look at her even if she couldn't touch her. "Computer, play back sections of tapes made earlier today containing Conner McVee."

There she was. Conner stood there watching the building. It started to rain, and Conner turned up her jacket collar and pulled her hat forward, but she didn't move. The computer played roughly an hour of Conner doing nothing more exciting than standing around in the rain, and yet Elantra was not bored.

She watched as a red car pulled up. There was a conversation that the antiquated audio equipment hadn't picked up, and then there was a gun blast that it caught loud and clear. Conner was knocked into a wall, and she slid down it. It was like a horrible nightmare. Elantra felt her heart roll in her chest, but then Conner got up. She stumbled into the street, fired at the retreating car, and then she turned to the building and cursed Elantra's father.

And Elantra hoped God would.

Her father had lied to her, even breaking his promise. He was still trying to kill Conner McVee, and from the way Conner was moving as she stumbled to her car, he just might have succeeded.

"Computer off." Elantra tried to sit down hard in her father's chair, but of course it didn't let her. She started to cry. Her father hadn't called the hit off. He'd never had any intention of calling the hit off. He had lied to her about that, just like he had lied about everything else in her life.

Conner had tried to tell her the truth about her father, but she wouldn't – couldn't believe it. Now Conner was hurt, maybe dying, and she was hunted. Elantra knew medicine. If she could find Conner she could help her.

Elantra knew now that she couldn't trust her father to cut a square deal with her. He wanted Conner McVee dead, and he wasn't going to stop until he had what he wanted.

She had to get to Conner; she had to help her. No matter what that might mean.

CHAPTER 13

Once again Conner found herself in Jakelord's basement abode.

"You've got brass nuts, Hammer McVee," Jakelord swore through clenched teeth.

"That's what I keep tellin' everyone." Conner was shaking, cold and hurt. "You owe me, Jakelord," she said through chattering teeth.

"We all owe each other," Jakelord hissed back.

"Yeah, well, till now I've done all the payin', and you've done all the gettin'." Conner looked up at him, met his gaze and held it. He stared back for only a few seconds and then looked away. "You owe me, Jakelord. Come on, man, I need your help."

One of his "boys" grabbed him and pulled him a ways away.

"Man, Jakelord, Tarent Powers is offering two million dollars for her head. I bet Mishy would pay damn near that much. We ice her and we could be wealthy, wealthy men. We help her and one of the big boys is going to take us out."

"Tell your stupid little buddy that I can hear him, and even fucked up I could kill every one of you dumb fucks before he could blink," Conner hissed, lifting the nail gun she held in her hand.

Jakelord punched the man in the face so hard that he fell to the floor with a thud and didn't move, then he turned to look at Conner. "You giant pain in the ass!" He walked over to her and started taking her jacket off. "One of you dick wads find something that approaches sterile and get me some clean water and rags."

Hammer smiled at Jakelord. "Thanks, Jake."

"Yeah, yeah, don' rub it in. I'm sure I'm gonna hate myself in the morning." He took her shirt off slowly, then took a step back and made a face.

"What?" Conner looked down. The bullet, an all-powerful big motherfucker, was stuck into the vest and obviously into her body. "Well, fuck."

"It could have been worse," Jakelord said. "That big mother fucker could be floating around in there somewhere. So... is it true you screwed Tarent Powers' little girl?"

"She's hardly a girl," Conner defended.

"Yes or no?" Jakelord asked with a smile.

Conner smiled and nodded. "Yeah."

Jakelord laughed and shook his head. "Ya always were a crazy bitch, Hammer."

A man walked in with a bowl of water and a bunch of rags. They both knew that when he pulled the bullet out it was going to gush even more blood. Jakelord stared at the bullet for a minute.

"So... what ya wanna do, Hammer?" Jakelord asked. "By the way... if you die I am taking your head to Tarent and collecting that damned reward."

"Why wouldn't you?" Hammer took a deep breath, and looked down at what she could see of the wound – which was actually nothing. "I think the mother fucker is hanging in one of my ribs."

"Beautiful," Jakelord said. "Sammy, go get Doc Parker."

"I need it out now. I've got to get back..."

"Shut the hell up, ya ain't worth shit to anyone dead... Oh, except for me." Jakelord shook his head, then added in a low, almost scolding tone. "You stupid fucking dyke. You're gonna get yourself killed over a piece of ass."

Conner smiled crookedly. "It is an exceptionally fine piece of ass."

"And you are exceptionally fucking stupid," he spat back. "I mean what the hell's wrong with ya? Ya got some weird thing for gangsters daughters, or what?"

"Peg was Mishy's sister..."

"Speaking of Mishy, he also wants your head on a platter, and if he comes in here..."

"You're going to defend me with your last ounce of blood because that's the kind of really swell guy that you are."

"I'm going to die like a big dog because that's the kind of stupid fuck that I am... So you want to wait for Doc Parker?"

"I think I'm leaking my blood all over. We have to stop the bleeding."

Jakelord nodded. "All right. Bullet out first or vest and bullet all at once?"

Hammer thought about it for only a second. "Better pull the bullet out first, then the vest off quick."

Jakelord took a pair of pliers out of Conner's tool belt. "These ought to do the trick." He looked into her eyes, then leaned over and whispered right in her ear, "All I have to do is push instead of pull, Hammer, and this goes right into your lung. You croak, and I get two million dollars. Why do you trust me?"

"Because I'm the only person that does, and you know that," Hammer said.

Jakelord pulled the bullet out. Then he jerked the vest off. He stuffed the gushing wound with rags. He had done this enough times that he knew what he was doing, and that this time it wasn't enough.

Hammer wavered, the pain had almost knocked her out. She rocked in her seat, damn near dropping her weapon, and Jakelord steadied her.

Doc Parker wasn't really a doctor, but he was the closest thing this part of Slum Town had. The only one of Willie's kids who couldn't hack a computer, he'd earned his keep by stuffing people's guts back in and stitching them up. He'd been good at it, a natural, and it made him a good and almost legal living in Slum Town. He ran over to Hammer, bag in hand. He smiled as he looked at her bare chest.

"You know, Hammer, seeing you like this I almost forget that you're one of the boys." He pulled the packing out, and more blood gushed. He shoved it back in. "Oh, that wasn't a good idea." He took a tool out of his bag that Hammer knew only too well, and she flinched. He smiled sadistically. "Yes, it looks like we're going to have to zap all those naughty little capillaries." He pulled the packing out again, sprayed the wound with a purple spray, and then started to cauterize the wound. The spray was supposed to sterilize the area and numb it. Hammer hoped that it did a better job sterilizing things than it did numbing them. "Your rib is broken, but not bad."

"Your rib can be... broken... *good*?" Conner ground out through gritted teeth.

"Still a smart ass, hey, McVee?" He finished and put his tool away. He looked up at her and smiled, sadly this time. "You've sure got yourself in a mess. Hammer, for God's sake... You deflowered Tarent Powers' little girl. What the hell were you thinking?"

Conner managed a smile.

"Yeah, that's what I thought. You need some blood." Doc Parker looked with meaning at Jakelord.

Jakelord rolled his eyes, then rolled up his sleeve and flopped on the table next to Conner. "Shit a damn brick, woman, if you aren't the biggest damn pain in the ass."

She coughed, and it almost killed her. Parker set up the transfusion tube – not for the first time, but this time Jakelord was giving blood to Hammer instead of Hammer giving it to Jakelord. Doc knew everyone's blood type and all their compatible donors. He dressed Hammer's wound with clean rags and duct tape as he transfused the blood. When the transfusion was complete he pulled the needles out and applied bandages with cotton balls to both arms.

"Thanks, Jakelord... Doc." Hammer got shakily on her feet. "I won't forget this."

"Where the hell do you think you're going?" Doc Parker asked.

"I have to go back," Hammer said.

Parker started to protest.

"It's better for all of us if she gets out of Slum Town before Tarent or Mishy finds out she's been here," Jakelord said.

"You at least need some dry clothes, Hammer," Parker protested.

"Sammy, find Hammer some dry clothes," Jakelord ordered.

"Thanks, guys," Conner said.

"Yeah... Well, you owe me forever. Don't fucking forget that," Jakelord said.

"I won't," Conner promised.

Sammy set the clothes down by Conner, and she started to trade her wet clothes for dry ones. When she was done, she started to leave.

"Hammer...Don't go back there, man," Jakelord pleaded.

She smiled at him, an all-knowing smile, and he spat back, "I can't collect on this favor if you're dead."

She put her nail belt back on and checked her weapon. She put in a new charge. "See you guys later." She kissed them both and left.

Elantra had started to just walk up to the front doors and demand that they let her out, but good sense had kicked in and she realized that wasn't likely to happen. She knew that the computer that hadn't been told that she wasn't allowed to go into her father's office and dig through his files *had* been told that she wasn't allowed to leave the floor, much less the building.

She sat on the bed in her room staring towards the window, trying to think of a way out. As if she hadn't had enough to worry about, while snooping through her father's files she ran into a transmission he had made earlier that night in which he talked to a doctor about having part of her brain erased tomorrow.

He wasn't happy to separate her from Conner. He wasn't even happy with simply killing Conner. He wanted to erase any trace of Conner from her mind. To remove those memories of the time they had spent together.

Time was running out. Conner was hurt and in danger, and if she didn't do something quick it wasn't going to matter anyway because her loving father was going to have her brain partially erased. By tomorrow evening she wouldn't know what real food tasted like, or what it was like to run in the ocean. She wouldn't remember even knowing who Conner McVee was, much less what it was like to be touched by and touch her. She'd forget what it was like to breathe real air and feel the water against her skin. She'd forget what it was like to love and to be loved. She wondered how removing those memories was going to effect the burning hot sensation she felt in her chest whenever she thought about Conner.

She was trying to think of solutions, but all she could think of was how hopeless the whole thing was.

She'd tried to call Conner, but the computer apparently had a lockout on transmissions to and from Conner McVee.

She wiped the tears from her eyes. There was only one thing left to do. She'd never done it before, and she was sure she had no idea how, but she was desperate.

"Hey God, this is Elantra. I'm in a real mess down here. Maybe You could help me out... This isn't working. I don't feel anything but stupid." She thought for a minute. Conner had said something, what? Something about you had to have a tool to get a blessing. She got up and rummaged through her room till she found the clothes she'd worn home. In the pocket of the pants she found what she was looking for. She sat down on her bed again and looked at the screwdriver. "OK,

God, I have my tool now, so here's the deal. I want Conner McVee to be all right, and I want to get out of this building before they wipe my brain out, and if You'll do that for me I'll... build something... I'll even build a baby," she made a face. "If that's what it takes. Just please let me get back to Conner."

She waited. She didn't feel anything, and no ideas came to mind. No lightning flashed, no thunder rolled. She looked at the screwdriver and started to throw it against the wall, but she stopped. As she stared at the screwdriver, a tingling went up her back, and she knew what she was going to do. She changed into the clothes she had brought with her from Wrench Town and shielded herself with all she had learned there. She grabbed up the clothes she had been wearing that day. When she walked out the door of her room she was a Constructionist.

She saw the camera turn to monitor her movements. She threw the blouse she was holding up so that it covered the camera completely, then she walked on down the hall, stopping only to throw her skirt over another camera. She skipped past the elevator to the staircase. It was an emergency thing, and in all probability it had never been used, except on the two occasions Elantra herself had used it to sneak out of the building. The door was like the doors in Wrench Town, manual, part of the emergency precautions. Down the hall she saw one of the drones patrolling. She tried to open the door quietly, but it squeaked. The drone turned just as she ducked into the stairwell. Registering that this was all wrong, it sounded the general alarm.

Elantra pushed the door closed quickly. There was no latch on it. She started to panic, and then she saw the light. It had come on when she entered the stairwell. She could reach it if she climbed up on the rail, which is just what she did. She took her screwdriver in hand and stabbed at the light till it broke and the stairwell was dark. As she climbed down, one of her father's men ran in the door, and the light from the hallway backlit him. Elantra jumped on him and started stabbing at him with her screwdriver. She was surprised to find that she easily overpowered the man who was twice her size. Her time in Wrench Town had made her strong. Of course, it might have just been that the poor bastard was still half asleep. After all, he was still in his pajamas.

She must have stabbed him in the right spot, because he fell to the ground and didn't move. Elantra heard men running down the hall. Now a louder siren was blaring – no doubt a full out alert. Who knew? It might have been a special *Elantra is trying to leave the building!* alarm.

"Great, I really am in a prison." She closed the door again and pulled the body of the guard in front of it. She found his gun and took it.

She smiled in the dark. "Now I have *two* tools." She took off down the staircase, using the rail to guide her in the dark. She heard the men trying to get in the door behind her, so she doubled her pace. On the next floor the light came on, and after a few seconds she figured out how to shoot the gun, aimed and fired. The light busted with one shot, but the gun jerked in her hand, which was a bit of a shock and she almost dropped it. She swallowed hard and went on.

Having gauged the distance between the stairs she now practically ran down them, and on the next floor almost into her father's men. She stopped short. The two men heard her and turned, but they were in the light and she was in the dark. There was a brief moment of moral dilemma. She was a doctor, and doctors saved people, they didn't shoot at them. But one of them had shot Conner, and at that thought her moral dilemma ended, and she shot at them. One of them fell, and the other ran into the hallway. She shot out the light, shoved the man in front of the door and took his gun, too. This one she tucked into the top of her pants. The other twenty-five floors down no one bothered her, and that made her wonder what would be waiting for her. No doubt they would have all gone to the bottom to wait, knowing that was the only way for her to get out of the building. But she had two guns and her screwdriver, and while she could shoot them, her father wouldn't let them shoot her.

At the bottom of the stairs there was a doorway that led outside. It was locked. There was another door that she knew opened into the lobby of Power's Tower. She stopped and thought. They could either be both places, or just one. The one door lead directly outside, that would be their biggest fear – that she would get out of the building. The other door led to the hallway, which would leave her with only one more door to go through.

She put her ear to the exterior door, a trick she had learned from Conner McVee. She could hear voices. She smiled and walked out the other door carefully, gun at the ready. She walked down the lighted hallway towards the front doors. She moved against the wall at the end of the hall, and looked carefully around the corner. There were two men there. She stuck her screwdriver in her pocket and pulled the other gun. Guns at the ready, she strolled out of hiding. They turned towards her and started to say something. No doubt to announce to the world that they had found Elantra.

Elantra smiled, aimed the guns at them, and shook her head no. She waved her guns slightly, motioning for them to move away from the front doors. They looked at each other for a second, each one waiting for the other one to come up with a better plan than moving away from the doors without saying a word and letting the boss's daughter just walk out. She shook the guns menacingly at them, and they moved away from the door silently.

She walked up to the access panel and poked at the buttons, but her code had been lifted from the memory. She had figured that it was, but there was no harm in trying. She turned to check quickly that the guards hadn't moved, then she put one gun back into the top of her pants and grabbed her screwdriver out of her pocket. She used it to pry the cover off the panel. There were sparks, but the door didn't open.

"Tarent, she's in here!" one of the men screamed. Then he made a run for her.

"God damn it!" Elantra screamed. She turned and shot the man, and the other man immediately put his hands up and started backing away.

She held onto the handle of the screwdriver, shoved it into the door control box and started twisting it around. There was a huge shower of sparks, and then the doors opened. She ran out just as five of her father's men ran around the corner of the building, and her father and half a dozen more men poured into the lobby behind her. She swiveled back and forth, trying to keep her guns on all of them as she walked slowly away from the building. She was momentarily shocked as even her father followed her out of Power's Tower.

"Get out of my way, or I'll kill you!" she screamed.

"Elantra, think about what you're doing..." her father started. He moved closer. "I'm your father. I'm the only one who can protect you."

"You can't protect me from you! You had Conner McVee shot... I saw it!" Elantra screamed. "You want to have my brain erased... The only way you are going to stop me is to kill me."

Tarent stopped in his tracks. He looked at his daughter in the light of the street lamp. Dark, beautiful and determined, she was no longer a weak-willed, innocent girl, but an independent, determined young woman, hell bent on having her own way. Driven by passion and by love, her only allegiances were to herself and the Constructionist cop that was Tarent's worst enemy. "OK, kill her."

"What!" Elantra screamed.

"Are you sure, boss?" one of his men asked. Elantra was already running towards the road.

"Yes, I'm sure," Tarent said.

Suddenly the night erupted in gunfire. Not just from behind her, but from all around she realized, though she didn't have time to think about the ramifications of it. It seemed to be coming from everywhere, and a lot of it wasn't aimed at her at all. She shot wildly in all directions. Suddenly a car pulled between her and her father's men, the door opened, and Conner screamed, "Get in!"

Elantra was already in the car and had the door shut before Conner had finished speaking. Conner roared off amid a spray of bullets. Elantra threw herself at Conner, kissing her over and over again, and making it almost impossible for Conner to drive. Three cars were already in hot pursuit.

"Damn it, there he was. Out in the open," Conner mumbled as she pushed Elantra gently away. "I'm glad to see you, too, honey, but if we want to stay alive you're going to have to let me drive."

"Conner McVee, why did you take me back there?" Elantra asked, suddenly angry.

"What! You *made* me take you back there..."

"You knew what kind of person my father was. You should have refused."

"Oh yes, like that would have worked," Conner mumbled. She swerved and just barely missed a car that had stopped at a light – one that she didn't stop at. Horns blared and cars automatically stopped before they could hit her. Unfortunately the computers didn't work fast enough, and two of the cars that were chasing her hit the confused cars standing in the middle of the road. The third car got through though, and started firing on them. Hammer turned sharply and headed down a side street.

A car roared out in front of her and stopped, effectively blocking her way. "Hang on!" Conner spun the car around and started back down the street she had just come up, heading straight at the car that had been following her, and into oncoming traffic. She wove expertly in and out of oncoming cars.

Elantra sat back in her seat and relaxed. She felt safe for the first time since she had returned to Freight City. "I was never so happy to see anyone in my life, Conner McVee, and not just because my father and his men were trying to kill me..."

"Your father! I thought it must be Mishy's boys."

"No, I think they were shooting at Daddy. There were bullets coming from everywhere..." She stopped, suddenly remembering that she had been shot at. She started checking herself for bullet holes and found none. "Wow! I didn't get hit, not once." She took her screwdriver out of her pocket, held it up and said. "Thanks, God."

Conner put the strange action down to stress and concentrated on driving, jerking in and out of traffic. Elantra looked back. They seemed to have lost their tail, and she told Conner so. They started down another street, and up ahead of them they saw a roadblock.

Conner spun around, and they picked up another tail. She swerved to miss an on-coming car and didn't quite make it. There was a crunch of metal, and they were thrown sideways. Conner hit the accelerator hard and sped away, the mess she left behind stopped their pursuer, but it would only be a matter of time before they picked up a new one, and the car was making dying noises and spewing steam. Every road out of Freight City or into Hammer Town was blocked, and not always by thugs. More and more the roadblocks ahead were police agents.

If the car was in bad shape, it was just a little bit worse off than Conner was. If she had been a hundred percent, she never would have hit that other car. The situation was desperate. She wondered where all the cops had come from and why they were helping the bad guys instead of her.

"What the hell is going on?" Elantra asked when they had

seen their sixth roadblock.

"They're keeping us from going into Hammer Town. We have to lose the car. It's on its last leg, and it's like a beacon out here among the self-driven models." They seemed to be alone for the moment, so she pulled into an alley, turned the lights off and parked. "The only thing I can't figure is how they got the police involved. Maybe the computer can enlighten us. Computer, run police bands." She sighed and leaned back in her seat.

Elantra moved closer to Conner. She noticed even in the dim light that Conner's face looked strained, and there was sweat on her brow. "Conner, I saw you get shot. How bad are you hurt? Should we go to a hospital?"

"I had on a vest, I'll be OK." She took Elantra's hand and held it tight. "Everything will be OK now that we're together, if we can just stay alive long enough to get out of town."

"I have guns," Elantra said. "I stabbed a guy, and I shot some guys and took their guns, and I have two..."

"You did what? You have what?" Conner said in disbelief.

"I have guns," Elantra said, holding up the one she was still clutching in her fist.

"How did you..?"

"It's not rocket science, you basically point and pull the trigger," Elantra said shrugging.

Conner smiled. It was the first time Elantra had answered one of her unfinished questions.

"What's wrong with your computer?" Elantra asked.

Conner looked at the blank screen and sighed. "I'm being scrambled."

"By who?"

"It's a Brakston Agency computer, so that means it could only be one person. James Rank."

Earlier that day...

James Rank entered the code that would scramble Hammer McVee's computer just as Jason Hunter walked in.

James looked up at Jason with utter contempt. "Did you shoot Hammer McVee?"

"I figured she'd come whining to you..."

"Yes or no. Did you shoot Hammer McVee?"

"McVee shot at me first. It was self defense..."

"That ain't the story Hammer tells. Be warned, Hunter,

Hammer's promisin' to kill you in a slow and painful way, and if she thinks I had anythin' ta do with it, she's goin' to kill me, too."

"Did she say so?"

"No I made it up! Of course she said so. Why else would I scramble her computer? I don' want her to be able to find me. I don' mind telling ya that I'm scared shitless. If ya done or said somethin' that implies that I wanted Hammer killed..."

"All I tried to do was talk to her. I told you, she shot at me first."

"You better pray to God that yer tellin' the truth, because if yer not and you have brought the wrath of Hammer McVee down on our heads..."

"You'll what, Rank? Slap my pee-pee till it's red! Fire me!" Hunter laughed. "This agency is *dead*, man. The Corporation's going to pull your charter. Don't you get it? Hammer McVee has made you a laughing stock, Rank. We're all going to be looking for work anyway." Rank yelled something at him, but he didn't really hear what it was because he was already heading out of the building and making plans.

Jason Hunter looked across the parking garage at the entrance to the Brakston Agency. He cradled the weapon in his arms. He had been a little surprised at the ease with which he had purchased it, but then it wasn't meant to be a weapon, it was meant to be a tool, and in Hammer Town when you wanted to buy a tool they were only too happy to oblige. He waited for Rank to step out of the building and fired once, twice, three times just for good measure. Rank went down, and he roared off.

"Computer on... Computer! Alert to all agency bands. Am in pursuit of Hammer McVee down North towards Towsend. She just shot James Rank."

In less than five minutes every police agency in the area was combing the streets with a shoot-to-kill order on Hammer McVee, while James Rank lay in an area hospital fighting for his life, and his assailant traveled through the city unmolested.

They had left the car a half an hour ago. Hammer had put on a long jacket that successfully covered her tool belt, but was thin and not very warm. Elantra wore Conner's jacket, which was soaking wet. The rain didn't look like it was going to let up, either. They ducked into a parking garage and snuck into the shadows. Elantra had been helping Conner walk the last fifteen minutes, and now Conner all but collapsed against the wall of the garage. Elantra grabbed her arm and managed to stop her from smacking into the floor.

"Conner!" Elantra knelt down beside her. Conner looked up at her, an unhealthy glaze in her good eye. Her teeth were chattering, and she was shaking all over. Elantra touched her. "My God, you're burning up." Elantra tried to think, but it was harder than it sounded after all she'd been through in the last few hours. "Conner... where are we heading?"

"Slum Town. I have lots of contacts... friends there," Conner answered. "Just give me a few minutes to rest."

"Conner, you're sick... are you sure... Slum Town?"

"I know the streets there. How they work. Places to stay, people who will help me. Help us, no questions asked."

Elantra nodded and sat down beside Conner. A car went by. The lights hit them for a minute, and she almost came out of her skin. Conner put an arm around her shoulders. "I'm sorry."

"No. I'm the one who's sorry," Elantra cried then. "This is all my fault. We could have been happily tucked away half way across the country by now."

Conner mustered a smile. "You said it, not me." Conner released her and started pushing herself up the wall. "Come on, we'd better go."

"Conner, I think..."

"We have to go, Elantra. Come on, just help me."

The woman opened the door a crack with a crowbar. "Hammer!" She forced the door open, grabbed Hammer by the collar of her jacket and pulled her in. Elantra followed. "Don't just stand there, girl! Hit the button half a dozen times hard and kick the door. It will close." Elantra did as the woman ordered.

She was a short, large woman with huge tits and little bitty feet. But she had the same sort of sleazy charm that Dedra had, and Elantra was sure that she was meeting yet another of Conner's old girlfriends.

The woman pulled Conner over and set her on one of four couches in the room, each one covered in a different floral print.

Conner started to introduce them. "Pinky Widefronts, this is..."

"I know who she is, baby, and I know what kind of trouble you're in, so just lay back and let mama take care of you." She started taking Conner's boots off. "Oh, child, you're soaked to the skin. Doc Parker told me he pulled a bullet out of you. Told me all about your problems, too." She gave Elantra a compassionate look, and Elantra relaxed a little.

Pinky apparently saw the gun sticking out of Elantra's waistband. She'd stuck the other one in a jacket pocket.

"You might want to put that some place safer," she said, pointing.

Elantra nodded, pulled the gun out of her pants and stuck it on the end table. She took the jacket off and lay it on the floor.

Elantra moved closer to look at Conner. "You told me you had your vest on..."

"I never said the bullet didn't go through it," Conner said with a smile.

"Poor baby," Pinky cooed, and started to help Conner off with the rest of her clothes.

Elantra coughed. "I can do that."

"Good, then I'll just go put the kettle on." Pinky ran off towards the kitchen. Elantra knelt at Conner's feet and helped her get first her jacket and then her tool belt off. Their eyes met.

"I... I thought I'd never see you again," Elantra said with tears in her eyes.

"I knew you would," Conner said through chattering teeth. "I'm so *cold*."

As if on cue Pinky ran in with a couple of blankets. "Young love," she cooed, and then ran out of the room again. Elantra took the rest of Conner's clothes off and wrapped the covers around her.

Elantra had tried to ignore the dressing on Conner's ribs. Some sort of gray tape had been wrapped all the way around her, and the cloth beneath was obviously soaked. The dressing needed to be changed, but that could wait till Conner stopped shaking. Conner probably needed a shot of antibiotics, at the very least some sort of pain and fever reducer. Elantra wondered if those things were going to be available here.

Pinky walked in with hot tea. She handed a cup to Conner

first.

"Thanks for everything, Pinky," Conner said.

"My pleasure, honey." She smiled at Elantra. "You really ought to get out of those wet things, sugar. The bathroom's that way, and you can wear one of my robes. Pretend like it's a tent and wrap it around a bunch of times. Goodness knows you're not big as a minute." She turned back to Conner. "We're going to have to put some meat on that girl's bones."

"I'm not really worried about me right now." Elantra got up and walked a little away, giving Pinky a meaningful look and Pinky followed. "As soon as she warms up I need to change the dressing on her wound. I was wondering what sort of medical supplies you might have."

"All that I have is in my medicine chest in the bathroom. You can check it out when you go to change. I have some old rags you can use for gauze. I'll just go get them. God knows I'll never be that size again anyway."

"Thanks," Elantra said and started towards the bathroom.

Elantra allowed herself a quick hot shower before she got into the huge floral print robe and started going through the medicine chest. She found alcohol, cotton balls, some aspirins and a bottle of antibiotics obviously left over from an ear infection Pinky'd had. Elantra was glad that Pinky hadn't bothered to follow the instructions that said to take them all. She found no tape, and hoped that Pinky would have something that would work. It wasn't what she had hoped for, but it would have to do.

When she carried the items into the living room Conner was sipping at the tea and appeared to have quit shaking. Elantra put the things on the coffee table as Picky walked in with a stack of rags and set them on the table as well.

"Have you got any medical tape?" Elantra asked.

Pinky smiled helplessly. "All I've got is duct tape." She apparently noticed the lack of recognition on Elantra's face. "Like the stuff she's wrapped up with now."

Elantra started to protest. "That will be fine," Conner said.

Pinky went to get the tape.

Elantra pulled the cover off Conner and knelt on the floor beside her. She kissed Conner gently on the mouth, and Conner kissed her back.

"Everything you said about my father was true. I'm so sorry. I'll believe anything you tell me from now on, so I have to ask... Do you love me?" Elantra asked, close to tears.

Conner smiled. "Of course I love you. Would I sit in the rain and get shot just to get back at your fucking father?" She sounded angrier than she wanted to.

"He killed Peggy. He admitted to me that he had her killed. How can you love me when I come from..." She did start crying then, "...from *that?*"

"Baby, if I don't blame you for all of this, and I don't, why would I blame you for that? Now either change my bandage or cover me back up, you are freezing me to death," Conner said.

Pinkey came in with a pair of scissors looped on one finger, a sponge floating in a bowl of warm water in her hands, and a roll of duct tape around her wrist. Seeing this Elantra immediately knew that Pinky Widefronts was a very resourceful person.

Elantra was glad that the rain had loosened the tape in spots, because where it hadn't it was stuck tight. She pulled at it gently, loosening it a little at a time in spite of Conner's constant protests that Elantra should, "Quit farting around and just rip it off." Elantra wasn't about to do that and risk pulling the wound open, so it took her fifteen minutes just to get the tape completely free. Then she carefully pulled the dressing away from the wound. She let out a screech and made a face in spite of herself.

"Oh, baby, that is nasty," Pinky said making a face to match Elantra's.

"Tyetheyl gabardine!" Elantra breathed in shock.

"Huh?" Pinky and Conner said at the same time.

"That purple stuff," Elantra said in horror.

Conner and Pinky looked at each other and smiled.

"Purple gack," they said.

"They use this stuff on farm animals," Elantra said in disbelief. "You're not supposed to use it on humans. It's not sterile it's... and what the hell have they done here? It looks like he cauterized the entire area! That only damages the whole area so that it will take longer to heal. Who are the butchers that did this?"

"Calm down," Conner said. "Pinky can take care of it if you don't have the stomach for it."

Elantra was more than a little disgruntled. "It's not that. It's just... who ever did this has done more harm than good." She started to clean the wound and the surrounding area as well as she could with the meager supplies she had on hand.

"If they hadn't done it, I would have bled out," Conner said.

Elantra only then noticed the tiny red spot on Conner's arm. She pointed at it. "What the hell is that?"

"They gave me a pint of blood," Conner said shrugging.

"Please tell me you're kidding!" Elantra all but screamed.

Conner smiled and looked at Pinky. "Did I not tell her that I was bleeding to death?"

"Do you have any idea how many diseases you can get from blood? How many hundreds of thousands of blood born pathogens there are?" Elantra asked hotly.

"No, and I'm hoping that you aren't going to tell me, because I'm starting to feel queasy. Could you please not scrub so hard? I'm not a virtual patient, you know," Conner begged.

"Sorry." Elantra was more careful. The purple "gack" was not going to come off, so she gave up. She redressed the wound and reapplied the tape. Then she looked at Conner's wrist and shoulder. These wounds were all but healed, still despite Conner's protest, she put salve on them both and dressed them. She gave Conner a sponge bath with the warm water, and by the time she was finished drying her off Conner seemed to be almost asleep. Pinky had run to get a glass of water at Elantra's request, and Elantra handed the glass, an antibiotic, and two aspirins to Conner. "Honey, are you allergic to aspirin or any antibiotics that you know of?"

"I'm not allergic to shit. Are you kidding? I've had dozens of complicated surgeries. If I was allergic to anything I would have died by now." Conner sat up and took the pills. Pinky helped her slip on a loose – fitting floral print shirt. "I'm tired."

"Well, I can't imagine why," Pinky said. "Come on, I'll help you. I've already fixed up the guest room for you."

Pinkey showed them to a bedroom that was – as you might have guessed – decorated in twenty different floral prints. "Maybe you should sleep alone," Elantra said as she helped Conner into bed.

Conner grabbed Elantra and dragged her into bed. Elantra had to move quickly to keep from landing on Conner's wounded body.

Pinky laughed. "Well, I'll just leave you two alone, then. Good night."

"Good night, Pinky, and thanks for everything," Conner

said.

"Anything for you, baby," Pinky said and closed the door.

Conner looked over at Elantra. "I never want to sleep alone again."

Elantra felt Conner's hands working at the knot that was holding the three layers of robe closed. Elantra took Conner's hands and held them.

"You're wounded and you're sick," she protested with a laugh.

"But I'm not dead," Conner said.

"Come on, Conner. You are way too sick for this. Being close to you is enough." She ran her hand down Conner's arm. "I never thought I'd even see you again, so just this is wonderful... I'm so sorry, baby..."

Conner put a finger over Elantra's lips. "Shush." She moved her finger, and kissed Elantra gently.

"I love you. We're together, and we're going to stay that way, come hell or high water." Conner moved to lie on her back, trying to get comfortable. She was obviously in pain.

"I wish there was something else I could give you besides aspirin," Elantra said gently.

"It's all right, I'll go to sleep and I'll be fine." Conner promised. "I'm too tired not to sleep."

Elantra snuggled against Conner, pulling the covers up over both of them. "Honey... is Pinky... well, is she one of your old girlfriends?"

Conner laughed then. "Is that what's bothering you? Pinky's not one of my old girlfriends." She laughed again. "Pinky's not any sort of *girl* at all, at least not physically."

"What do you mean?" Elantra asked.

"Honey, Pinky's a man, physically."

Elantra was completely confused.

"But she looks..."

"She's dressed like a woman because she feels like a woman. The boobs are real... well, sort of, and he prefers that you treat him like a she when she's dressed like one. You might say that me and my generation of street thugs are the children Pinky never had. She's always been very good to us. She makes a lot of money as a performer; she could live like a queen. She lives here in this dump because she spends all her money taking care of building brats who wind up in Slum Town. If Pinky sees a kid who's lost and afraid, she makes sure they have a place to sleep, a meal, and if they want to go back home she makes sure they get there. If they want to stay here she tries to make sure they don't get a rough deal."

"We're safe here, at least for the time being. Pinky would never turn us over, and no one would ever rat Pinky out."

Conner moved, trying again to get comfortable and not having much luck.

She lay her head on Elantra's chest and lay her arm over her. She sighed, as if finally finding a place where she was comfortable "Don't move," she told Elantra.

Elantra brushed the hair out of Conner's face. "I won't move. Do you feel better?"

"Yes." Then she asked in a voice suddenly filled with doubt, as if afraid of the answer she might get. "Elantra... Do you... Do you still love me?"

"Of course I do," Elantra said.

"Say it."

"I love you, Conner McVee."

Conner was almost asleep. "Elantra?"

"Yes."

"The minute I saw you, I knew that I was supposed to find you."

"And the first time I saw you... you took my breath away."

Elantra watched Conner go to sleep. She wasn't really comfortable, but Conner was, and that was more important right now. Whatever they threw at them they could handle together.

She thought of how she had broken out of Power's Tower, and felt smug. She had worked, she had used her tool, and she had escaped. She thought of how her father had ordered Conner shot, and anger boiled inside her. For the first time in her life a red-hot hatred that demanded to be fed burned inside her, and she understood why Conner had worked so hard to avenge Peggy's death.

But Tarent hadn't stopped there. Her own father had ordered her shot. But with all she now knew about her father, this wasn't shocking, and therefore not as traumatic as it probably should have been. And for some reason the fact that he had ordered her killed didn't make her as angry as the fact that he wanted Conner dead – had in fact gotten her shot.

Right then nothing seemed as important to her as the fact that she was no longer her father's captive, and that she was back in Conner's arms. She wasn't stupid; she knew this wasn't over yet, that they were still in danger and that things were likely to get a whole lot worse before they were clear of Freight City. But Conner had assured her that they were safe here, and so she fell asleep dreaming of the ocean, the sky, and her lover's touch.

Jason Hunter was starting to sweat. He hadn't counted on Hammer's nail gun being a beefed up version of the one he had purchased. He'd seen Hammer's gun shoot nails through cars and bricks and shatter a man's head. He had assumed the one he had purchased to kill James Rank would do the same thing. It hadn't.

James Rank was in bad shape, and he still wasn't conscious, but he was by no means dead. To make matters worse, no one had a bead on Hammer McVee, which meant she had successfully gone underground.

They had found her car abandoned, the front end of it smashed in one of the twenty crashes that had occurred in the city that night. It was a record in Freight City since the invention of the computer-driven car.

Conner McVee was out there somewhere, and no one had any idea where. They had set up roadblocks to Hammer Town, but she could have gotten there anyway. If she got to Hammer Town, no one would be able to pull her out till she wanted to leave. If she had gotten into Slum Town it wouldn't be much better. Slum Town was her turf. She had contacts there. While money could usually pay those scum to sell their own mothers out, they probably wouldn't sell out Hammer McVee.

Hammer had a rep in Slum Town. She didn't go after the small timers, in fact rumor had it that she would actually cover for them, and it was a fact that she had bailed a couple of the more seedy members of Slum Town out of jail on more than one occasion. Then there was that other part of her rep. If Hammer was after you, she caught you, and she had a record of bringing most of her collars in dead. This also was completely true.

The scum in Slum Town lived by two rules. Money buys happiness. Dead people can't spend money. So no amount of money is worth getting killed for.

In short, the only people who were trying to hit Hammer were those stupid enough to think they could kill her.

People like Jason Hunter.

Jason had made things harder for Hammer by framing her for the attack on Rank, but just having all her rights and privileges removed and having every police agency in the city after her wasn't likely to root her out.

And then there was Tarent Powers. At one point he had ordered his daughter killed, and in the next breath recanted the order. He'd doubled the price on Hammer's head and promised to kill anyone who so much as touched a hair on his daughter's head. Since Elantra was now with Hammer it made killing her that much harder. Then of course there was Mishy, who had apparently decided that if Hammer and the girl got killed that would be good. But Tarent dead was better, and that was where he was putting all his manpower and his money.

Jason was caught in the middle of a giant squeeze, and it seemed that any way things fell, he wasn't likely to walk away unscathed.

He was running out of time. At any minute James Rank might wake up. He'd tell everyone that Jason was the one that shot him, and that Jason had shot Hammer McVee. They'd guess then that he was a double agent working with Tarent Powers. Every agent in town would be combing the street for him the way they were now looking for Hammer, and he didn't have Hammer's connections.

His only chance of coming out of this alive was to find Hammer McVee and finish the job that he had started, return the girl to her father, and then hide under Tarent's protection.

But first he had to get to James Rank and finish the job he had started there as well.

CHAPTER 14

Elantra woke to the sound of snoring and the sun in her face, and knew immediately that she wasn't in Power's Tower and who she was with. She felt a sudden elation, which made her want to laugh out loud. She was free! She was free and she was with Conner. In that moment when she wasn't quite awake, it was easy to forget everything else.

Conner had flopped onto her back during the night, but seemed to be sleeping peacefully. Elantra touched Conner gently on her arm, and was relieved to find that she wasn't running a temperature. She carefully pulled the covers up over Conner where she had uncovered herself. She was out cold, and Elantra was glad. In the absence of modern medicine, sleep would help her heal as quickly as anything else they could realistically provide.

Burning the living hell out of my baby and then spraying her with tyethel gabardine. What the hell were those idiots thinking? Then as she watched the happy rhythm of Conner's chest as it rose and fell, she knew that her life was more important than some more scars. *They saved her, probably the only way they knew how, and with what little they had. I have to remember where I am.*

Elantra smelled food, real food, and she smiled. She could hear Pinky working in the kitchen, and she was suddenly aware of something that should have been painfully obvious last night. Pinky was a Constructionist. The clues had been all around her, the water shower, the aspirin in the cabinet, the doors you had to open and chairs you had to sit in.

Everything was so surreal last night it's a wonder I was able to think at all. Besides, in the short time I lived with Conner in Wrench Town I got used to all those things. In all the confusion it never dawned on me that I was back.

Elantra wondered if Pinky had introduced Hammer to the cult.

The sound of the sink, the whirl of a mixer, all were music to Elantra's ears.

She lay there and just watched Conner for a long time, happy to be alive, and even more happy that Conner was alive and there with her. She was painfully aware that her foolishness had almost gotten them both killed.

They weren't safe yet, and as long as Mishy and her father were after them she wondered if they ever could be. What kind of a life could they possibly have if they were constantly on the run, always looking over their shoulders? She might not know her father as well as she thought she did, but she did know one thing about him. When he wanted something he wasn't likely to stop until he got it.

And he wanted Conner dead.

Elantra looked at Conner and frowned; she was sure that the rib under the wound was at least cracked. Of course with that purple crap everywhere it was impossible to see if there was any bruising. She began wishing she had the doctor back in Wrench Town's antiquated x-ray machine.

She wished there was some way she could take Conner to the hospital. At the very least she hoped that they could stay here long enough for Conner to heal, but was afraid even that was probably too much to ask for.

The more she thought about what she had done the night before, the more it seemed like it had been someone else who did it. She had found courage in that moment that she hadn't known she possessed. She now felt like she was ready for anything they could throw at her. Even if at that moment every muscle in her body hurt and she tensed up at the slightest movement.

A thought suddenly hit her like a fist. *I shot people last night! I might have even killed them.* She tried to reconcile the magnitude of this with the fact that she had just now thought about it, and that try as she might she couldn't find any guilt to go along with her realization. *They would have killed me. They were all trying to kill Conner. It all happened so fast... My father's a crime lord, a murderer who kills people for profit. If I killed anyone it was because they didn't leave me much choice. I don't feel guilty, so why should I pretend at an emotion that I really don't feel? Conner kills people, killing people doesn't mean you're bad. If you're killing the right people.*

Conner had pegged her right at their first meeting when she had called her a building brat, but Elantra wasn't a building brat anymore. She had taken a long drink of life outside the building, and it had changed her. She had resisted change at first, and then she had embraced it, welcomed it. Now there was no going back.

In that building her imagination had been stifled by machines. In there she had been nothing more than a piece of her father's life. Someone to marry off to Buddy so that Tarent could join in a lucrative partnership – no doubt in criminal activities – with his family.

Out here Elantra had her own identity, separate from her father, separate even from Conner McVee.

Elantra had been kidnapped from her father's prison. She'd gone back of her own free will, thinking that there was something that she had left there that was worth having. Now she knew the truth, and she would never go back there again. Not alive anyway.

Conner the Hammer McVee had become a legend among her people, and Elantra knew that she was about to become a legend among hers.

She got up, careful not to disturb Conner, and went to the kitchen where Pinky was busy cooking.

Pinky smiled at Elantra. "How's she doing?"

"Better, she's sleeping soundly, and there's no fever," Elantra said. She started to sit down and then had an odd thought. "Ah, do you need some help?"

"No, but if you'd like to worship go for it," Pinky said. "There's a stack of dishes over there needs doing."

Elantra walked towards the dishes and looked at them. Pinky seemed to read her mind.

"Have you ever done dishes before, dear?" Pinky asked gently.

"No... I've watched Conner do them. It's water and stuff, and rubbing the dishes," Elantra said.

"Very good," Pinky said, flipping a pancake on the grill. "All right then, run the water till it's hot, then plug up the sink... yes, that's the thing there. Plug the sink and add some soap. I start doing the dishes right away, rinsing in the water as it comes in the sink. That saves water."

It wasn't very hard, and Elantra felt good working. She and Pinky made idle chatter till Elantra finished the dishes. She wiped her pruney hands and sat at the table. Pinky set a plate of pancakes in front of her, and she poured syrup on them and started to eat. Pinky joined her.

"I think it's better to let Hammer sleep, don't you?" Pinky asked.

Elantra nodded. "She can eat when she gets up." She stopped eating for a minute and looked up. "Pinky... do you think we'll be able to stay here till Conner heals?"

"That's a good question," Pinky said morosely. "I would hope so, but... I heard from one of my kids on the street that your old man doesn't want you dead anymore, but he's doubled the price on Hammer's head to four million dollars. For that sort of money... I don't know too many people who will remain loyal when that sort of cash is hanging in the balance. Right now, as far as we know, only the three of us know Hammer's here, but... someone might have seen you come here. We can't be sure, and then there is all that money. People are going to start thinking. They know that Hammer and I have been friends a long time. They could put two and two together. I just don't know, and then there's the other problem."

Elantra sighed. "I'm not sure I want to hear that there is another problem, but maybe I'd better anyway."

"Well... it seems the cops had a reason for going after Hammer last night. Word on the street is that Hammer's clearance has been revoked and she's been accused of shooting her boss, James Rank," Pinky said.

Elantra didn't know whether Conner had shot Rank or not. She didn't really care. If Conner had shot him, she no doubt had a damn good reason to, except... "I wonder when she had time to do that."

"I didn't shoot Rank," Conner's voice made Elantra jump. Conner walked in, limping slightly and sat down at the table carefully. Elantra leaned over and kissed her on the cheek, just because she could, and Conner smiled at her, and then frowned. "Why the hell would they think I shot Rank?"

"He was shot with a nail gun," Pinky said quietly.

"If I had shot him, he'd be dead," Conner said taking the cup of coffee Pinky slid towards her. "Someone wanted it to look like I shot him. Now who would that be.... that fucking weasel, Jason Hunter. The same scum sucking shit muncher that shot me," Conner hissed. "Rank must have told Hunter that I called and what I told him. It's almost brilliant. Jason's been working for Tarent Powers and Brakston Agency at the same time, which isn't legal in any way, shape or form. He shoots me, but he doesn't kill me. I tell Rank, I even threaten him if he sent Hunter after me." She looked thoughtful. "So Jason buys a nail gun and shoots Rank. With Rank dead, no one knows that he shot me, and no one will be able to figure out that he works for Tarent Powers. With me framed for the shooting he's successfully put me on all the agency hit lists as well." She took a sip of the coffee and made a face. "That's how Tarent has stayed ahead of the law all these years. He's probably got guys inside all the big agencies. These guys aren't just on the take. They're on his payroll. Although I've suspected as much, I've never been able to prove anything. These guys are slick. Of course, in a computerized push-button society it isn't too hard to escape detection."

"Amen, sister," Pinky said, and Elantra couldn't tell if she was kidding or sincere.

"Of course, I still feel like a grade-A number one idiot for working with this bastard all these years and not knowing he was working for Tarent. Hey, Pinky! Where are my pancakes?"

Pinky got up and came back with a platefull, and set them in front of her. She started eating, making little pleasant noises as they disappeared down her throat.

"What are we going to do?" Elantra asked gently.

Conner swallowed before answering. "Well, a lot of that depends on whether Rank is still alive or not," Conner said.

"They said he was hanging on, but in a coma," Pinky offered.

Conner frowned. "If he dies it will be damn hard to prove I didn't shoot him."

It had been years since Tarent Powers had actually been on the streets. Today was no different. He paced his office as reports came back from his boys cruising Slum Town looking for any sign of Hammer McVee or his daughter. But people in Slum Town were normally tight-lipped, and with the cops everywhere roughing them up, they'd die before they gave anything up. Slummers weren't as weird as Constructionists, but they were just as freewilled and hardheaded. He had hoped that the promise of huge amounts of money would loosen their tongues as it normally did, but word had gotten around that Hammer had been knocking off some of his top men for the better part of a week now, and if any of them knew where she was, they weren't in any hurry to incur the wrath of the infamous Hammer McVee. The fact that she had apparently shot her boss at the agency only proved to them that she had already been pushed over the edge.

When he first heard that Hammer McVee had shot James Rank he had been a little shocked, but after seeing the evidence he was fairly sure that Hammer didn't have anything to do with it. First off their case was just too good. Second off he'd seen what bodies looked like after they'd been hit with Hammer's nail gun. Heads exploded, legs were shattered, and James Rank was still alive. If Hammer meant for him to be dead, he had no doubt the man would be dead.

The only answer was that someone was trying to frame Hammer McVee. He had a good idea that it was his boy Jason Hunter. Of course, knowing that the cops were doing nothing but making it harder for Tarent to find his daughter, Jason wasn't likely to confess to Tarent any time soon. He would have done it to save his own ass, and if and when Tarent found out for certain that Jason had done it, he was going to take that boy out of the game. Tarent didn't need anyone working for him that wasn't a team player.

Of course there was one more suspect, Mishy. Mishy wanted Hammer and Elantra dead. Mostly he wanted Tarent dead. Siccing the cops on Hammer McVee would leave Mishy free to pursue Tarent, and only Tarent. Meanwhile, every available man Tarent could spare was on the streets looking for Elantra and Hammer, their efforts muddled by cops everywhere doing the same thing. Tarent was feeling increasingly vulnerable, and for the first time in his life completely without any real game plan.

He was frightened and confused.

For a second last night he had thought that he wanted Elantra dead, but as soon as he realized that Mishy's goons had started firing on them both, he knew it wasn't what he wanted. Elantra was his, his blood; she belonged to him. He had to keep and protect her, or lose face forever with his business associates and his enemies.

Elantra was a disobedient, defiant brat, but she was *his* disobedient, defiant brat, and if he wanted to kill her that was one thing, but no one else had better try it. He was glad that his rash words hadn't caused her death, and he was determined not to let Hammer McVee keep her or let the cops or Mishy kill her.

Squat's face filled his screen. "I'm telling you, boss. It's like they just disappeared."

"Well keep looking! Ask around, find out who Hammer's contacts are. She's a police agent for God's sake! There have got to be people in Slum Town that hate the bitch!"

"Problem is them what's hate her is afraid of her," Squat explained.

"Then you make them more afraid of you, Squat! They are street scum. Intimidate the hell out of the little bastards," Tarent said.

"Boss, lots ah these guys... they work for Mishy. Even if they wanted to, they ain't gonna tell us nothin'."

"So now we're afraid of Mishy's street thugs!" Tarent screamed. "I am Tarent Powers. Do you hear me? I'm Tarent Powers! I'm not afraid of Hammer McVee, I'm not afraid of Mishy or his inbred minions. I'm asking you for simple things, Squat. A few simple things. Kill Mishy. Kill Hammer McVee. Bring my daughter home in one piece! Now... is that too much to ask for?"

"No sir, boss," Squat answered.

"Then quit talking to me and get your ass back to work. Transmission closed."

Squat and Dacker looked at the blank screen on their consol and then each other.

"This fucking sucks," Squat said. Dacker nodded. "Tell me again why we put up with this shit? We ain't rich, we don't get any respect, hell, I can't remember the last time I had any pussy."

"We do it so the boss don' kill us," Dacker reminded.

"Big deal! When's the last time he killed someone? Hell, he killed his old lady, that's it. Right now I ain't as afraid of him as I am Hammer McVee, or Mishy, or even his fucking daughter." He rubbed at his side. "That little bitch stuck me good. I should be laid up in the hospital healin' for a few days, but oh no, it's run the doctor in, have him glue the fucker together, slap a bandage on it and then *boom!*, I'm back at work. I say screw it."

"What are you gettin' at, Squat?" Dacker asked.

"You owe Tarent Powers one damn thing?"

Dacker thought about it for a minute, and smiled. "I don't reckon as I do. What you got in mind?"

"Well... you an me been pickin' up the money from his drops for years now..."

"We could give up all this lookin' for a quick ride to the

morgue, go make our usual pickups..."

"An instead of loadin' them inta Tarent Powers already bulging accounts, we load them inta our computer, head out of the country, and then load them into our new accounts. It would be more than enough money to get us started someplace else, and by the time he figured out we hadn't been killed by either Mishy or Hammer..."

"If he ever did," Dacker laughed.

"We'd be so far away he'd never find us," Squat finished. "So... what do you say? We wouldn't be rich, but we ain't rich now. We might have ta get real jobs, but hey! at least it won't be shit like *track down this psychopathic cyborg and get your ass nailed to a wall*."

"Let's pick up the loot and get the hell out of here," Dacker said. "I'm beginning to agree with all this scum around here. I'd rather be poor than dead."

Suddenly Squat started laughing.

"What's so damn funny?" Dacker asked, no doubt fearing a double cross.

"Calm down," Squat slapped him on the back. "I think I just figured out how we can get rich and stay alive."

"How's that?" Dacker asked.

Squat didn't get to answer. A red light started flashing on the dashboard. "What the hell is that?"

Tarent watched his screen as the interior of the car seemed to be sucked into a vacuum with the two men in the car, and then the screen went blank.

"You can't get good help these days," he mumbled. "Computer, switch to Fred and Gorge's car."

"Hey boss!" Gorge said, rubbing at his neck, obviously uncomfortable.

"You're behind Squat and Dacker's car, aren't you?"

"Well yes, boss... Something happened... something bad..."

"Yes, something awful. They pissed me off, and so I killed them. Do you want to piss me off, Gorge?"

"No. No sir, boss," Gorge said quickly.

"They were talking about double-crossing me, can you believe that Gorge?" Tarent didn't stop talking long enough for Gorge to answer, and Gorge knew he didn't expect him to. "All you idiots, listen up. Computer, send to all my employees... This is Tarent Powers. There is nowhere in this city that you can go where I can't see you. Where I can't hear you. That's what your loyalty implants are all about. Anyone else tries to double-cross me, and they'll end up just like Squat and Dacker. Now all of you quit farting around and find Hammer McVee, kill her, and bring Elantra home. I don't want to hear any more of your feeble excuses."

Tarent's paranoia had just been doubled. Squat and Dacker had been with him from the beginning. He would and had trusted them with his life. If they would turn on him, who could he trust?

The answer was easy. There was no one he could trust.

"Computer, issue this command. All humans are to leave this floor of the tower immediately. Their functions will be performed by droids. Deploy eighteen security droids on this floor, programed with the instruction that they are to kill anyone other than myself that walks onto this floor. The elevator is to be programmed not to stop on this floor. Do you compute?"

"Yes," the computer droned.

"This will be in effect until such time as I shall order you otherwise. Is this also understood?"

"Yes."

"Then initiate the program now."

Tarent sat back smugly in his chair. He didn't need people. They had all out-smarted themselves, Mishy, Hammer, the cops, any of his men who were thinking of taking him down for the money Mishy offered. No one could touch him now. They had played their hand one too many times, and now he was all locked down. No one could get to him. He could stay here indefinitely. He'd just proved to his boys that he could handle them without leaving the building. It was bad for business, but he had enough money to ride it out for years if he had to.

He might lose face, but he'd be alive to worry about it. Sooner or later someone would kill McVee, and Mishy. They'd bring Elantra home, and things could all return to normal.

He'd think of this time as a holiday, he'd relax and enjoy it. Kick back and just let the problem take care of itself.

He was Tarent Powers, the most powerful man in Freight City. He had nothing to be afraid of. He heard something and he jumped, his chair jumping along with him.

"Computer, what was that noise?" Tarent asked.

"My sensors detected no strange noise," the computer droned. "All personnel have now left the floor, and the droids have been programmed as you specified and are currently entering. After that the elevator will discontinue opening on this floor as you have commanded."

"Good." He felt suddenly cold. "Computer, make the room warmer."

"Done."

Tarent's stomach felt strange, and when he looked down at his hands they were shaking. He knew there was nothing the computer could do about that.

CHAPTER 15

They had finished breakfast and moved into the living room.

"How soon?" Pinky asked carefully as she sat down in a huge overstuffed chair, covered in the ever-popular floral print.

"The sooner we leave, the safer you'll be," Hammer said sitting on a couch across from Pinky with an effort normally reserved for trying to squirm into a place two sizes too small for a human body. She was obviously in a great deal of pain.

Pinky shook her head emphatically. "Don't you worry about this old girl. I can take care of myself, Hammer. You stay as long as you need to."

"It will be safer for us, too," Hammer said. "Everyone knows we're old friends. Someone will spill their guts, and it will be better for all of us if we're not here when Tarent, and/or Mishy's men come looking."

Pinky nodded.

Hammer saw where Pinky was looking, and answered her unanswered question. "She isn't used to the sugar."

Elantra was pacing back and forth behind the couch at a quick pace, looking determined. She stopped when she realized they were talking about her and looked at Conner. "I'm thinking," she protested.

"About what?" Hammer asked with a sly smile.

"Well, for one thing, how you think we're going to go anywhere, when you can hardly walk," Elantra said.

Conner looked at Pinky. "We'll leave as soon as it gets dark. I'll need you to go out first and make sure things are clear."

Pinky nodded.

Elantra had started pacing again. "What if they aren't?" she asked nervously.

"I'll call some friends and have them make a diversion," Pinky said, then added, "You know that might not be such a bad idea anyway. Just to be on the safe side."

"Good idea," Conner said nodding. "I'm going to need wheels."

"I'll call Justin, have him bring up something from Hammer Town and park it in the alley out back."

"That'll work," Conner said, turned her head and just watched in silence as Elantra paced back and forth. They were together, and now she wondered why she had been so convinced that they would be. After all that had happened it was a wonder that they were both still alive. The fact that they were both still alive and together was nothing short of a miracle. The implant suddenly kicked in, and she knew why Elantra was pacing. It had very little to do with either the sugar or any thinking she was doing. Conner got up, displaying less effort than she had sitting down. The pain was suddenly kicked back by a more urgent need. She walked over, grabbed Elantra by the hand and started pulling her back in the direction of the guest room.

"Conner McVee, I swear you aren't going to be happy till you jerk my arm right out of the socket."

"So you keep saying," Conner mumbled.

"What on Earth has gotten into you?" Elantra asked.

Conner turned and fixed her with a stare.

"Oh! Are you sure you're..."

Pinky laughed, and Conner just growled and pulled Elantra along.

"Are you all right?" Elantra asked, placing a gentle hand on the dressing on Conner's ribs.

"I'm wonderful, what about you?"

"Yeah?" Elantra said with a sigh. "I suppose we better make some sort of plan."

Conner didn't know how to explain to Elantra that there were certain things that you couldn't plan for. Hoping you were prepared for anything they threw at you was sometimes the best you could do. Most of her life she'd just flown by the seat of her pants and hoped for the best. It was easy when you had no one to worry about but yourself. This wasn't just about getting herself out of a scrape, though. This time she had someone else to protect. She had to get out of this dragging Elantra with her the whole way, and what plan could she possibly have?

"Conner?"

"It's not that easy," Conner said. "Everyone in this city who has a gun wants one or both of us dead. Pinky's right.

With the kind of money your daddy's put on my head, there's basically no one we can trust."

"The Constructionists..."

"They aren't going to make it easy for us to get out of Freight City, much less to Hammer Town." Conner was thoughtful then, because saying all that made it sound completely hopeless, in which case maybe the best thing to do was just stay put and have sex till someone came and killed them.

"Conner, tell me what you're thinking. It's my life, too."

She was right of course, but Conner was reluctant to tell Elantra just how screwed they were. Suddenly like an epiphany the answer came to her. "They expect us to try to leave, so we won't. We have to attack them before they can attack us."

"What?" Elantra asked, not understanding.

"We have to go on the offensive," Conner said. "There are too many of them. Running and hiding isn't going to work. They'll run us till we get tired, and then they'll kill us."

"So we're going to attack them?" Elantra asked in disbelief.

"Exactly," Conner said.

"With you all busted up, and me knowing nothing more than point, pull the trigger, and hope for the best?"

"Yeah. You wanted a plan, and now I've got one. So you want to hear it or not?"

Jason Hunter easily gained access to James Rank's room. A nurse was busily working at the computer that was basically taking care of Rank. She was a problem, because she didn't seem like she was in any hurry to leave.

Jason moved to Rank's bedside like a concerned friend. "So, Buddy, how you doing?"

"He ain't none too good," a familiar voice said from behind him. Jason felt a needle slide into the flesh of his ass, and then he felt nothing.

Conner made sure the nurse's uniform she had acquired still covered all her weapons. The wheel chair had followed her into the room on her request, and now upon her command it rolled out of the corner and over to the unconscious man. Conner searched Hunter, found both of his pieces, and hid them in her tool belt under the nurse's smock. Then she stripped him naked, put him in a hospital gown, and loaded him into the chair, not without a great deal of effort and pain. Then she told the chair to take Jason to the parking garage. She followed. If anyone noticed anything amiss, they didn't say so. Still, she didn't start to breathe again till she had loaded Jason into the trunk of the car, got in and drove away from the hospital.

"Could I please sit up and look about? I feel like a total idiot down here in the car's floor." Elantra looked up at her from where she sat with her knees curled up in the floor and her head on the seat. "The windows are smoked, no one can see in..."

"They can with the right equipment..."

"With the right equipment they could detect my body heat, not to mention the guy you just threw in the back."

"Point taken. You can sit in the seat."

"Good." Elantra popped into the seat. "Seat belt on," she ordered, and it slid into place over her.

Justin had found them the perfect car. It looked just like all the other self-drivers on the road and had all the amenities, but it could still be driven manually if the need arose, and it would arise where she needed it to go.

"How did you know he'd show up there and then?" Elantra asked.

"I hacked into the hospital computer and planted a false report that James Rank was coming to. I knew Jason couldn't risk that," Conner said.

"What are you going to do with him?"

"Use him."

CHAPTER 16

Gorge and Fred had been on the streets of Slum Town all day. Walking, of all things. Forcing guns in every lowlife hood's face and questioning them. Barely avoiding the dozens of police agents who were doing the same thing. They were exhausted, and God only knew what germs they'd been exposed to.

Slum Town's small-time hoods, while easily intimidated by their size and their firepower, were tight lipped for the most part, but by the afternoon they had hit pay dirt. Hammer had several good friends in Slum Town. Most of them had seemed to have miraculously disappeared. However, she was apparently in very tight with a crossdressing Constructionist who was something of a celebrity. She had been easy to find, as she did three shows nightly in one of the more popular clubs in Freight City, a place called Down Lows. Which was good, because when they'd showed up at her apartment building to accost her, a bunch of queens had started a huge bitch fight, screaming and throwing pieces of their drag at each other.

Fred and Gorge wanted no part of that, so they went to the club and waited for the guy to show up. They decided it was time to show a little muscle, so when the aging drag queen took the stage to perform to the packed house, they and six more of Tarent's top men stormed the stage. Fred and Gorge punched the queen and knocked him to the ground while the others stood at the edge of the stage, weapons drawn pointing at the audience. Gorge had straddled the guy, and had him by the collar.

"So, freak, where's Hammer McVee?"

"Boy, did you just make a big mistake," Pinky said.

"Hey!" someone screamed in a shrill voice. "They hit Pinky!"

Fred watched in amazement as weapon fire erupted, and the six boys watching their backs fell like lined-up dominos. He hit the floor, and when he looked up the old queen had Gorge by the front of his shirt and was pounding the living shit out of his face. Fred thought he should probably help his buddy out, so he jumped up, lifted his gun, and watched as it was kicked from his grip to go spinning across the floor. Then the flower-wearing fairy was pummeling his ass.

Gorge and Fred barely got out of the club and into their car alive. "Car drive, drive!" Gorge ordered.

"Fuck!" Fred said. He looked over at Gorge, whose face looked like it had been hit by a truck. "You think he knew where Hammer was?"

"I don't give a fuck!" Gorge said.

"What the hell happened?" Tarent's angry face glared at them from the console on the dash.

"They... they must have been waiting for us," Gorge said quickly. "They killed six of our guys, Fred and I barely made it out of there alive."

Tarent's rage was so apparent that you could almost feel his hot breath coming off the monitor. "You mean to tell me that you two morons and six of my best men got your asses kicked by an aging drag queen and a room full of fairies?"

"He was a really big old queen, an the fairies had guns," Gorge said helplessly.

It was an old abandoned building in the middle of Slum Town. It was in such bad disrepair and so rat infested that not even the residents of Slum Town thought it was a good idea to inhabit it. A flashlight in one hand, and Jason in the other, Conner headed for the basement. Elantra had Jason's other arm and was helping Conner pull him along.

"If you're not careful, you're going to open your wound," Elantra scolded.

"I'm fine," Conner assured her.

Elantra took a deep breath then asked, "You sure there's no other way?"

Conner nodded silently. She walked directly to the old elevator where she dropped Jason unceremon-iously to the floor and handed Elantra the flashlight. "Point it on the control panel."

Elantra nodded and did so. Conner used her tools to remove the panel cover, and then wired in her keyboard. In seconds the doors opened to reveal a pristine elevator obviously in good repair and in full working order. Conner stuck her foot in the door and undid the keyboard. Together she and Elantra pulled Jason Hunter into the elevator, the doors closed, and they were going down.

"Conner McVee," a voice hissed at her.

She looked up at the camera and smiled. "Listen, Mishy..."

"Are you committing suicide, or are you finally going to give me the girl?"

"Neither. I'm not going to beat around the bush here, Mishy. You want to kill us, then do it, and let us have some peace. Mishy, Tarent isn't you, and he's not me. He doesn't give a damn about Elantra. Hell, he ordered her killed himself rather than see her go off with me again. I know your people were there and that you heard him do it. There's only one way to make Tarent pay, and that's to kill him."

"Short of nuking Power's Tower you can't get at Tarent Powers."

"I can, with your help. All I ask is that you hear me out. Otherwise it will be a race to see who kills who down here, and I don't want that."

"Hammer, if you try to doublecross me..."

"We both want the same thing, Mishy, because if you'll admit it, you know I'm right. Killing Elantra isn't going to make you feel any better about William or Peggy."

There was silence as the elevator came to a stop. Conner pulled her weapon, leaned over and kissed Elantra. Elantra kissed her back.

The doors slid open, and two of Mishy's men stood there with their weapons pulled.

"Put your weapons down," the bigger of the two said.

"No. Why on earth would I do that? So that it would make it easy for you to kill us? No, you want to kill us, you're going to have to deal with the fact that we're going to be trying to kill you, too."

"Boss?" he asked, seemingly of the air.

There was a moment of silence, then, "Bring them on back," Mishy's voice said.

"Mind carrying my luggage?" Hammer said, pointing to Jason where he lay on the floor. The two men grumbled, but grabbed him and brought him along. Hammer took Elantra's hand and led the way. After all, she knew right where Mishy's office was.

Unlike Tarent, Mishy didn't like to hide in a building and run everything by computer. Mishy liked to occasionally get down in the trenches. This had at one time been a secret government laboratory, built to do experimentation in germ warfare. After the great plague all such installations had been closed. Mishy had bought the decaying building above it for a song, knowing what gold lay beneath it, and had turned it into his private lair. It was where he went when he needed to be close to the business at hand, or when things were hot like they were now.

The door opened before them, and they walked in. The two men dropped Jason unceremoniously on the floor.

"What may I ask is that?" Mishy asked of Jason.

"That is Jason Hunter, a police agent who works for Brakston Agency. He shot me, then he shot James Rank and got every agent in the city breathing down my shirt. See, the bastard *actually* works for Tarent Powers."

Mishy looked Elantra up and down and snarled. "So... I'm curious. You're not stupid, so why did you bring the girl with you? You know I'm packing heat. I could kill her right now. You'd probably kill me, but I think you know I don't really care about that."

"Because you aren't stupid, Mishy. You must have figured out by now that I need Elantra alive to get to Tarent. Besides, there was no place I could have left her where she would have been any safer."

"You know... when I saw you in bed with her, I wanted to see you dead."

"Yes."

"But the truth is," Mishy laughed then, cutting the tension of the moment, "the bloodthirsty bastard wouldn't have been nearly as pissed off if you'd killed her as he was because you fucked her. Then you took the bitch back and just gave her to him, and I *really* wanted to kill you then, but then what does she do? She runs away from him to be with you. Which totally destroyed the bastard. I think you've actually caused the bastard to suffer, and now I think I'm ready to have all this finished permanently, so..." He stood up slowly and stuck his hand out. Hammer walked forward and shook his hand. "How can I help?"

"I need you to kill me."

Tarent watched again as Mishy's men mowed a limping Conner "the Hammer" McVee down. Her body lay limp and bleeding on the ground. He looked at the other monitor where

Jason Hunter sat in his car with Elantra on the seat beside him, crying and screaming obscenities. Her hands were cuffed.

"We'll be there in about fifteen minutes, and ya got ta let me in, boss," Jason was begging. "Mishy's men are on my ass, and the cops are everywhere."

"I'd heard that Rank had come to and fingered you as the shooter. The door will be open. Bring Elantra straight to my office. I'll have the doctor waiting, and he can take care of all those horrible memories clouding Elantra's judgment."

Tarent called the doctor and ordered his presence. He told the computer to undo the lockdown on his floor, and prepared to deal with Jason Hunter and his daughter. Jason would have to be killed, Elantra deprogrammed, and then finally life could get back to normal. With no more Hammer McVee, the only fly in his ointment would be Mishy. With Hammer out of the way he could easily deal with Mishy.

He watched in the monitor as Jason's car pulled up out front, and as ordered, his men went to escort Jason and Elantra into the building in a cone of protected firepower. His computer glitched. There was a flickering on all his monitors, but then it was back on, and everything seemed to be going as planned. In mere minutes Elantra was standing in front of him, still handcuffed and in tears, but alone.

Tarent's brow furrowed. He'd been watching on the monitor. "Where's Jason? The others?" He started to stand, and his chair helped him to do so. He hit the security button on his desk as he watched the cuffs fall off Elantra's hands. Then behind her Hammer McVee strode in the door, weapon in hand.

"All drones! Kill Hammer McVee!" he screamed.

She laughed at him. "In case you haven't figured it out yet, Tarent, your security system isn't exactly working."

She took aim, and he knew she was going to fire. "Elantra... I'm your father."

"You're a murdering creep," Elantra said, still crying, though only now he realized the tears weren't for McVee.

He did the only thing he could think of – he moved quickly to put Elantra between himself and McVee. Knowing what he was doing, McVee fired, but the nail barely missed him, hitting instead the window behind him. It hit just right, too, because the "bulletproof" glass behind him shattered, and then blew out in a shower of shards, each no bigger than a dime.

Tarent grabbed Elantra and slung her towards the now open window. As he expected, McVee slung her weapon down and made a mad dash across the room. Tarent made a run for the door of his office and ran out, only to find Mishy standing there flanked by his men.

"This one's mine, boys," Mishy said, and the last thing Tarent Powers heard was Mishy laughing.

Conner jumped, throwing herself at the window. She barely caught Elantra's hand as Elantra went through the broken window. She crashed to the floor with enough impact to reopen her wound. Elantra's hand gripped hers tightly.

"Hang on," Conner ordered.

"Like I was thinking of letting go!" Elantra screamed back.

Conner pulled Elantra in the window and into the safety of the room. She hugged her tight. "You all right?"

"No," Elantra cried. She held Conner tightly with her one good arm. "I knew eventually you'd pull my arm out of the socket."

James looked up at the cyborg cop and the mobster's daughter and smiled. He wasn't actually expecting a visit from them, and said as much.

"We were here anyway," Conner said nodding towards the sling on Elantra's arm.

"And they wanted to *keep* you," Elantra said in a scolding tone.

"I feel fine. Hell, they even managed to get most the purple gack off," Conner said, shrugging.

"So... how'd ya do it?" Rank asked.

She told him first how she'd captured Jason Hunter, after which he thanked her for saving his life.

"Yeah, yeah, anyway. We made a tape of Mishy's boys pretending to shoot me and me dying. Then I told Jason if he didn't make the tape with Elantra for us to show to Tarent, I'd make good on my promise to kill him, which was a hell of a lot worse than jail. I'd never had any luck hacking into Tarent's systems, but Elantra had hacked her way out and past his security on more than one occasion using stuff she'd gotten through the access on her tutorials. See, it's an open-ended link. So we hacked in easily using that access, and fed the images to Tarent when we wanted them fed to him. When he loosened his security to let "Hunter" in, we used that link to take his security systems entirely offline. We used a loop so that he only saw what we wanted him to see. So we killed all his goons, and then we just walked right into the building. It was easy. Except for him throwing Elantra out the window, which wasn't part of the plan."

"So what ya gonna do now? I'm sorry, I can' tell ya how sorry I am. If ya wanna come back ta work for Brackston…"

She interrupted him with her laughter. "You're kidding, right? You know I got all the shit ta prove how dirty Tarent was now. Mishy can't take credit for taking him down, so it's my collar. Since I did it as an independent agent, that means I'm going to make a fortune. Hell, I might buy Brakston and you can work for me."

Conner put her arm around Elantra, and she put her good arm around Conner and rested her head on Conner's shoulder as they walked out of the hospital.

"Tired?" Conner asked.

"Yes… Conner, what are we going to do now? I mean… we don't even know where we're going to sleep tonight."

"Well, then I guess the first thing to do is rent a hotel room."

"Then what?" Elantra asked.

"Then we'll do whatever you want to do."

"What about what you want?"

"That *is* what I want."

ABOUT THE AUTHOR

Selina Rosen lives in rural Arkansas with her partner, her parrot, Ricky, assorted fish and fowl – both inside and out, several milk goats, an undetermined number of barn cats and her dogs, Spud and Keri. Besides writing, editing, and taking care of the farm, she's a gardener, carpenter, rock mason, electrician (NOT a plumber), *Torah* scholar and sword fighter. In her spare time she creates water gardens, builds furniture, and adds to her on-going creation of the "Great Wall of Kibler".

Selina's short fiction has appeared in several magazines and anthologies including *Sword and Sorceress 16*, *Such A Pretty Face*, *Distant Journeys*, three of the MZB Fantasy Mags, *Tooth and Claw*, *Turn the Other Chick*, and *Anthology At the End of the Universe*, just to name a few. Her critically acclaimed story entitled "Ritual Evolution" appeared in the first of the new *Thieves World* anthologies, *Turning Points*, and her second *TW* story, "Gathering Strength," appeared in the new *TW* anthology, *Enemies of Fortune*. *The Bubba Chronicles* is a collection of her short fiction which features – strangely enough – bubbas.

Her novels include *Queen of Denial*, *Recycled*, *Chains of Freedom*, *Chains of Destruction*, and *Strange Robby* from Meisha Merlin Publishing, and *The Host* trilogy, *Fire & Ice*, *Hammer Town*, *Reruns*, and novellas entitled *The Boatman* and *Material Things*.

Bad Lands, a gonzo-mystery novel co-written with Laura J. Underwood, is due out from Five Star Mysteries in 2007, and *Sword Masters*, the first full-length fantasy novel by Selina is also due out in 2007.

In her capacity as owner and editor in chief of Yard Dog Press, Ms. Rosen has edited several anthologies, including the award-winning *Bubbas of the Apocalypse*, *The Four Bubbas of the Apocalypse: Flatulence, Halitosis, Incest and... Ned*, *International House of Bubbas,* and two collections of "modern" fairy tales – the Stoker-nominated *Stories That Won't Make Your Parents Hurl* and *More Stories That Won't Make*

Your Parents Hurl.

You can contact Selina through her personal website www.selinarosen.com, or write her at selinarosen@cox.net.

ABOUT THE COVER ARTIST

Brad W. Foster is an award-winning artist who has had work published in over a thousand books, magazines, comics, and indefinable small press publications—the man needs a hobby!

Brad has created three covers for Yard Dog Press publications—*Illusions of Sanity*, *Wolf's Trap*, and now *Hammer Town*.

Brad draws to live, and finds it interesting that he also lives to draw. You can find out even more about Brad and his work at www.jabberwockygraphix.com.

Yard Dog Press Titles As Of This Print Date

Turn Left to Tomorrow, Robin Wayne Bailey
Wandering Lark, Laura J. Underwood
Wings of Morning, Katharine Eliska Kimbriel
Zombies In Oz and Other Undead Musings, Robin Wayne Bailey

*Double Dog
(A YDP Imprint):*

#1:
Of Stars & Shadows,
Mark W. Tiedemann
This Instance Of Me,
Jeffrey Turner

#2:
Gods and Other Children,
Bill D. Allen
Tranquility,
Tracy Morris

#3:
Home Is the Hunter,
James K. Burk
Farstep Station,
Lazette Gifford

#4:
Sabre Dance,
Melanie Fletcher
The Lunari Mask,
Laura J. Underwood

#5:
House of Doors,
Julia Mandala
Jaguar Moon,
Linda A. Donahue

*Just Cause
(A YDP Imprint):*

Death Under the Crescent Moon
Dusty Rainbolt

The Ghost Writer
Selina Rosen

*It's Not Rocket Science: Spirituality
for the Working-Class Soul*
Selina Rosen

Not My Life
Selina Rosen

The Pit
Selina Rosen

*Plots and Protagonists: A Reference
Guide for Writers*
Mel. White

Vanishing Fame
Selina Rosen

Non-YDP titles we distribute:

*Chains of Freedom
Chains of Destruction
Jabone's Sword
Queen of Denial
Recycled
Strange Robby
Sword Masters*
Selina Rosen

Three Ways to Order:

1. Write us a letter telling us what you want, then send it along with your check or money order (made payable to Yard Dog Press) to: Yard Dog Press, 710 W. Redbud Lane, Alma, AR 72921-7247

2. Use selinarosen@cox.net or lynnstran@cox.net to contact us and place your order. Then send your check or money order to the address above. *This has the advantage of allowing you to check on the availability of short-stock items such as T-shirts and back-issues of Yard Dog Comics.*

3. Contact us as in #1 or #2 above and pay with a credit card or by debit from your checking account. Either give us the credit card information in your letter/Email/phone call, or go to our website and use our shopping carts. If you send us your information, please include your name as it appears on the card, your credit card number, the expiration date, and the 3 or 4-digit security code after your signature on the back (CVV). Please remember that we will include media rate (minimum $3.00) S/H for mailing in the lower 48 states.

Watch our website at
www.yarddogpress.com
for news of upcoming projects
and new titles!!

A Note to Our Readers

We at Yard Dog Press understand that many people buy used books because they simply can't afford new ones. That said, and understanding that not everyone is made of money, we'd like you to know something that you may not have realized. Writers only make money on new books that sell. At the big houses a writer's entire future can hinge on the number of books they sell. While this isn't the case at Yard Dog Press, the honest truth is that when you sell or trade your book or let many people read it, the writer and the publishing house aren't making any money.

As much as we'd all like to believe that we can exist on love and sweet potato pie, the truth is we all need money to buy the things essential to our daily lives. Writers and publishers are no different.

We realize that these "freebies" and cheap books often turn people on to new writers and books that they wouldn't otherwise read. However we hope that you will reconsider selling your copy, and that if you trade it or let your friends borrow it, you also pass on the information that if they really like the author's work they should consider buying one of their books at full price sometime so that the writer can afford to continue to write work that entertains you.

We appreciate all our readers and *depend* upon their support.

Thanks,
The Editorial Staff
Yard Dog Press

PS – Please note that "used" books without covers have, in most cases, been stolen. Neither the author nor the publisher has made any money on these books because they were supposed to be pulped for lack of sales.

Please do not purchase books without covers.